Not everything that is faced can be changed, but nothing can be changed until it is faced.

—JAMES BALDWIN IN *REMEMBER THIS HOUSE*

Savannah Secrets

Savannah Secrets

Sapphire Secret

MARLENE CHASE

Guideposts

Danbury, Connecticut

Sapphire Secret

Chapter One

MEREDITH BELLEFONTAINE RAN A HAND through her short blond curls, which the sun turned to warm silk against her fingers. She made the short jaunt to Magnolia Investigations, buoyed with enthusiasm. It was a new day. A new week. Anything could happen.

In the eighteen months since she'd reopened her husband's agency, a lot of water had flowed down the Savannah River. Like the river, which was sometimes wild and dangerous and sometimes benign as a doting mother's smile, days had never been dull.

She sighed happily as she joined Julia in the agency's parking lot behind Whitaker Street. "On a day like this, you can't think of November as bleak or cold like some fierce prophet, warning of winter. Magnolias are still blooming, and even this early in the morning I hardly need this jacket."

Julia Foley rolled expressive gray eyes at her best friend and partner as they lingered by their cars. She smiled. "That's why our fair city is so full of festivals and art fairs—and marathons—this time of the year. And you, Mrs. Bellefontaine, look ready to run one—a marathon, that is."

Meredith returned the smile. She and Julia had arrived for work at the same time, but neither seemed anxious to go inside. Julia's long arms were crossed over her forest-green suit jacket that contrasted perfectly with her silver hair. Tall and formidable, whether in a judge's robe or dressed for a day at the office, she looked every bit the sharp-minded and adventurous woman that she was.

They had met in college and become fast friends. Then life had swept them along in divergent currents until they discovered each other again. Meredith blessed the day she had convinced the former juvenile court judge of Chatham County to join her at Magnolia Investigations. She had surprised even herself when, after Ron's death, she decided to reopen the business which he had so conscientiously built up.

"Well, I don't think I'm ready for a marathon," Meredith said, "but there's no denying that this is one gorgeous Savannah day. November is one of my favorite months. And Thanksgiving will be here before we know it."

Julia followed her gaze, glancing up at the sun that gilded the tops of trees. A nearby strip of woods had been preserved in the historic district amid stately homes and office buildings. "You're right," she said. "November in Savannah has plenty of warmth for comfort and just enough briskness to energize a person."

Meredith breathed in the freshness of the morning. Not knowing what the day would hold was part of its mystique, but there was a certain knowing, an awareness that "the mercies of the Lord were new every morning." She let out a big breath. "I'm not sure I'd survive a marathon, but an easy stroll in the park would be tempting on a day like this. What do you think?"

"I won't be running any marathons today either," Julia said with a groan. "I spent Saturday taking some of the youth from church on a hike at Skidaway Park. You've no idea how twenty-two junior high kids can wear a body down."

Julia was a high-energy gal who thrived on hard-hitting action and solving dilemmas. Only her critical thinking skills kept her from jumping into something with both feet before she put on her shoes.

"But it's Monday," she said with resignation. "And somebody's got to open the office. Carmen's not coming in until ten this morning, remember?"

"That's right."

Carmen had said she needed to keep an important appointment for Harmony, the little girl she mentored from the Boys and Girls Club. Their assistant, who had struggled growing up, was now encouraging others.

"Stars and garters! What do you make of that?"

Meredith spun around at Julia's exclamation.

A young woman—a teenager, perhaps—was running their way. Her feet barely touched the ground as she sprinted toward them. She was thin as an arrow, wearing jeans and a white shirt. Blond hair bobbed behind her and drizzled around her face as she came closer. Her breath came in quick, short gasps.

Meredith stared as she kept coming, not slowing down at all. Would she run straight into them? The girl's eyes flashed, scanning the parking lot and buildings as she advanced on soundless feet.

"Good heavenly days!" Julia muttered, lurching forward.

And then the girl stopped inches away. "Miss Bellefontaine?" she panted in a high-pitched voice that was childlike and urgent. Deep blue eyes—nearly black—flashed, oddly discordant with her light skin and hair.

"I'm Meredith Bellefontaine," Meredith said. "Can I help you?"

"Please!" She clasped small hands at the bare spot between her shirt and jeans and bent over to catch her breath. "I—I need your help. And—and I can pay you!" The disturbing eyes flashed left and right then over her shoulder.

Meredith scrambled through her memory. Did she know this girl who seemed to know who she was? A waitress from one of the cafés in the area? Maybe she was a retail worker from one of the shops nearby. Meredith searched the heart-shaped face, which was very pale, making her eyes pop like black marbles. Her chin trembled. There was a small design on the pocket of her white shirt, which appeared to have been hastily tied at her waist.

"What's wrong?" Meredith asked. "How can we help you?"

"Please! I can't talk long. I have to get back, but I have to find out why—" She froze suddenly and then jerked her head to the left. Her mouth formed a startled O. "Someone is following me!"

Meredith scanned the area but saw no one. It was not yet eight thirty in the morning, and the parking lot was deserted. "Who? Who is following you?" she urged. She took a step toward the girl, who quickly backed up like a skittish cat, flashing those glistening eyes around the parking lot yet again.

Julia too went toward her, hands outstretched. "Try to calm down. No one can hurt you here."

She shook her head violently, locked eyes with Meredith. "I need to hire you. I've got to know. Please!"

Know who was following her, Meredith supposed, scanning the area but still seeing no one. "Calm down and tell us what's wrong."

Her head bobbed again—left, right, before focusing once more on Meredith. "I can pay you!" She reached into the pocket of trendy

4

designer jeans, fished out a wad of bills, and thrust them into Meredith's hand.

"Wait!" Meredith said, closing her fingers over the bills before they could spill onto the ground. "Our office is right behind us." She gestured with her free hand. "Why don't we go inside and talk—"

"I can't right now!" came the abrupt refusal. The young woman shifted from side to side in a quick rocking motion, her canvas shoes making no sound. The dark eyes flashed. "I have to get back! Please… I have to go!"

Meredith took a sustaining breath. "Go where? Who are you? How do you know us?"

The young woman looked behind her frantically then reached up to push strands of damp hair from her forehead. "I—I know who you are. My grandma—"

A crack in the bushes several yards to their left brought a startled gasp to her pale lips. Before Meredith or Julia could react, she bolted like a frightened gazelle. She streaked away in the opposite direction from the sound, her hair streaming behind her like a tattered flag in the wind.

"Wait!" Meredith yelled as Julia took off in the direction of the bushes.

The young woman fled around to the front of the building. Meredith ran after her, chasing her onto Whitaker and then into Forsyth Park, but her heels were no match for the fleet-footed young woman's sneakers. She ran for several yards without catching sight of her. Likely she had detoured into the brush, but in what direction?

Besides, there were thirty acres of walking trails in the famous park. People were taking advantage of the lovely green space still fragrant with late-autumn flowers.

Breathing hard, Meredith stopped, the money still clutched in her hand. She crammed it into her purse. There was no point in trying to catch the girl, so with an embarrassed shrug for the curious watchers, she headed back the way she had come. The fleeing young woman would return—if for no other reason than to claim her money.

"I couldn't catch her," she gasped upon rejoining Julia in the parking lot. "You see anything?"

"Someone was there all right," Julia said, brows drawn together in a silver line. "He went racing through that strip of woods and disappeared. Unfortunately, there are plenty of buildings to sneak into and back gardens to hide in. All I got was a glimpse of two skinny legs and a pair of cowboy boots."

Meredith held her aching side. "So much for my marathon readiness," she gasped. "Let's get inside. I need a drink of water."

Julia opened the door to the agency's rear entrance. Meredith veered to the right and stepped into the warm kitchen with its comforting gray walls. She dropped her purse on the island counter and pulled a glass from the cupboard.

"Who do you think she was?" Julia asked, nearly knocking over the vase of orange mums Carmen had brought in on Friday.

"I've never seen her before," Meredith said after a restoring gulp of water. "I've been racking my brain, trying to think of some connection we might have had." Meredith felt a tightening in her chest. What was happening to the young woman? "She was just a girl, Julia. What would you say? Seventeen, eighteen?"

Julia pulled a glass down for herself. "Maybe," she mumbled, "but there was something about her eyes—like maybe she had seen a lot more than high school." She frowned. "I don't know, but she was sure scared out of her wits. Wish I could have caught that guy—whoever he was."

"She was really frightened—almost hysterical," Meredith murmured. At least whoever the girl thought was following her had fled in the opposite direction and not gone after her. The girl's large eyes in the heart-shaped face burrowed into her mind, engraving their dark pathos there. Her heart lurched as she recalled the desperate plea for help. Why hadn't the girl gone to the police instead of running to the first stranger she thought might help her?

I know who you are, she had said. Meredith chewed the inside of her cheek. No, she hadn't come to a stranger. She had come to someone she knew—or knew of. And what was that about a grandma? Meredith searched her mind for any tie that made sense.

"She came prepared to pay for help," Julia said, breaking into Meredith's scattered thoughts.

"Yes! The money!" Meredith scrambled to open her purse and retrieve the wad she had stashed there when the girl had bolted out of sight. She folded out the roll, saw a hundred-dollar bill on top. Where had a teenager come up with that kind of money? She began thumbing through the notes with growing amazement.

"Those are hundred-dollar bills!" Julia exclaimed.

Meredith caught her partner's startled gaze. "Yes. Every one of them. Jules, there's a thousand dollars here."

"Where would a kid like that get a thousand bucks? Do you suppose that's what the guy in the bushes was after?"

Meredith shook her head, unable to articulate her own surprise. She'd expected a few sweaty tens in the crumpled wad, but a thousand dollars? The frightened young woman had left it behind. It made no sense at all.

Julia released a long breath. "Surely she'll be back. She's not about to let all this money get away with nothing to show for it."

What if she can't get back? Whoever was lurking in the bushes had run away in the opposite direction. He hadn't gone after her. But suppose he did later?

"I wonder why she ran. Whoever was following her wouldn't have tried anything right in front of our agency," Julia said. "But we'd better report it." Julia punched in some numbers on her phone and described the young woman who had come out of nowhere asking for help and then run away.

Julia told the dispatcher of her unsuccessful attempt to catch the man wearing cowboy boots. No, they had no idea who he was or who the young woman was. "They'll send someone to patrol the area," she said after ending the call and tucking her cell phone away, "but I don't really expect anything will come of it."

Meredith set her water glass down. She looked up at Julia, who was twirling a strand of hair around her ear. "What do you think we should do now?"

Julia raised her eyebrows and let the strand of hair fall away. "Just wait, I suppose. Surely she'll be back to claim her thousand bucks. I bet she won't let much grass grow under her feet either."

Meredith nodded. There was little else they could do for the moment. They had no idea where to find her—or how to keep her safe. She drew in a sharp breath, haunted by the small pale face. So young, so vulnerable. Kinsley a few years hence perhaps. What—or who—was she running from? And how could they help her?

As she headed for her office, another ripple of concern marred the bright November day. Something was going on with her own sweet granddaughter, Kinsley Faith. She hadn't been her usual chatty self during their last virtual get-together. She'd been temperamental and pouty. She had even moved away from the camera, causing her mother to gently rebuke her for not paying the proper attention to Gran.

Kinsley was usually ready with a dramatic catalog of her activities. She'd been a girly-girl from the beginning. It was such fun to find the perfect pink dress or a new animal figurine for her collection. It was lovely to have a little girl to love. Of course, Kinsley's interests were changing. Gran would have to be sensitive to them—and perhaps to new moods and reactions.

Carter's two children, Kinsley and her brother, Kaden, were growing up so fast, but every mother and grandmother felt that way, didn't they? Kaden, eleven going on Einstein, loved all things science—especially astronomy. Meredith had been itching to give him a real hug—not a virtual one. Kaden's Asperger's syndrome kept him wary of close contact—even hers.

What would they be like later, when they were the age of the frightened young woman who had split the morning? And if they were in trouble—heaven forbid—who would reach out to them with a loving hand?

She whispered a prayer that God who witnessed the tiny sparrow's fall would keep His eye on the children of this world, especially the frightened young woman who had run to them for help.

Chapter Two

IT WAS WELL PAST FIVE thirty when Meredith sped upstairs to change, leaving the baby red potatoes to simmer gently in butter sauce. The salmon steaks were prepared, warming on the counter for twenty or so minutes before they were ready for the pan. Asparagus spears purchased from the outdoor market would round out the meal she and Carter would soon share.

"I invite a lady out for dinner, and what does she do but turn the tables on me!"

Her son's voice on the phone had surprised and delighted her. Carter had been called to a last-minute business meeting in Savannah, and he wasn't going to head back to Charleston without a chance to see his "best girl." She had convinced him she'd much rather cook for him than eat out. "This way I can have you all to myself," she had told him.

Carter was a successful banker and the father of two rapidly growing children, but he was still her child—her little boy with the tenacity of a bulldog when he had hold of something important. His family, his job, his duty to God and country. He'd embraced all these, and the older he grew, the more he resembled his father—from principles down to his chestnut hair and trim physique.

He had not championed her plan to reopen Ron's detective agency, however. His vision for his mom included something less challenging—like finding another man to share her life with. Not just any man, of course. Search the bushes for the best candidates and enjoy her life. Practical, she supposed, as she put on her favorite lounging pants and a pink cotton blouse with buttons shaped like rosebuds. Maybe even romantic. Carter wasn't without his soft side. But she loved being involved with people—usually people with a problem for which her help was needed. The element of danger existed, of course, and perhaps that too had its allure.

On the dating front she had taken his advice. Well, to some extent. It was hard to think of caring for someone else the way she had cared for Ron, the finest man she'd ever known. There hadn't been anyone to make her look twice. Well, not until Quin, that is.

She secured the final rosebud button. Catching her reflection in the mirror, she realized she was wearing the same blouse a few weeks ago when Quin had driven her to Charleston for Kaden's science fair. His eyes had admired her, and during the four hours traveling to Charleston and back she had experienced a closeness that surprised and unnerved her.

He had offered to take her after she sprained her ankle and feared she would have to disappoint Kaden. Julia couldn't get away, and Meredith hadn't had the heart to ask Carmen, who had plans with someone that Saturday. Quin said it would be a pleasure to attend Kaden's event. He'd already become something of a hero to her grandson, who had warmed to him the moment the two had met. Quin had one child. Jamie, with her husband and daughter, lived in Columbus, where for years Quin had practiced law.

Meredith had kept him at arm's length for many months and wasn't sure why. Except maybe it was simply that her heart hadn't been ready. *And now?* She turned to see GK sitting a few feet away peering at her from the hallway. "Don't look at me like that."

The Russian Blue assumed a proprietary pose, tail wrapped neatly around his feet. Named for theologian G.K. Chesterton, the cat had been a great comfort to her since she'd been widowed. He knew when she was feeling down and stayed nearby, watchful but giving her space. Now he did a demure pirouette and resumed his pose.

"I know, as long as you get your warm milk and tuna bites, you're good."

GK's ears suddenly pricked, and the tip of his tail twitched. Then he scurried down the stairs—a full thirty seconds before the doorbell rang, announcing her older son's arrival. Right on time. Carter was never late and seldom early.

"Come, sit with me in the kitchen," Meredith said after hugging him and hanging his coat in the foyer. "Salmon steaks take only a few minutes in the pan, and we'll be ready. Hope you're hungry."

"When did I ever dawdle when it came to your cooking?" he asked with a wink, the corners of his eyes crinkling just like his father's. "Especially when there are homemade rolls to go with it." He lifted his chin in hopeful inquiry.

"Uh—no, sorry," she said, leading the way into her newly remodeled kitchen with its white cabinets and beautiful butcher block island. "Got the rolls at the bakery. Probably better than mine. Besides, a girl can't spend all day over a hot stove. She's gotta work, you know." The day's events came filtering through her mind.

She and Julia spent considerable time going over the footage from the agency's security camera. They lingered at the office longer than usual, waiting to see if the frightened young woman would return. She didn't. And the police hadn't had any success locating her.

At six thirty, the sun had already set. She liked to serve her occasional guests on the deck, but it was too cool, so she had set two places in the dining room. When she remodeled the house, she had made the dining and living areas one, resulting in an airy great room with high ceilings, wainscoting, and two grand fireplaces.

Carter pulled a stool up to the kitchen island and gazed out on the deck, where brass lanterns affixed to the rail lit up the comfortable outdoor furniture and plethora of potted plants. The stucco Italianate house was beautiful, but it was likely the remarkable view of Troup Square that held the real allure with its charming gravel paths and lush greenery.

"Grandfather always had an eye for good property," Carter remarked. "And for homes with good bones like this one, still strong after a hundred and fifty years." He cast his gaze around the kitchen and through to the great room. "But you must rattle around in this big place all by yourself."

Meredith smiled over the sizzle of the steaks. "I don't have time to 'rattle around' much. Besides, you're just used to those two charming rowdies filling up your house." While Kaden was a quiet sort, his science projects were a dominant feature in the family, taking up lots of room and bringing them all into his fascination for how the world worked.

Ten-year-old Kinsley was Kaden's opposite, keeping up a nonstop chatter and planning the next sleepover with her friends. Well, usually. Meredith frowned, remembering their virtual visit two days ago. "How are they doing?" she asked, placing a bowl of leafy green salad on a tray.

"They're fine," Carter said, fixing his gaze beyond the glass doors. "You never can tell about kids, though. Sometimes I think they enjoy confusing me and Sherri Lynn." A little knot perched between his brows, and a vein in his temple pulsed. "Kaden insisted on wearing a bow tie to school this morning like Bill Nye, the Science Guy."

Meredith lifted the salmon steaks onto a delft blue platter and studied her son's frown.

Several seconds passed before he added, "Kinsley didn't want to go to school at all."

"Really?" Meredith couldn't hide her surprise. "She loves school. She even plays school when it's a holiday. Did something happen?"

Carter let his breath out in a sigh. "Not that we know of. She's just going through a phase, probably." He got up, pushing back the stool. "This ready to go?" He picked up the tray holding the salad and condiments. "I'm starved, actually. We worked through lunch."

Meredith nodded. She grasped the platter of parslied potatoes and steaks and carried it into the dining room. She didn't resume the mention of Kinsley until after grace and they had placed their napkins in their laps.

"Did she say why she didn't want to go to school today?" Meredith asked, passing the salmon to her son.

"Stomachache," he said simply, forking a mouthful of the tender salmon. "Last time it was a headache."

Meredith felt a ripple of concern. "Has she been sick—had a cold or something?" She'd always been grateful that Carter was tuned in to both his children and spent a lot of time with them.

"She hasn't." He picked up his glass of lemonade and swirled it a bit before taking a drink. "Kinsley's growing so fast. Before you know it she'll be off to college. Besides, women—even the little ones—are hard to figure." His wry smile didn't quite reach his eyes.

Meredith thought to tell him not to worry, that he was probably right about a "phase" or a mood, but how helpful was that? She held her glass in midair. "You and Sherri Lynn will get to the bottom of it," she said softly. *And this grandma has just moved Kinsley Faith up higher on her prayer list.*

They finished their dessert and coffee in the comfortable togetherness. Over the weekend she had made Carter's favorite chocolate chip cherry bars.

"You've still got the touch," he said, settling back in the easy chair that faced the fireplace.

"Have another."

"Nope. Don't have the time for a double workout at the gym." The smile wrinkles at the corners of his eyes deepened. "But thank you for dinner and for taking the time to bake this incredible dessert."

"I'm sending some with you for Sherri Lynn and the kids. Promise you won't eat them on the way home."

Carter groaned. "Couldn't if I tried," he said, rubbing his hand over his flat stomach.

Meredith nodded toward the remote on the coffee table. "Want the news? Or something else?"

Carter shook his head. "Just your company. We don't often get to just sit and talk." He angled his head. "So how are things going? Is it all work, or are you taking some time for yourself?"

Translation: Getting out? Meeting anyone of the male persuasion? Meredith smiled. "You're so predictable!" she teased.

A little thrust of his jaw. "How's Quin?"

She'd introduced Carter to Quin a year and a half ago when her son was helping Maggie Lu with the transfer of the Besset Mansion she'd inherited to the historical society. They had talked again at Kaden's science fair.

She shrugged, tidying dessert crumbs and napkins and placing them on the serving plate. "He's good."

He eyed her from his relaxed position—fingers locked behind his head. "You two do anything special over the weekend?" He closed his eyes lazily.

Meredith gave him a sardonic grin, hoping the warmth she felt creeping up her neck didn't show. "No," she said evenly. "He took his granddaughter to an equestrian event in Columbus. Grace is learning to ride. So I've had the weekend to just relax."

Carter opened one eye. "Well," he said, releasing a breath. "At least you weren't off chasing some society deviant."

"We leave that sort of thing to the police," she said, snapping her linen napkin at her son's socked foot resting on the coffee table. "Actually…" She pursed her lips. "This morning I did chase a young woman through Forsyth Park." She dropped down on the couch across from Carter. In her mind's eye she again saw a pair of blue eyes dark and deep as inkwells. Was the girl all right?

"Oh?" Carter narrowed his eyes.

Meredith sighed. "She came running at us out of nowhere. Julia and I were just chatting in the parking lot before going inside." She frowned, trying to recall everything in proper sequence. "She stopped just short of slamming into us and said she needed help. That someone was following her. Said she had to know something." *Yes,* Meredith mused silently. *She wanted to know why.* "Then she shoved a fistful of money at me and took off."

Carter sat up, flung his feet off the coffee table. "Do you know her?"

"Never saw her before. Julia hasn't either. She looked like a teenager. Just a child really."

"That's it? And she gave you some money?"

"Yes." Meredith caught her lower lip in her teeth. "Ten big ones."

Carter's brow knit. "How big?"

"They were hundred-dollar bills, Carter. Ten of them. I couldn't believe it when I discovered what she'd given me."

"Where would a kid get money like that?" Carter studied Meredith's face, and then something dark passed over his own. "Drug money, probably. Kids get up to some serious stuff sometimes. Bet she's a runaway too."

Somehow, Meredith didn't think drugs were involved. She hadn't seemed like the type. But how could you tell, really? She'd seen only a frightened face, curly blond hair, and a white blouse tied at her midriff.

"Get anything from the security camera?" Carter asked.

"Not much. The angle was all wrong. She was facing away. We'll work on enhancing the footage, but our system is old. We should have updated to one of those sophisticated types that tilts every which way and zooms in on faces. Just haven't really had a good reason to do it until now." She paused. "And it didn't pick up anything of the guy in the bushes."

"The guy in the bushes?" Carter's eyes widened. "Mom—"

"Julia went after him, but he was too quick. She got a fleeting image of skinny legs and cowboy boots." Meredith knew Carter's blood pressure was rising. "No harm done," she said with a shrug. "We thought surely the girl would be back for her money, but she didn't show up. We reported it to the police, and they sent a cruiser but didn't find her—or him. I'm really worried about her."

"And I'm really worried about you."

How long was it going to take for Carter to get used to the idea of his mother doing investigative work? She squeezed his arm. "Don't worry. My guess is she won't waste too much time before returning for her money." But she wasn't sure at all. What if she wasn't able to come back?

Carter stood up and began to jingle the keys in his pocket—something he did when he was troubled or frustrated. "Strange that she knew who you were. That you and Julia were investigators."

Meredith nodded. "Yes. Very strange. 'I know who you are,' she said, and then something about her grandmother. I've been racking my brain, but I'm coming up empty."

After a few seconds of nervous jingling, Carter said in an ominous tone, "Well, if you don't know this girl, then Dad must have known her."

Meredith locked eyes with her son. She hadn't thought of that, but it made sense. *Dear husband, what do you know about a frightened young woman with blond hair and a heart-shaped face?*

Chapter Three

Eager to get to the office the next morning, Meredith pulled into her parking space behind the agency. Julia's car was already there, as was Carmen's, complete with a Chihuahua bobblehead in the back window. She headed inside. But not without a furtive glance around the parking lot.

Would the frightened young woman who had run toward them yesterday make another appearance? She found herself scanning the wooded strip beyond the parking lot where someone had been watching until spooked. She exhaled. All quiet. Another grand autumn day with a chill not wholly to be blamed on the weather.

"Well, if you don't know this girl, then Dad must have known her."

Carter's words echoed in her mind. If they had a name, Meredith could look through Ron's old case files—at least those that remained after the fire destroyed, among other things, several storage boxes. But they didn't have a name, nor did they have a good photographic record.

"Good morning, Carmen," she called, rushing through to the reception area at the front of the agency.

"*¡Hola!*" Carmen's head bobbed up, releasing a light fragrance from her shining dark hair. Her complexion glowed, perhaps reflecting her fuchsia blouse that ruffled slightly at her neck.

Their assistant had clearly been engrossed in something on her computer screen. And Meredith recognized the something—video footage from the outdoor camera. A glance showed little improvement over the initial reading. But Carmen had an uncanny way with all things digital. She also knew how to navigate the information superhighway in inventive and surprising ways.

Meredith leaned in, laying a hand on Carmen's shoulder. The picture on the screen caught only a partial image from behind with just a sliver of the young woman's profile. Yesterday had been a sunny day, but the image was dark and blurry. "Able to clear it up any?"

"Not much," Carmen said, pushing back a strand of dark hair from her temple. "But I'm working on it." Her lips turned up in a jaunty smile, and she winked one brown eye. "*Un minuto.*"

The young woman, originally from Guatemala, might not need more than a minute. She was an indispensable part of their daily work. Wily and street-smart, with a warm heart, she was a hard worker. She had become a ward of the state after her parents were killed, and she had learned to get along in a world that was often hostile.

Julia appeared, mug of coffee in hand. "Thought I saw you breeze by."

It was Julia who had seen the promise in Carmen, whom she met in the course of her judicial duties and recommended for a position at their newly formed agency. Canny, perceptive Julia had become Carmen's mentor and more.

"How was dinner with Carter last night?" she asked, looking across at Meredith over her mug. "You get home in time to whip up something marvelous as usual?"

"Salmon steaks, baby red potatoes, asparagus. Pretty simple. But it was great seeing him. I don't usually get to have a quiet evening with my number-one son." Meredith peered over Carmen's shoulder again. "Wish we had updated our camera before yesterday's events," she said glumly.

"Yep," Julia said, coming closer to Carmen's desk. "That's something we better look into soon. Maybe one of those sophisticated ones that does everything but cuff a prowler and arrest him."

"I was reading up on those cameras," Carmen said. "They have these PTZ ones—that means pan, tilt, and zoom—so you can move fast and get up close on objects or people. With the optical zoom feature, you can catch details like faces and license plates. ¡Fantastica!"

"Faces would have been good," Julia remarked, glancing at the blurry image again. "Might as well go whole hog and get color night vision and ultra HD 4K recording." She narrowed her eyes. "Won't help us now though. I see we didn't get anything on our stalker either—not even a pair of boots." She laughed. "Nice shot of me streaking into the bushes though."

Carmen looked up at Meredith. "So she really slipped a cool thousand into your hand and took off?" She tossed her abundant hair.

"Pretty much." Meredith sighed. "I'm just surprised she didn't come back or call. She just left the money behind. No call from the precinct yet?"

Carmen, still bent over the image on the screen, gave a negative shake of her head. "She looks young to be carrying that kind of cash around."

"Carter suggested it might have something to do with drugs," Meredith responded glumly. "Carmen, have you ever seen her around Savannah before? Maybe at the market or a concert or..."

"No." She wagged her head, eyes still glued to the screen. "Nothing strikes me as familiar at all. *Nada*. But I'd like to have a friend who could toss around a grand."

Meredith straightened. "Well, stay with it. And make a copy, will you please?" She looped an arm in Julia's. "Give me a minute. I'll get my coffee and meet you in your office." They needed to talk about yesterday's strange confrontation further and decide what to do about it.

A few minutes later Meredith pulled out a foldable whiteboard and placed it strategically between Julia's desk and one of the two Louis XV chairs. There were lots of ways to brainstorm, but she'd decided to make notes the old-fashioned way for a change. Something about seeing details clustered together in black marker might help them work things out.

Julia perched on the edge of her desk and picked up the marker. "Why not?" she announced, studying the pen briefly. "This is the way it was done before the digital age. So, let the case begin."

"It's not exactly our case," Meredith said, "but we do have the young woman's money...."

"Tucked away in the safe," Julia interjected. She wrote *$1K* on the board and circled it.

"The young woman," Meredith mused, "we'll call her A."

Julia put a big *A* on the left side of the board then a hyphen for listing details. She thought out loud: "Age?"

"Should we say seventeen to twenty?" Meredith suggested. "I thought she was on the low side of that, but you estimated she might be older." Meredith had learned to trust her partner's instincts as well as her own.

The marker squeaked as Julia wrote in the numbers. They went through their recollections of physical details, including the time of the meeting in the parking lot and what had been said.

"What do you make of that design on Miss A's pocket?" Meredith asked. The camera hadn't picked it up, and even Carmen's ministrations hadn't been able to zero in on it.

"A logo maybe. It looked like an *R* was part of it," Julia said. "It could have been a *P* or a *B*, but I'd go with an *R* if I had to guess."

"Mm." Meredith caught the inside of her cheek with her teeth. "There was something else, kind of like a circle around it. Rats! I wish I had been closer. It could be a real help in locating her."

Julia drew the letter *R* inside a half circle, another one with a full circle, and *P* and *B* with a question mark. "A camera with a zoom might have given us the scoop. I suppose we could drive around the neighborhood looking for business names and logos, but we could spend months trying to find her that way."

Meredith wondered if the young woman could wait that long. Though the watcher in the bushes had fled the opposite way from her, suppose he was a real threat?

The hider in the bushes was labeled *B*, but the only thing under his physical details were *thin, 5'10"–6'1", jeans,* and *cowboy boots.* "There was something unusual about those boots," Julia mused. "Besides the fact that you don't see them around here much." She twiddled the marker between her fingers, her brow furrowed. "So maybe he ain't from 'round here."

"You don't see cowboy boots much in the city," Meredith agreed. "But there are a lot of riding stables—mostly along the coast or toward the southeast. And some guys who don't work on ranches or own a horse still dress like cowboys."

Julia suddenly locked eyes with Meredith. "Silver toes! I remember the way they flashed when he ran. I was behind him, but I'm sure those boots had a shiny metal of some sort at the tips." She put that little detail under *B,* and they continued their brainstorming until they had exhausted their short supply of "facts."

Julia capped the marker and pushed the board to the corner. When she returned to her desk, she picked up her mug and put it to her lips. "Yuck!" she said, grimacing. "Nothing's more insipid than cold coffee."

Meredith grinned. "Whip up some froth and put an ice cube in it. You could sell it for five bucks."

"Thanks, Mere. You're a genius." She gave her partner a mock evil eye and sighed. "Well, I don't know what else we can do about Miss A—or should do—but I have an appointment with the delightful Mrs. Arbuckle to photograph her jewels."

Meredith groaned. "Oh yes." Her conscience, though, still rankled. "I know it hasn't been forty-eight hours, and Miss A is not technically missing...but we do have her money, and I'm worried about her. I think while you pacify Mrs. Arbuckle, I'm going to have a talk with Wally and find out if the cruiser had anything to say about the runaway girl or the cowboy."

Wallace "Wally" Parker was a detective and Ron's partner when Ron served on the police force. Wally retired early but hated retirement life. A former Georgia Tech defensive lineman, he fought crime with the tenacity of a bulldog and, though no longer a young pup, was gladly reaccepted back on the force. After Ron left the force, the two had remained friends, despite rooting for rival college football teams.

"He could tell us about any recent runaways in this area or…" She drew in her breath. "Or drug heists. I'll take a copy of the camera footage, though I doubt he'll be able to make any more out of it than we have."

When Meredith arrived at the Central Precinct Police Station, she marveled anew at its improvement over the old headquarters on Bull Street. In 2019 the city had cut the ribbon on the 13,000-square-foot building with its expanded briefing room, community space, offices, and interviewing room. The structure with its variegated brick facade had been built on 34th Street near the Montgomery and MLK corridors, a short drive from Magnolia Investigations.

She was ushered into Wally's office and greeted with his generous smile and open arms. "Meredith!" he exclaimed. "You're a sight for sore eyes."

His dark hair had gone mostly gray, but it was thick and trimmed neatly around his ears. He stepped back to look her in the face, blue eyes twinkling. "Wait until I tell Em. This morning we were just talking about you—and Ron. Man, how I miss that guy." He quickly reddened. "I'm sorry. If I miss him, you must—"

"It's okay, Wally. I welcome hearing my husband's name. It's just really good to see you." He looked weary and had grown a little thinner. As long as she'd known him, he had never been careful about his diet. He might even be a poster boy for the donut-eating street cop. She hoped his slimming down didn't portend illness or trouble.

"Say, you want coffee? We may have some envelopes of cocoa mix. Won't be too long before it's cocoa weather. I heard we're going all the way down to forty something tonight."

"I'm good," Meredith said, taking the chair Wally indicated. It had been a long time since he and Em had been to the house. The last time was nearly a year ago when they'd come for a Christmas brunch. When Ron was alive the house had seen a fair share of guests. She didn't entertain much anymore—not because she shied away from company. It was just, well, different now that she was alone.

Wally pushed the sleeve of his shirt higher on his bicep as he moved around to his desk. "It's hard to believe that we've been in this facility almost two years already."

"It's quite the upgrade," Meredith said. "You probably don't know what to do with all this space."

"Well, nature abhors a vacuum, and all that. And sadly, there's no lack of criminal activity to deal with." He gave her a lingering look. "The report says there was no sign of your fleeing young woman yesterday. Also, I checked those serial numbers you gave me. Nothing's coming up, so the cash isn't stolen, so far as we know now."

"Ah," Meredith said. "That's good, I guess, but we don't know what to do with this girl's money." She pulled a jump drive from her shoulder bag and described in as much detail as she could what the young woman looked like. "Here's what we got on the security camera."

He slid the drive into his computer port and silently studied the screen over dark-rimmed readers. His ruddy face seemed to pale momentarily as the heavy brows knit together. His blue gaze flickered, and his usually placid mouth twitched.

"Not much help here, Meredith," he said after staring at the screen for a long moment. "It's pretty grainy."

She searched his face, disappointed. "I was hoping you might have seen her or…"

He cleared his throat. "Sorry, but we'll be in touch if anything turns up that might help." The strange expression she'd imagined earlier had disappeared. In its place a warm smile spread.

She pondered his reaction to the camera footage. Maybe something about the girl had put him in mind of his own troubled granddaughter who had run away to Atlanta when she was sixteen. Was she all right now? She didn't dare ask, to stir up more sadness. She said gently, "We're not sure what we should do with the money."

"Maybe she'll come back for it," he said. After a moment, he brightened and tapped something on his keyboard. "I have some pictures of runaways and missing persons you can look at for comparison." He pulled a chair close to his desk and gestured for her to join him.

Meredith settled close to the screen and clicked through the sad parade of young female faces. When there were no more to peruse, she sat back, shaking her head. None had the same heart-shaped face and delicate brows or brooding eyes wild with some unnamed fear. She crossed her arms over her waist. Why had this girl come to them in the still of Monday morning, calling her by name? Why was someone following her? What was happening to her now?

Wally's voice broke in. "You—uh—said the camera didn't record a man in the bushes?"

"No. Julia lit out after him, but he got away. All she saw was a pair of skinny legs and some fancy cowboy boots with silver tips."

"Huh," he said, and then, after a pause, "Try not to worry too much. I'll call you if we hear something."

"Thanks, Wally," she said, standing.

Wally touched her arm gently. "Always a treat to see you, Meredith. Em and I have missed you. We'd like to have you over, but..." A shadow crossed his face, and an odd little silence ensued before he gave her a quick hug and stepped back toward his desk.

She drove back to Magnolia Investigations, thinking of the times she and Ron had enjoyed with Wally and Emily. He hadn't explained why they hadn't called. He had left the sentence hanging. She knew, of course, that things changed—even your circle of friends—after you became single. It was sad, and she was as much to blame as he. However earnestly they might want their friendship to continue, the urgency of daily life and business had a way of swallowing good intentions.

As she turned the corner to head around to the parking lot, she noticed a car parked along Whitaker Street a few yards from the agency. Someone was behind the wheel of the idling Jeep with a mottled paint job—a cross between green and gray. The camouflaged look seemed out of place along the historic tree-lined street. She drove around to the back of the agency, parked, and headed inside.

Julia was passing in the hallway when Meredith came in the back door. "There you are," she greeted her. "How did it go with Wally?"

Meredith sighed. "Good, but I learned nothing about our mystery guest. Wally says there were no reports of anyone dashing through the area yesterday morning. He suggested that we hold on to Miss A's money and see if she makes another appearance." She walked along with Julia toward the reception area, pondering Wally's reaction to the security footage. "Carmen still at it?"

"Think so. In between phone calls." Julia paused at the wide front window. "That guy in the Jeep's still there!" she said with surprise. "I passed it fifteen minutes ago, and he was just sitting there."

Meredith joined her at the window. "That's the vehicle I saw when I was driving up."

Suddenly the door of the Jeep opened. A blond-haired man in a denim jacket unfolded himself and stepped onto the sidewalk. The sun caught the gleam of silver at the toes of his cowboy boots.

Chapter Four

"It's him!" Julia gasped, staring as the man moved tentatively toward the agency, his thin blue-jeaned legs slightly bowed. He glanced up furtively, hesitated a step, and then kept coming.

"It's the guy in the bushes!" Julia exclaimed. "Look! I'd know those legs and those boots anywhere."

Meredith gaped. The stranger who had outrun Julia was now coming up the stairs to the porch. She watched him approach. He had curly hair the color of sun-ripened wheat and a square, boyish face that might one day be described as rugged. One long arm reached for the door.

Julia had already leaped into action, reaching the double glass doors before Carmen could even look up from her computer.

Meredith scrutinized the visitor's suntanned face as he stopped just short of the threshold. He had a straight nose, a strong chin with a hint of gold shadow. Clean-cut with a small scar above his left eyebrow, he might be a vision of the boy next door. A boy with sky-blue eyes who had clearly grown into a man.

A man who spied on young women and hid in the bushes. Meredith felt a chill pass through her.

"Is there something we can do for you?" Julia's voice was professional but firm. Her gray eyes narrowed as she searched the blond visitor's face.

"Miss Bellefontaine?" he asked.

The voice was a mellow baritone, hesitant. His eyes met Julia's, darted away to Meredith, who stood just at her left a few feet away.

"That would be my partner," Julia said, her tone stern. "I'm Julia Foley. You know, the one who chased you after you scared that young woman in our parking lot."

His eyes fell away, and his chin dropped briefly to the edge of the denim jacket that Meredith saw was weathered but clean and unbuttoned over a white tee. "Yes," he said simply, raising his chin.

Meredith stepped forward, more curious than wary. "Maybe you'd better state your business." From the corner of her eye, she saw Carmen lift the phone off its cradle, ready to summon assistance if needed. "Your name would be a good start."

"Gage," came the quick response. "Gage Gallagher." Color rose in the tanned plane of his face. "Yes. I was there yesterday, but I meant no harm to her." His eyes roamed between the two women, coming to rest on Julia again. "I'm—sorry, I didn't mean to cause any trouble."

Julia folded her arms over her chest. Formidable in her stance, she was only slightly shorter than he was. "Hiding in the bushes and running away doesn't inspire confidence."

His eyes flashed briefly then settled. He spread his hands in a gesture of submission. "I came here hoping you would give me a chance to explain."

"All right," Julia said, "we're ready to listen."

"Why don't we sit down out there," Meredith broke in. She gestured beyond the glass doors to the porch where a swing hung from four chains bolted into the ceiling. A roomy rocking chair was next to it with a table between them, on which a pot of wax begonias bloomed. The group would be visible enough for safety and still private enough for conversation.

Gage Gallagher walked to the rocker but didn't sit until Meredith and Julia had taken their places on the swing. *He may be a stalker, but he has manners,* Meredith thought, taking a place closest to their quarry.

He placed his elbows on the rocker's arms and then, changing his mind, clapped his hands over his knees. His booted feet made no movement on the wooden plank floor. A car made its way down Whitaker Street, its motor the only sound close enough to be identified.

Meredith felt rather than heard Julia's impatient breathing next to her as she waited for Gallagher to lift his face. His ears behind curling sideburns lay flat against his head. There was a slight crease across his forehead. *Hat hair,* she thought, realizing that a cowboy hat probably accompanied the denim jacket and boots.

He pressed his lips together, and then he opened them only to close them again as though finding it difficult to frame his explanation. Finally he looked up and across at Meredith. "It's true I was watching her, but only to protect her."

"So, you know her," Julia said, prompting.

"Are you related to her?" Meredith asked.

"No. She's a friend. Her uncle is my boss, which is how I got to know her. I haven't worked there long, so I don't know a lot. And it's none of my business, really, except…" He took another break in his explanation and flexed rough knuckles against his knees. "I work at the Riverton Ranch."

"The old Riverton property south of Richmond Hill?" Meredith asked. The stately home had never made it to the list of historic sites, but she knew of it. In its heyday—long years past—it had been the home of wealthy planters and, no doubt, many enslaved people who worked the land. The property had been turned into range land and was located some twenty-five or thirty miles south of Savannah near Richmond Hill. An elegant mansion on the site had been destroyed in a fire.

He glanced up, perhaps surprised that his place of employment was known to the investigator. "Yes, ma'am," he answered. "I'm the barn manager and groom in charge of the horses."

"I was the historical society director for a few years here in Savannah," she said. She'd never visited the site, and Richmond Hill was off the beaten path for most tourists to the area. She knew nothing of its present owner or owners. "How long have you worked at Riverton, Mr. Gallagher?" she asked.

"Just Gage, ma'am," Gallagher said, his mouth curling into a hint of a smile. "Everyone back home calls me Gage. They call my father 'Mr. Gallagher.'"

"Back home?" Julia asked.

"Texas, ma'am. San Antonio, but I'm working my way through A&M." He leaned back a little in the rocker and cast his gaze out to the street where a motorcycle was passing. "Veterinary School," he continued. "Taking a sabbatical of sorts. Ran out of funds, so I took some time off to earn next semester's tuition. Riverton needed someone experienced with horses. So that's what I'm doing here."

"Let's get back to the young lady you were following," Meredith said after a pause in which she had been studying his face for clues that would enforce truth or its counterpart.

"She's Mr. Riverton's niece." Gage pursed his mouth, rippling the fine blond hairs of an almost-mustache. "Theodore Riverton." His lips morphed into a straight line. "You have probably heard of him—he owns a lot of franchises in these parts...including the Riverton Clinic."

Meredith's memory clicked in. *Riverton Clinic.* A private institution that served people with mental health difficulties, nervous disorders, various addictions. Those who could afford it, of course. She exchanged glances with Julia.

"Sapphire works in a shop in City Market—just across the park. She designs silk flower centerpieces that are sold in the shop. Downright beautiful—and they bring a pretty penny. It's one of those specialty places owned by her family."

"Sapphire?" Meredith had never known anyone by the unusual name.

"She's called 'Sapphie' sometimes. She's—" Once more he hesitated. "I followed her into town because she was—uh—she wasn't doing so well." He rubbed his hands over his knees. "She has what Mrs. Riverton calls her 'spells.'"

Meredith watched him clench his hands over the arms of the rocking chair. "When she gets that way, they check her into the clinic. There's a private bungalow reserved just for her." His jaw tightened. "For all the good it ever does her."

"So you followed her in from the ranch?" Julia asked. "How did she get into the city?"

"She drove. She's no kid. She'll be twenty-one in a few weeks." Gold-fringed lashes any woman would envy fluttered briefly. "She parked at the shop where she works, but she didn't go in. She just took off running through Forsyth Park and headed straight here. I was worried about her, so I got out of my car and went after her." He paused, frowned. "She had told me she was worried—said she had to talk to someone who could find out who was following her—she didn't mean me—and…" He clamped his lips shut for a few seconds before going on. "And why she can hear her mother calling."

"Her mother?" Meredith tried to remember any reports about the owners of the Riverton Estate—male or female.

"Her mother's dead. A long time ago, but the thing is, she feels responsible. All those extended visits to the clinic don't do her a lick of good!" He set the chair rocking then stopped it abruptly and stood up. "They wouldn't like it if they knew I came here. They don't want any of us getting into their business—especially Sapphire's. But sometimes when Sapphie comes to ride Mandolin—her chestnut bay—we talk."

"Please," Meredith said. "Where is she now?"

"I don't know. Could be at the clinic. Maybe checked herself in again—or her uncle did." His lips closed over any further explanation.

Was Gage Gallagher interested in Sapphire out of friendship? Pity, perhaps? Or maybe the Riverton fortune, which according to rumor was considerable.

"I don't know why she came here, but she's in some kind of trouble. She thinks someone is following her. She really needs your help, ma'am."

"Gage, Sapphire said she knew who we were and then something about her grandma." Meredith studied the young man's frown. "Do you know what she meant?"

"No, I don't, ma'am. I think there's a lot I don't know about Sapphie and her family." He shuffled his feet nervously, the metal tips of his boots clicking on the plank floor, then moved toward the stairs. "I've got to get back. If they knew I came here, I'd be run out of Dodge, for sure. Wiley—he's the foreman—made that clear from the get-go. He says the Rivertons don't like strangers prying into their private business. I think Wiley's made himself Sapphire's personal watchdog. Reporting to her uncle Teddy, most likely." He handed Meredith a slip of paper. "My cell phone if you need to find me." He tipped an imaginary hat, hurried down the porch steps, and headed for the Jeep parked at the end of the block.

Neither Julia nor Meredith spoke until the Jeep had disappeared. Squirrels chattered, birds twittered in the trees, mingling with subdued traffic noises. Gage Gallagher had been a larger-than-life presence strangely out of context.

"Did I imagine it or was that Tex Ritter sitting in that rocker?" Julia asked.

"It's quite a story," Meredith said, replaying in her mind the nuances of the tale—or hint of a tale. Who were these Rivertons? Who was the young woman who felt responsible for something that happened to her mother and who had a private cottage in a health clinic owned by her uncle? Was Gage Gallagher who he said he was? Who knew what his intentions or motivations might be?

"What do you think we should do now?" Julia drew a deep breath and released it slowly.

"The sixty-four-thousand-dollar question," Meredith said. *She really needs your help, ma'am.* Gallagher's words echoed in her mind. "Sounds as though she needs the help of psychiatrists, not detectives."

The glass door opened, and Carmen popped her head out. "All quiet on the western front?" she asked, grinning and peering into the distance where the mysterious cowboy had evaporated.

"All quiet," Julia said, rising.

"Good. Because Maggie Lu is here."

Charlene would have brought her mother, since Maggie Lu didn't drive, and they must have parked and entered the agency around back. Meredith jumped up, always eager to see the smiling face and the bright spirit that was Maggie Lu Clement King. The unofficial member of their little sleuthing company had helped them solve their first case. In truth, it had been all about her, since she'd turned out to be the heir to the Bessett Estate they had been hired to investigate nearly two years earlier.

"She and Charlene are in the conference room," Carmen said. "Just came about five minutes ago. I brought them some coffee and said you'd be there momentarily." Carmen stepped back to usher her and Julia inside. "Some hunk!" she said, winking one sparkling brown eye and gesturing to the unseen Gage Gallagher.

"Down, girl," Julia quipped.

"Maggie Lu!" Meredith slid in beside her at the conference table. She put an arm across her shoulder and leaned in to touch Maggie

Lu's cheek with her own. "And Charlene, how are things at the diner?"

"Buzzing—even at this time of the year." The elegant woman in her fifties set a cup down on the table across from Meredith and eased into a chair with athletic grace, her cap of iron-gray curls clinging close to her head. Instead of her usual hoops, she wore bright red diamond-shaped earrings that matched her blouse. "We're headed there for lunch, and then I'll drop Mom at the library. She's filling in for another volunteer this afternoon."

"Lunch means I'll eat, and she'll be running from kitchen to dining room taking care of business!" Maggie Lu said with a mock pout. "Can't get that girl to slow down and smell the roses!"

Meredith laughed. Charlene did work hard, but the Downhome Diner was her dream, and as its entrepreneur and owner she'd been enormously successful. With no little thanks to her mother's sacrifice and encouragement. "I bet she takes plenty of time for little Jake. Nearly a year now, right, Charlene?"

"One year going on kindergarten!" Charlene said.

"Jacob Philip Beasley's a wonder, that he is," proud great-grandma Maggie Lu said. She chuckled. "He keeps our sweet Clarissa on the move, for sure."

Maggie Lu was especially close to Jake's mama. In turn, Clarissa loved Maggie Lu and never tired of listening to stories from her grandmother's amazing life. Seventy-seven years old and still ramrod straight and sharp as a tack.

"I hope we didn't keep you from something," Maggie Lu said, perceptive eyes meeting Meredith's.

"We saw you had company out there on the porch," Charlene added.

"No, Tex was just about to ride off into the sunset," Julia said. She shrugged. "Or back to his horses at the Riverton Ranch."

"Riverton. Hmm, that's a name I haven't heard in a while," Maggie Lu said. "Riverton as in Riverton Estate?"

Meredith angled her head to one side. "Probably, though no one calls it that anymore. New buildings and a lot of range land. Horses, apparently, considering our visitor this morning."

Maggie Lu fingered the handle of her cup meditatively but waited.

"Gage Gallagher," Julia said. "The cowboy we were chatting with. He's—what did he say, Meredith? The barn manager?"

Meredith nodded. Over the next few minutes she outlined the events of yesterday that led up to the surprising reappearance of the man Julia had chased from behind the parking lot.

"So your frightened young woman is connected to Riverton," Maggie Lu murmured. She shook her head gravely. "I recall hearing about a woman who died there years ago."

"Gallagher said our young woman—he said her name is Sapphire—needs help," Julia put in. "She says someone is following her, and according to Gage, she feels responsible for what happened to her mother."

"Sapphire." Maggie Lu spoke the name softly, drawing out the second syllable so that it seemed to drift into space and waft upward like sparks.

A fitting name for her, Meredith thought, recalling the cobalt of the girl's eyes that might appear more blue than black if she were not frightened. A precious gemstone, sapphire was typically blue but some so-called "fancy" varieties could be yellow, orange, or green. She'd had a friend in college whose engagement ring, an oval sapphire, had cost fifteen thousand dollars. She'd always wondered how she knew its cost and if her fiancé had proudly proffered a bill of sale while on bended knee.

"I remember something about a woman with a gemstone name," Maggie Lu said just above a whisper. "Wasn't Sapphire." Her forehead wrinkled in thought. "It was such a long time ago."

Meredith watched the perceptive eyes beneath the still smooth forehead. Maggie Lu had seen a lot in her seventy-seven years.

"The woman I'm remembering was much older," Maggie Lu mused. "She couldn't be your girl's mother. Grandmother, maybe. I used to see her on 32nd Street that crossed LeGrand. She worked there as a hairdresser, as I recall. It wasn't far from the old Spencer Elementary. We always said hello when we passed and chatted there on the street. Pleasant woman."

"I believe the original mansion burned in a fire," Meredith said. "I'll have to check the record, but it had to have happened some fifty years ago—back in the seventies." She paused, arrested by the nostalgic look on Maggie Lu's face. "I didn't pay a lot of attention during my historical director years, since Riverton never was classified as a historic site."

Carmen, who was never far from some electronic device, suddenly held out her tablet with a look of triumph. "June 3, 1970, to be exact. That's when the mansion burned down."

Chapter Five

"Thel! You going to leave me under this thing till my head explodes, or what?"

Thelma Chambers shut her eyes against Ellie Peever's high-pitched quaver mingled with the raucous plaint of Elton John and Kiki Dee singing "Don't Go Breakin' My Heart." She turned to her daughter, who fidgeted excitedly in the vinyl-backed chair in the beauty shop's tiny break room.

"He asked me to marry him, Mama! He wants me, Mama." Her eyes glowed with such brilliance Thelma thought they must light up the entire city of Savannah.

Thelma's heart swelled looking at her beautiful child whose cornflower-blue eyes were twin fireflies in her cherubic face. Thick hair the color of summer wheat fell to her shoulders—bare but for the spaghetti straps of her red-and-white-checkered sundress.

"Cora June," Thelma shouted over her shoulder loudly enough so the beautician on the other side of the wall could hear. "Brush out Miss Peever, will you? I got to see to my girl here!"

She'd been an extraordinary beauty from the day she was born. Thelma had pinched herself over and over, wondering what star had found its way that winter morning to the dingy apartment in 1979 where it shone upon Garnet Georgianna Chambers.

"Oh, Gigi," Thelma whispered, feeling the love and fear in her heart like a knife thrust deeper and deeper through flesh and bone.

"It's true, Mama. And it's not because he doesn't know that we're—" She lowered her eyes, the lashes so gold and thick you could comb them. "I mean, it doesn't matter that we're not rich or important or anything."

She was "Gigi"—not for the famous film character but for the two "G's" in her name. Garnet Georgianna. One couldn't go on calling a child by such a sophisticated couplet forever. She'd named her only child for the beautiful gemstone—maybe because of her bow mouth that was like a ripe cherry. It was the first part of her baby she had seen. She'd been alone in the sterile hospital room, except for a nurse with pity in her eyes every time she looked at the solitary laboring mother. Jimmy Ray had split at the first sign of her pregnancy, and there had been no one else to care. No one to care that life had become even more complicated for Thelma Chambers than ever. Which was saying a lot.

She had chosen the name Georgianna for her own father, whom she had never met. One of three million war fatalities *of the Korean Conflict, he'd died before ever seeing his child. Shortly afterward, her mother had succumbed to pneumonia, leaving Thelma orphaned. So much for her pedigree. But Jimmy Ray had loved her—at least for a while—and she bore him no grudge, though she had not the slightest idea where he was now or where he had been for the last nineteen years of Garnet's life.*

Thelma poured herself into the life of her daughter, working as many jobs as it took to keep her in school and dress her in nice clothes. Not like high society, by any means, but Gigi never complained. She was sometimes so good and sweet that Thelma marveled. An angel on loan to planet Earth?

Of course, there had been boys fluttering around Gigi since she was twelve. She would make any man proud. Thelma had bought her party frocks, prom dresses, whatever would delight her. She told her stories of knights and ladies, of glass slippers and princes. They'd laugh together over dreams of golden carriages, white horses, and castles. All the while she worried. No one must hurt this lovely girl. Was it right to fill her head with visions of grandeur?

For Gigi believed she had at last found her prince. An heir to the Riverton Mansion, no less, who had rescued her when she'd fallen on a slick sidewalk downtown and sprained her ankle. He'd taken her home to the small apartment where she lived with her beautician mother. It had happened only a few months ago, but how quickly the romance had deepened.

"He's so kind, Mama—and so good—better than Sir Galahad"—who had been her favorite knight since Thelma

began reading stories of swashbuckling heroes to her little girl. "You'll see, Mama. We'll be so happy. And he says you could come to Riverton too. You will not be alone. I don't want to leave you alone!"

"You're ruining it!" Mrs. Peever's shrill voice rang out. "Thelma, get out here and fix this nightmare Cora June's made of my hair!"

Someone had turned the radio up again. It droned on as she stared into Gigi's glowing face. "'You put the light in my life. Oh, you put the spark to the flame. I've got your heart in my sights—so don't go breaking my heart!'"

Thelma felt the thrust of a knife drive deep into her heart. She could fix Ellie Peever's stiff gray curls. But what was to become of her beautiful Garnet Georgianna if Preston Riverton III should break her heart?

Meredith woke to see GK studying her from the doorway of her bedroom, his elegant tail wrapped around his paws. GK seldom begged for his breakfast except in this backhanded way of staring at her until she felt guilty enough to get up.

"All right, Mr. Chesterton," she said, rolling out of her comfortable four poster. She'd slept a bit longer than usual after the eventful day at the agency. And somewhat fitfully perhaps, as she pondered the visit of Gage Gallagher and what they had learned. Something about the young woman who had pleaded for help and run away had gotten under Meredith's skin. She was haunted by those dark, secretive eyes and the thought that the young woman might not be quite sane.

Why had Gage come to the agency? Everything he had told them had reinforced their thinking that Sapphire Riverton needed the help of psychiatrists not detectives. Still, Gage had gone out of his way, even risking his job, to ask them to help her if they could. *They don't like strangers prying into their private business*, he had said, and something about getting run out of Dodge by the ranch foreman.

For that matter, why had Sapphire come to them? *"I know who you are...my grandma...,"* she had said. Gage didn't know what that meant any more than they did. At least, he said he didn't.

Could they be certain that Gage was telling the truth? Why had the veterinary student seeking a barn manager's job come all the way to Georgia? Weren't there opportunities in his home state of Texas—probably more than were available in this part of the South? Maybe it signified nothing beyond a chance to earn the next semester's tuition at university, like he said.

Who was this grandmother Sapphire had mentioned? How did she know the name "Bellefontaine"? A search through Ron's old files after Maggie Lu's departure had revealed no reference to the name "Riverton." If there was some connection, it had been lost in the agency fire.

Well, in a little while they would head to the once famous Riverton Estate—or Ranch as it was now called. If there was nothing they could do for Sapphire, they would return the money she had left behind and get on with business. There were other cases to attend to. "A lady has to make a living," she said aloud to GK, who was up on all fours now, tail swishing impatiently. As clear a plea for breakfast as he ever made.

Her cell rang just as she was ready to leave the house at eight forty-five. Sherri Lynn's number. She accepted the call with a hand gone suddenly tense.

"Hi, it's me, Sherri Lynn. Sorry to bother you so early—"

Meredith's daughter-in-law rarely phoned during the week except perhaps to confirm a visit. Or if she happened to be coming to Savannah to shop. She had a few favorite places she liked to browse on her own without Carter or the children along. "No problem, honey. You all right?" Had something happened to Carter or one of the kids? She swallowed a lump just beginning to form.

"We're fine," she said. "Sorry to alarm you. I just—well, I just wanted to chat for a minute."

"Great. It's always good to hear your voice. And I'm so looking forward to you all coming for Thanksgiving this year. I'm going to have all our traditional favorites, but I'm planning a new stuffing recipe, and I hope you're going to bring your special scalloped oyster dish. The kids won't like it, but Chase and I will fight over it. And don't forget your honeyed-lime fruit salad that everyone likes so much. Wouldn't be Thanksgiving without it." Meredith pictured her daughter-in-law with phone in hand. Straight honey-colored hair pushed back from her ears. Soft brown eyes serious, soulful.

"I can't believe how quickly the holiday is coming," Sherri Lynn said. "It seems like the months fly past, and you can hardly see them go."

Meredith laughed in agreement, and the conversation lapsed. Sherri Lynn seemed to want to say something. Or was Meredith imagining it? The fifth of seven children growing up on a farm, Sherri Lynn had learned to cope. And more than cope—she was a wonderful mother to Kaden and Kinsley. Meredith glanced at the clock on the wall. Her grandchildren would have boarded their school bus by eight. "Kids get off to school all right?" she asked into the silence.

Meredith heard an intake of breath and something that sounded like a sigh. "Actually, only Kaden went today." Sherri Lynn allowed a lengthy pause before adding, "Kinsley isn't feeling well. It's nothing serious," she added quickly. "She has a little stomachache, so I thought it best…" Another pause.

In a flash, Meredith was back in her living room finishing coffee with Carter after their salmon steaks. *Kinsley didn't want to go to school. Last week it was a headache…a phase she's going through.* She remembered the knot of worry on Carter's forehead and her own quick concern. Kinsley was usually full of stories about things she was learning in school, the games they played at recess, and the teacher she thought walked on water.

"Sherri Lynn," Meredith said carefully into the phone, "Carter told me Kinsley's been a bit difficult lately. Do you think something happened at school that's worrying her?"

There was a slight tremor in the soft voice. "I don't know. She won't talk to me about it. Just clams up when I ask her, and you know that's not like her."

No, indeed it wasn't. But then again, things changed as children grew. Sometimes kids seemed to sprout up right before your eyes. Kinsley had decided last month that her favorite color was no longer pink. If Gran bought her new curtains for her room, she wanted blue ones now. "Have you talked with her teacher?"

"I did. She says Kinsley's work is really good, that she's attentive in class, though a little quieter than usual." Sherri Lynn's voice tapered off, and the silence lingered a bit too long.

"Honey, I'm sorry. Maybe she just needs a little time...." Meredith stopped, sensing that Sherri Lynn had something more to say. "Do you want me to talk to her? Maybe she and Gran should have a playdate—just the two of us. What do you think?"

"That would be great." Relief echoed in Sherri Lynn's voice. "Actually, she doesn't have school on Friday. Teachers are having an in-service day. I planned to take the kids with me to Savannah to see my sister, but Kinsley would much rather see you than her aunt Bella. I could drop her off for a few hours. Do you think that would work for you?"

"I'll make it work," Meredith said. "You know how much I love spending time with that sweet girl."

"It means a lot to me," Sherri Lynn said. "I mean *you* do. You're such an important part of her life. Of all our lives." She hesitated, and Meredith guessed Sherri Lynn was thinking of her own family. Since her mother's death seven years ago the family had grown distant—especially since Sherri Lynn and Carter had moved to

Charleston. None of the family had approved of Sherri Lynn moving away from Savannah, but her sister Bella had always been the most difficult and critical.

Meredith wished she could put her arms around Sherri Lynn through the phone. She was such a devoted mom and loved keeping their home beautiful and comfortable. She also loved entertaining, whether for a planned party or for an impromptu business meeting for Carter's boss. Meredith couldn't have wished for a better, more loving daughter-in-law. "I'll see you Friday. And just know that I'm praying for her, for the right way to help."

Sherri Lynn's voice grew stronger. "Your prayers are the best gift of all. Thank you so much."

***

"So, do you think we should have called ahead? Made an appointment maybe?" Julia asked later that day after she and Meredith pulled away from the agency parking lot, picked up Highway 17, and were traveling south on 144.

"We agreed that the element of surprise might be the best way to see life as it is at the Riverton Ranch, didn't we?" Meredith asked, adjusting her seat belt across her lap.

"Just second-guessing," Julia said with a shrug. "I confess I'm a little nervous about how we're going to handle this when we get there."

"We're there to see Sapphire Riverton and return something that belongs to her, that's all." Meredith patted her pocketbook, which contained the ten one-hundred-dollar bills. "Mohammad won't come to the mountain, so the mountain is going to Mohammad."

"Well, let's hope Mohammad is up for a visit," Julia said.

"According to Google Maps, we can keep following 144 along Blackbeard Creek past Fancy Hall, then hit those small back roads until we get to the ranch," Meredith said. "Forty-five minutes. A bit of a commute between home and the shop where Gage said Sapphire works."

"And to her uncle's clinic," Julia added, gazing appreciatively on the landscape. "But this isn't so bad. There's lots of serene countryside to calm the nerves."

Meredith obeyed yet another directive from the insistent GPS. "That property isn't exactly on the beaten path," Meredith said. "Their place isn't something you'd just happen upon. Guess the Rivertons like their privacy."

After several more turns, they rounded a bend and followed a road bordered on both sides by thick cottonwoods and pine. Branches groped across the expanse as though trying to touch each other. When they reached a clearing, Meredith saw miles of traditional rope fencing and browning pastureland spread beneath a topaz sky. Horses grazed with tails swishing, their beautiful, muscled necks bending to nip spare blades of grass.

"They're magnificent, aren't they?" Meredith said. "Those are some of the finest quarter horses I've ever seen. And there's an Arabian. I can tell by its distinctive head shape and the high tail carriage. Arabians have great stamina and win a lot of competitive trail and endurance rides."

"I didn't know you were so well informed about the equine species," Julia said, following Meredith's pointing finger to a beautiful white horse tossing its elegant head as it gamboled across the field.

"Even city girls love horses, especially when they're teenagers. I had trading cards of every known breed. On my fifteenth birthday I talked Dad into taking me riding along the coast. And Ron and I took the boys on trail rides."

"Maybe that's where your Kinsley gets her fondness for horses." Julia smiled as they whizzed along past fields of corn and pecan groves as well as what looked like soybeans.

The road forked at a sign with an arrow pointing to the right that read, RIVERTON RIDING STABLES. That was where they could find Gage, who had cautioned them that his job might be in jeopardy if Mr. Riverton knew he had contacted them.

"So, the left fork probably goes to the homestead, wouldn't you think, Jules?" Meredith asked. She turned at Julia's murmur of agreement and continued past sturdy outbuildings and fields where farm workers went about their busy activities. They saw gleaming farm machinery, a late-model pickup truck, and assorted other vehicles as the road wound upward. They came to another crossroad, this one overhung by trees and brush with a wooden gate closing it off to traffic.

"I bet that leads to that old garden I heard about, the one no one takes care of anymore," Julia said.

"Years ago, before I joined the historical society board, I read that it was a real showplace—a draw for tourists," Meredith remarked. "That was before the old mansion burned."

"It sure looks forlorn—creepy almost—with all those crumbling statues and weeds," Julia said, shaking her head. "In any case, it looks like Riverton hasn't spent any of his money keeping it up."

"He's put his millions into that instead!" Meredith exclaimed as they turned onto a wide, well-cleared road.

The two-story pebble-stone structure directly ahead was magnificent with gabled roof and sturdy walnut-stained columns. The house had a surprising number of windows from double-hung casements to charming dormers and broad bays. Two huge verandas—front and side—were overhung with ivy and wisteria. Around the side of the house, the turquoise glint of a swimming pool reflected the morning sun.

They parked in the handsome circular driveway and ducked under a decorative archway to the front door. Meredith locked eyes with Julia and lifted her hand to knock.

But the door was swung open, revealing a young woman with enviable curves and a bandana tied over dark cherry-streaked hair. She peered out at them through sharp, close-set eyes. She wore a butcher-style apron over jeans, and a dish towel was swung over one shoulder. The maid, Meredith thought with amused surprise, minus the stereotypical starched cap and white apron. The young woman looked from Meredith to Julia, discontent in her expression.

"Never mind. I will take care of this." At the maid's elbow, a woman appeared with glossy black hair parted in the middle and pulled into a chignon. Thick penciled brows arched above almond-shaped mahogany eyes. Her mouth lifted in a genteel smile. But wariness lingered in her face. "Yes? How may I help you ladies?"

Meredith guessed her age at fifty to fifty-five, her light accent Spanish. "Hello," she said brightly, reaching for a nonchalance she didn't feel. "We're looking for Sapphire Riverton. Is she at home perhaps?"

"Sapphire?" she repeated, as though testing an unfamiliar name. The brown eyes tinged with gold roved between her visitors. She cleared her throat and folded slim, jeweled hands over her waist, where a wide belt separated her embroidered white blouse from her dark blue skirt. The skirt had a slight ruffle at the hem just above her sandaled feet.

Victoria Montoya Cannon of *High Chaparral* fame, Meredith thought, surprised at the memory of the TV series from the late sixties, which still aired on retro TV. The woman before them was a little older than the actress, a little less ingenuous, but elegant, lacking only a lace tiara on her proud head.

"I see," she said after a slightly too long pause. "What is it you wish to see her about?"

"We just want to return something she left when we met on Monday," Meredith said, distracted by the luxurious surroundings beyond the entrance alcove. The place was palatial with a grand staircase and a glittering chandelier that might rival furnishings of the pre-seventies' mansion that had been razed.

"I shall see that she gets it," she said pleasantly, eyes unreadable.

"We'd really prefer to talk to Sapphire," Julia said evenly, her friendly demeanor intact.

A small sigh escaped the woman's carefully drawn lips, but the polite exterior remained. "Who are you, please?"

"Meredith Bellefontaine, and this is Julia Foley. We represent Magnolia Investigations."

Her eyes glittered slightly and settled. Detectives coming to the door seldom put anyone at ease.

From a doorway, the head of the maid suddenly appeared then ducked away. Meredith heard no sound of footsteps moving on, meaning the maid was likely eavesdropping. Meredith met the eyes of the older woman and waited for a response.

"I am Elena Riverton," she said, her chin rising. "Sapphire is my husband's niece. He is her legal guardian." She sighed again and this time stepped back from the door with a little sweep of one hand. "I am sorry if she has caused you some inconvenience...but you need to understand. Sapphire is fragile. This is not a good time to disturb her."

"We only want a moment," Meredith said hastily, glancing toward the winding staircase where one could imagine debutantes in voluminous skirts ascending and descending. "We won't keep her long, and we'll try not to upset her."

"She is not available just now. As I said, I will be glad to give her a message or whatever it is you say belongs to her—" She broke off, blinking, lips slightly parted.

Meredith waited, torn between giving the money to Elena Riverton or holding on to it until...*until what?* Sapphire wasn't yet twenty-one and was still living at home. A more than adequate home from all appearances. And according to Gage, she was receiving emotional and mental support. And yet... "I think we'd like to return her property to her in person," she said. "Could you ask her to call us?" She smiled and held out a business card.

Lines appeared around the ruby lips. "You will have to speak to my husband," she said without inflection. Her chin rose another inch or two. "Theodore Riverton—*Doctor* Theodore Riverton. Perhaps you are aware of the Riverton Clinic?"

So Gage had been right that Sapphire might be at the clinic, perhaps being treated for whatever troubled her, whatever had sent her running to strange detectives with a thousand-dollar retainer.

Before Meredith could respond, a door at the top of the grand staircase opened noisily, and a frenzied voice made everyone turn and stare, including the blue-jeaned maid lurking in the corner.

A thin woman in a red dressing gown, gray hair wild and twizzled, stood on the landing. In her arms was a doll, an oversized Raggedy Ann with one stuffed arm flopping outside a blue blanket.

"*Shh*!" the old woman hissed. "Go away! You'll wake up my baby!" She peered into the doll's face and began to hum a tune unlike any lullaby Meredith had ever heard. The haunting, infinitely sad singsong sent a chill rippling through her.

"Lara!" Elena's voice was a sharp whisper. "Go and help Granny T back into bed!" As the maid rushed up the steps, Elena moved gracefully toward the landing, looking up at the woman with the doll. "It's all right now, Thelma," she cooed. "It's all right. Lara will take you back to your room."

Meredith glanced at Julia, whose face reflected her own shock. She drew in a quick breath and turned to Elena. "We'll be on our way now," she said, backing up. "We're sorry to disturb you."

She wasn't sure whether she had said goodbye or not as she swept down the circular drive with Julia on her heels.

Chapter Six

"I KNOW THIS IS LAST-MINUTE, but any chance I can take you to dinner tonight?"

Quin's voice was just the tonic Meredith needed after the day she and Julia had spent, but it wouldn't do to sound too glad. If it had been anyone else but the handsome silver-haired lawyer who was winning her heart by degrees, she would have declined. She had thought to heat up leftovers from last night's supper and go to bed.

Quin had been away, and she would have missed him if so much hadn't been happening to keep her busy. Oh, who was she kidding? Of course she had missed him. Arthur Quin Crowley, attorney at law, had been often on her mind.

"You're back! How was your trip? How's Grace?"

"That's two questions," Quin said roguishly, "and it will take at least two hours to tell you. So, dinner? How's seven?"

She agreed and, after a little more chitchat, clicked off, remembering the first time she had met Quin. They'd run into each other while she was on a case. Well, to be truthful, she had run into him—literally. Irritation had been mixed with attraction for the handsome lawyer with arresting eyes who had moved to Savannah after the death of his wife. Their friendship might have ended when she learned that he was defending a miscreant trying to cheat Maggie

Lu out of her inheritance. As it turned out, Quin had ended up help-ing Maggie Lu defend her right to the Bessett mansion.

And now they would have dinner together. She dressed care-fully, her mind still busy with what she had seen and heard at the Riverton mansion. And then there was the matter of Kinsley's sud-denly not wanting to go to school. Meredith was worrying, and she knew worry could be exhausting—not to mention of little use to change situations. But she would give her best to helping these people whom God had placed in her path. She found herself eagerly looking forward to Quin's company.

Later as Meredith sat across from him at the restaurant that had become a favorite, she thought he looked more rested than he had in a while. Working hard was a trademark, though he could name his own hours and choose his own cases. He was taking things much easier now, he had told her. When his daughter was growing up, he had missed out on a lot, and his wife and daughter, Quin had wor-ried, had good reason to resent it. His wife had died six years ago. There could be no making up for the past with Andrea, and Meredith knew that was a source of regret for Quin. But for now, he was look-ing at her intently, admiration in his glance.

He lifted his water glass as though in a toast to her. There was real sparkle in his unique bicolored eyes that had first attracted her when he had emerged from his Land Rover nearly two years ago with a black umbrella in hand. He had demanded to know what she thought she was doing trying to park in the space he already occupied.

She had been distracted in the storm and bumped right into his back bumper. He had been rather smug about it all, and she had been embarrassed and angry, not so much because he had been right but because he had let her off the hook. *"No need to phone the incident in; no harm done really."* Except to her pride. But he had begun to win her over from that first moment.

"Grandfathering agrees with you," she said, noting the glow of good health in his face. As a lawyer, he spent a lot of time indoors taking depositions and holding briefings. But when he could, he enjoyed the great outdoors and was teaching his six-year-old grand-daughter to love nature too.

"My daughter says I spoil her," he said with a sidelong look at Meredith. Jamie was a busy real estate agent in Columbus whom Quin said he had neglected far too much when she was growing up. He had determined never to let his work bring distance between him and his loved ones again. "I probably do spoil her," he said, "but she's growing up so fast, and she's such a great kid. You should see her on that pony. Grace has named her Penelope."

Meredith laughed. "Penny, for short?"

"Well, you would expect that, wouldn't you? But Gracie is full of surprises. She says a penny is far too small and insignificant. The pony will be called Penelope and only Penelope."

Meredith liked the way Quin's smile softened when he spoke of his granddaughter. His heterochromatic eyes shone. At first glance, eyes of different colors might be distracting, but they worked together in amazingly unique balance, reminding her of shimmering water tinted by sun. His skin had the coppery glow of a man who liked the outdoors. He'd been a redhead, and now silver glistened in the thick strands of hair.

"The Welsh pony is the smallest of the riding ponies—forty-eight inches—twelve hands—and good for beginners, especially young ones. Penelope has a sweet manner and is more reliable than the temperamental Shetland. She's pretty too with a dark gray coat, four white socks, and a white blaze."

Meredith was thinking that Grace was a lucky girl to have a grandpa like Quin. A gentle champion of the underdog with a thirst for justice. A man of the world, perhaps, but ruled by a heart attuned to its Creator. "Penelope sounds perfect," she said, and from thoughts of Quin's Grace, she was catapulted to concern for Kinsley. What changes were going on in her life? What trouble caused her to suddenly make excuses for not going to school?

"A Penelope for your thoughts—or rather, a penny."

"Hmm?" Meredith looked up, realizing she hadn't heard what Quin had just said. "I'm sorry." She released an embarrassed breath. "I was thinking about my granddaughter."

"Ah, how is your Kinsley, and Kaden too? Great kids. You're rightly proud of them."

"Yes, I am. Like someone said, if I'd known how wonderful grandchildren were, I'd have had them first." She chuckled at the trite joke, but her heart was heavy. Grandparents might think they could spoil the kids for a day or two and send them back to Mom and Dad without worry. The truth was grandchildren made permanent imprints on the heart, and one felt their every footfall.

Quin was looking at her, a little frown perched between his eyebrows. A long moment passed between them before he said, "Something bothering you, Meredith?"

She paused as the waiter brought their entrees. Chicken and dumplings for Quin, who was, after all, an old-fashioned kind of guy. She had ordered shrimp and grits, a decidedly Southern specialty.

"It's about Kinsley. Sherri Lynn phoned this morning before I left for the office. She's concerned about her. So is Carter, though he says it's probably just a phase she's going through." She shrugged. "He may be right, but lately Kinsley hasn't wanted to go to school. She's been faking stomachaches and staying home."

"Ah, I used to pull that one every time there was an English test." Quin made a face. "It rarely worked, and when it did it always backfired." He sobered, seeing Meredith's frown, and cleared his throat. "Will she talk about it?" he asked.

"Sherri Lynn says she just clams up and won't say what's bothering her. It's not like her. She usually chatters on about school. Always loved it, and she's an excellent student." She smoothed her napkin over her lap and studied it a while before looking up. "Anyway, I'm going to spend Friday with her. Kids are off for teacher's in-service day or something. Maybe I can help. I sure hope so."

Quin reached across the table and laid his hand over hers where it was poised on the fork beside her plate. The comfort of it touched her, and she would have been happy to stay in that moment a long time.

"I'm not sure where we could go for a day of fun," she said, feeling her color rise. "She's a little past the doll and tea party stage."

"She likes animals," Quin said. "And nothing quite compares with enjoying them in the great outdoors. Einstein said, 'Look deep into nature, and then you will understand everything better.'" He angled his head. "Maybe you could go on a trail ride with her. You can get a gentle horse that won't scare you."

"Hey, I'll have you know I used to be a passable horsewoman back in the day."

"One more thing I'm learning about you," Quin said, tenderness in his gaze. "There's something about girls and horses, isn't there?" He gave her hand a squeeze before letting go. "They seem to have a natural affinity, and they don't grow out of it. I read somewhere that girls express their own power by identifying with the strong, dynamic horse."

She recalled the magnificent horses she'd seen in Riverton's pastures. There was a lot to dazzle the eye at that big ranch. As quickly came the image of a wild-eyed old woman holding a rag doll at the top of a grand staircase, pleading for them not to wake her baby.

Meredith looked up, aware again of her inattention. She heard herself sigh.

"Try not to worry too much," he said.

"I'll try," she promised, smiling across at him with profound gratitude for his gentleness, his caring heart. "I'm sorry I'm such a downer tonight, but this has been quite a day and not just personal stuff." She hadn't intended to, but she shared what had happened on Monday and how she and Julia had tried to visit Sapphire Riverton.

"Riverton..." Quin repeated the name, drawing his brows together. "Would that be Theodore Riverton, who owns that very elite spa and health clinic?"

"That's the one. I don't know much about it. Do you?"

"It's only been in operation a few years, so it doesn't have a long history. Where Savannah is concerned, neither do I. There's a lot I don't know about this city." He raised an eyebrow. "I heard, however, that there were a few legal hassles to handle before the opening." He frowned. "But money can find loopholes to crawl through."

Meredith had a quick flash of memory from her afternoon at the third precinct. Had Wally recognized Sapphire Riverton from her description as well as the grainy camera image? "Were you involved in any of those proceedings?" Meredith asked, studying his face.

"No. That's not the kind of case I want to handle—even if it was offered. Which it wasn't. Likely the Riverton Ranch has its own lawyers who have been handling their affairs for years."

"We researched the history of the Rivertons, of course," Meredith said, "but it was pretty sketchy by the third generation. The old Riverton Estate was built by Preston A. Riverton, a wealthy British immigrant, just before the turn of the century. It was passed on to his only son, Preston Jr., who managed it until the late 1980s, when Preston III inherited."

"So how did Theodore get mixed into all those Prestons?"

"He's the half brother of Preston III, whose father married again when his first wife died. It's all very confusing. In any case, since the death of Sapphire's father, Theodore has been managing the estate."

"Managing an estate in addition to a clinic here in town," Quin commented. "Not only a rich landowner but a licensed psychologist with his own private clinic."

"You should see the home that took the place of the mansion that burned down. I'm sure it's been through a few renovations since the nineties because it's state-of-the-art and nothing short of palatial." She took a swallow of her coffee. "Riverton Estate never made it onto the national register of historic homes, so when I was historical director, we didn't pay it much attention. By then it was a ranch, mostly breeding horses and quite a way south of Savannah, not on the way to anything. I never saw the house that replaced the mansion until today."

"I haven't seen it. Don't get down that way very often, but Theodore Riverton is a name that carries a lot of weight. Money talks, and he's got plenty."

Meredith saw that Quin's eyebrows hadn't yet unclenched. "Yes," she said. "I hear that he has his finger in a lot of pies—besides that posh clinic. Supposedly, his niece works at one of the boutiques he owns near City Market—when she isn't being treated at the clinic. That cowboy who came to the agency says she has her own bungalow where she goes to receive treatment."

"Family perks," Quin remarked.

"He also said he didn't think her uncle's health clinic was doing her much good. Seems to genuinely care about the girl, but we don't know a lot about him. Carmen trolled the social media sites for Sapphire Riverton and came up empty. It's hard to believe at her age that she has no personal life—at least that we found in our cursory checks."

"This sounds like a convoluted case. Is it a case?" Quin angled his head to consider her. "You said Gage thinks she wants to know something about her mother."

"There's really nothing to investigate on that score. The record clearly states, 'accidental death.' That was seventeen years ago, Sapphire couldn't have been more than three or four years old." She sighed. "That young lady needs the kind of professional help Julia and I can't give her."

"Supposedly she can get that kind of help from her own family, can't she?" Quin asked.

"I almost gave Mrs. Riverton the money Sapphire gave to me before she ran off. I didn't tell her it was a thousand dollars. She offered to return it for me, but something stopped me. I don't know what."

Quin studied her through serious eyes.

Meredith felt a shiver and rubbed her upper arms, remembering Granny T cradling a doll in her arms. She knew that some patients who suffered from dementia or Alzheimer's reverted to an earlier, happier time in their memories, even to early childhood. She replayed in her mind Granny T's plea not to wake her baby and Elena's crooning, *"It's all right now, Thelma. It's all right."* Was Sapphire as unstable as her grandmother appeared to be?

"What are you planning to do?"

"We'll do what Elena said we must if we want to see Sapphire. We'll go to the clinic and talk to Uncle Theodore."

Quin ran a hand across his jaw. "You and Julia do get yourselves into some unusual scrapes." He paused. "You will be careful, right?"

"You sound like Carter."

"Sorry. I know you can take care of yourself. But I don't promise not to worry about you." He closed his brown eye in a slow wink. "But you look like you need a good night's rest, so I think I'd better get you home."

It was comforting to ride next to Quin in his Land Rover, to watch his hands with their fine copper and silver hairs manipulate the steering wheel. The leather bucket seats had a console between them, but she was close enough to feel his warmth and strength. She closed her eyes, at ease, not wishing to be anywhere in that moment but beside him.

Drifting in a satisfied haze, she didn't realize at first that Quin had made a few unusual turns. Maybe there had been detour signs and she'd missed them. But when he sped up and swerved again, she turned to him in surprise. "What's wrong?"

He didn't immediately answer, and she saw that he was staring into his rearview mirror.

"Maybe nothing, but that truck behind us might be following us. I'm testing to see if it really is." He spoke in a low voice, as though fearing someone could overhear.

"What?" Meredith turned around in the seat and looked back at the road behind them.

A pickup truck drove several yards behind the Land Rover, its headlights obscuring detail on the dark vehicle. It slowed when Quin slowed and sped up when he did. "You think he's following us?" she asked incredulously.

"That cowboy you told me about—does he drive a pickup?"

"No." She pictured the slightly battered Jeep Gage Gallagher had parked near the agency when he'd come to see them the day before. There had been a pickup at the Riverton ranch—along with an assortment of other vehicles and farm equipment though. Company issue. Maybe Gage had borrowed one.

"The driver is wearing a big cowboy hat."

Gage Gallagher wouldn't be following them, would he? What would be the point? He had come asking for their assistance. He wanted to help. Didn't he? Why would he follow her?

Quin kept on driving, his eyes narrowed and watchful. But she saw he wasn't heading to her house. Instead, she recognized the neighborhood of the Central District's new police building. Twisting around again, Meredith saw the pickup make a left turn and speed away down the road.

"Do you really think he was following us?" she asked as he drew up along the curb a block or so from the precinct.

"It sure seemed like it. I noticed that pickup when we left the restaurant. Wish I'd gotten a look at the guy's face or the license plate." He grimaced. "Any reason you can think of why that cowboy might be tailing us? Tailing you?"

"None at all. Gallagher said he wanted us to help Sapphire. He seemed genuine."

"We're talking about a guy who hides in the bushes and spies on people," he interjected.

"Well, yes, he did at first, but he explained all that, and he did come and face us the next day." Meredith felt her pulse racing. *He's not the only guy in Savannah who dresses like a cowboy*, she thought. She expelled an exasperated breath. "But if he's pulling something…"

She whipped out her cell phone and punched in the number Gallagher had supplied. He'd given it to her freely, asking her not to divulge his interest in Sapphire to his boss.

Two rings and a recorded message. "Gallagher. Leave a message."

Okay, so he was busy or not picking up. Didn't mean he was out spying on her, did it? But if he was…

She tamped down a sudden flare of suspicion and cleared her throat. She knew exactly how Julia would handle Gage. "Meredith

Bellefontaine here," she said. "Call me ASAP. It's important." She ended the call and tucked her phone in her purse.

"Remind me not to mess with you," Quin said.

She took several deep breaths and felt herself calming. "I can't believe he'd do that, but I'll find out. He seems like a good guy, like he really wants to help Sapphire."

Quin reached over and put his hand over hers. She gave his fingers a squeeze. "Whoever that was, he probably wasn't following us," she said, more to assure herself than to Quin.

"Maybe not, but I hate to think of leaving you alone at your house tonight. Want to stop in at the precinct?"

"And say what? Someone might have been following us, but we don't know who, or even if? No, Quin." Weariness washed over her like a flood. "I think I just want to go home."

Chapter Seven

Garnet Georgianna stood in the doorway of the apartment where she had grown up. She radiated quality from the pale blue afternoon dress to the silken shawl draped over her shoulders. Her summer sandals had tiny rhinestones in them and showed off freshly manicured pink nails.

Thelma studied her daughter, watching her wave to the driver of the Rolls-Royce Special as it pulled away from the curb. After the visit, the chauffeur would return to take her home.

Thelma drew her close, loving the sweet fragrance of her. She smelled like honeysuckle, the wildflower that grew in chaotic profusion behind the shop.

"It's so good to be home, Mama."

"Of course, this will always be your home, Gigi, but you have your own now—a dream house like you always wanted. A home fit for a princess."

"I know, Mama, but sometimes I just miss being here. Most of all, I miss you." The mass of blond curls had been

tamed into a smooth pageboy so perfect that Thelma felt a pang of jealousy. Could she, a seasoned hairdresser, have done as well as the posh, uptown stylist Preston had engaged for his new wife?

"Oh, sweetheart. I miss you too!" She pushed back from the embrace to look into the guileless sea-blue eyes of her daughter and swallowed something that tasted like fear. Surely her little girl was happy, wasn't she? It was all Thelma ever wanted from life from the first moment she'd held her.

It had been four months since the fairy-tale wedding on the luxurious lawn where the handsome Preston Riverton III and Garnet Georgianna Chambers had taken their vows. The music of the orchestra had spun a magic rainbow over the small assembled group. The preacher had declared the couple one, and they had kissed beneath an arbor of pink roses and white magnolias. The bride's gown, a stunning creation of pearls and lace, flowed like a snow-spilled mountain stream to the ground. The satin train draped the manicured emerald lawn of the house that gleamed in the May sunshine. With its sleek lines, its columns and dormer windows, it was pure elegance, magnificence in every stone and beam.

The couple had honeymooned in Aruba, returning with glistening tans and a cargo of expensive souvenirs. Gigi's eyes had sparkled as she described the beauty that surrounded her, the affection of her new husband who loved to show her off, declaring that he had the most beautiful wife in the world.

"You look happy," Thelma said softly. "You are, aren't you, Gigi?"

"Of course, Mama. Dreams come true, just like you always told me. I have everything I ever wanted."

Indeed, there was a glow about her, the way a newlywed should look. And what mother could have asked for a better match? Her daughter would never want for anything—never forage in an empty refrigerator for something to fill her stomach, never be cold on a winter night. Maybe that was why Thelma had filled her daughter's mind with stories of wonder and possibility—hope for things she herself had never had. And still did not, for all her hard work, scrimping, and saving.

"I wish you would come back with me. There's lots of room in that big house." Garnet's forehead puckered. "I miss you."

Thelma was touched, but there was no way she would intrude on a young couple's new beginning. They needed to be alone, to learn the rhythm of the life they would create together. "You and Preston need this time for yourselves without relatives hanging around." She touched Gigi's cheek and the natural ruby-like lips that had inspired her name the day she was born. A garnet reflected light, created tiny rainbows that spun and danced. "Garnet"—precious gem. There must always be rainbows for her Gigi.

"But there's lots of people at the house," Garnet said, her lips forming a pout. "Lots of them, besides Preston's business

partner and the people who work there. Maids and a cook and..." She paused. "But sometimes..."

When Gigi's eyes dropped, Thelma tipped up her daughter's soft chin, inhaled the honeysuckle fragrance. "My work is here, Gigi. But you can call me anytime." She sensed her daughter wanted to tell her something. "What is it?" She found herself asking the same question again. "You are happy, aren't you?"

"Of course. It's just that I'm lonely. Preston is so busy now. He's gone a lot, and sometimes I just wish you and I could make peanut butter cookies together and..." She wrung her hands at her waist like she used to when a math problem didn't work out or when a picture she was coloring didn't meet her expectation. Her lower lip trembled almost imperceptibly. Thelma never missed the slightest nuance when it came to Gigi.

"I'm right here, sweetheart. I'll always be here for you." Thelma brushed back the pale hair from Gigi's forehead, suddenly hearing in the recesses of her memory as she had a few weeks earlier, "Don't go breaking my heart...."

"Oh, Mama. I'm just being silly. I know Preston's got to be away for his work sometimes and that I have to stay home alone, but I'm afraid." She shook her head as though to dispel her sadness. She turned up the corners of her mouth, and her blue eyes shone as though a candle had been lit. "I'm afraid because...I'm going to have a baby!"

Thelma blanched. Of course! What would be more natural? And yet the shock of it struck her. A baby! Gigi was so

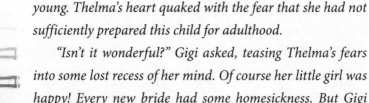

young. Thelma's heart quaked with the fear that she had not sufficiently prepared this child for adulthood.

"Isn't it wonderful?" Gigi asked, teasing Thelma's fears into some lost recess of her mind. Of course her little girl was happy! Every new bride had some homesickness. But Gigi was going to be a mother. And she, Thelma Louise Chambers, was going to be a grandmother!

"Wow! This is some place! Looks more like a private club. Do you think she's here now?" Julia stopped the car in a shady parking lot bounded by sculpted bushes and young trees carefully planted to enhance the elegant lines of a modern building that likely contained the offices. Situated on the beautiful acreage were some two dozen attractive cottages constructed of the same stone as the main building. Shrubs and flowers outside each cottage appeared carefully tended.

Was Sapphire Riverton in residence here? The tight-lipped Elena had been vague on the matter. Gage Gallagher, who hadn't yet returned her call, had said that Sapphire had her own private bungalow at her uncle's institution. "I can think of worse places to seek refuge from the world. Beautiful, isn't it?"

Julia pivoted to take in the elegant surroundings. "Impressive. Must have cost a fortune. From everything we read about Theodore Riverton though, he can afford it."

The sun, persistent even in November, was quickly warming the air. It glistened on the inlaid stone walkway that led to a sleek building with its natural stone veneer.

Glass double doors gleamed beneath an attractive wood-look canopy trimmed in dark blue. Meredith entered an upscale yet homelike waiting room that was split into smaller-scale seating zones. The cubicles were unoccupied, but people moved about in the hallway. She headed toward a mahogany reception desk trimmed in the same cobalt blue as the exterior canopy. A tall woman in a chic linen suit of cadmium yellow readjusted a vase of fall asters on the desk and smiled a welcome.

"We're here to see Dr. Riverton," Meredith said, extending a business card. "Meredith Bellefontaine and Julia Foley. I believe he's expecting us." There was no point in surprising him, for his wife had certainly outlined the details of their meeting at his home. So they had phoned for an appointment and now were right on time.

"I will let him know you are here," the receptionist said with a decided Jamaican accent. She pushed a button on her phone to announce their arrival.

Before Meredith could respond, an inner door opened, and a sturdy-looking sixty-plus man of medium height approached. He had white hair that curled at exaggerated sideburns and a smile that made deep parentheses on both sides of his face. Salt-and-pepper brows bushed over very dark eyes, giving him a weathered, out-doorsy look. Meredith could well imagine him in a gentleman rancher's flannel shirt and boots. His three-piece suit, however, clearly marked him as an executive, complete with a gold chain escalloped across his crimson necktie.

"Ladies, good morning. I'm Dr. Riverton." He reached his hand out to shake each of theirs in turn. "Follow me, please."

Bookshelves, certificates, and plaques lined the walls in the spacious office to which they were ushered. An uncluttered desk held an ebony pen holder and pen as well as a gold nameplate reading THEODORE RIVERTON with initials following in small print. The only other adornment was a costly-looking bronze statue of a stallion, hooves poised in the air. No pictures of loved ones in view, Meredith noted with some surprise as she and Julia took the chairs he indicated.

When he too sat down, he folded his hands on his desk in a casual pose. A practiced manner, perhaps, to put at ease guests who had issues for which they might seek his expertise.

Meredith had learned that Theodore Riverton earned his degree from the University of Pennsylvania. He was a psychologist, not a medical doctor as a psychiatrist was, and therefore couldn't prescribe drugs for a patient. After working ten years in a clinic in Philadelphia, he had stopped practicing and gone south to help his half brother run the ranch Preston had inherited. It would be interesting to know what led to such an abrupt career move. A move that now seemed to have come full circle to this clinic that catered to the wealthy.

He looked Meredith in the eye, his smile still in place. "And how is business at Magnolia Investigations?" he asked, holding her gaze.

How did one respond to such a question? She looked at him steadily. "Dr. Riverton, we're here about your niece, whom we met a few days ago. Actually, we'd very much like to talk to her."

"Ah." The parentheses widened. His thick fingers unfolded and refolded like thoughts seeking organization. "Elena tells me that my niece came to you with some frantic request for help. Something about her mother, yes?" But he didn't wait for an answer. He looked down at his hands for a quick moment and resumed. "You're not the first. She's been known to accost the mailman or a vendor near the boutique. Even a policeman. Yes, they know her down at the precinct, and to their credit they're very understanding and let us know when this happens so we can help."

Shocked by these revelations, Meredith's mind swirled with questions. Did Wally know Sapphire? Had he recognized her after all? She had come directly to Magnolia Investigations. She was looking for a Bellefontaine. It hadn't been a random reaching out. *"I know who you are…my grandma…"* Meredith pushed her questions aside and listened.

"Sapphire is a wonderful girl—smart and talented—and I couldn't love her more if she were my own daughter." He chuckled softly. "I practically raised her—even before the death of her father— God rest his soul." He shook his head slowly from side to side. "Sapphire suffers from an anxiety disorder that sometimes manifests itself in irrational behavior. She can be fine, able to function quite well for an extended period, and then…" He breathed heavily in a kind of half sigh. "Indeed, things have gone along quite smoothly until recently." He pursed his lips as though assailed by his thoughts then relaxed them. "Yes, quite smoothly, and then something happens to set her off."

Depression? Maybe something that triggered a clinical disorder?

A patient smile deepened the crevices in his cheeks. "As you know, psychology, like medicine in general, isn't an exact science."

Julia uncrossed one leg, crossed the other—her typical gesture of impatience, but like Meredith she did not interrupt.

Riverton leaned back, folded his hands in his lap. "It all began when she was quite young—after the death of her mother. In short, she's never really come to terms with it and somehow believes that she is to blame. Ridiculous, of course. She was only four years old when the accident happened."

Meredith remembered the scant details—a clear case of accidental death from a fall. There had been no mention of a child on the scene. She wondered if the doctor might elaborate on the tragic event.

"She has dreams in which she can hear her mother calling. And on occasion she suffers from somnambulism." The heavy brows lifted and fell. "Sleepwalking," he explained unnecessarily. "Sometimes patients can resolve whatever is troubling them through sleep, something the mind but not the will is trying to remember." He studied his hands briefly before looking up, his expression still affable but the dark eyes unreadable. "So you can see that it would not be in my niece's best interest for you to see her at this time." His broad smile remained fixed.

Meredith felt her pulse throb in her throat. Sapphire was twenty years old—of legal age. As such, they could speak to her directly if they chose to. But to all appearances, the young woman was not able to handle her own affairs. Her uncle was her legal guardian. What were the terms of that guardianship? Should Meredith and Julia simply turn over Sapphire's "retainer" to this man who, ostensibly at least, had her best interests at heart? *Who couldn't love her more if she were his own child?* Still, something kept Meredith from mentioning the money Sapphire had left with her.

"It may not be long before she feels ready to receive visitors," Theodore said in the vein of a doctor wishing to reassure a patient. "We are hopeful that she will be able to return home soon. She may contact you then if she wishes to, but if her behaviors mimic past episodes, she may forget all about approaching you."

Julia's legs were crossing and uncrossing with increasing frequency. She was clearly agitated. "If we may ask," she broke in, "does the woman we saw at your home suffer from a similar malady as Sapphire's? I believe your wife referred to her as 'Granny T.'"

Theodore released a slow breath. "Sapphire's maternal grandmother suffers from vascular dementia following a stroke. Sadly, it has left her with permanent damage, but Elena and our personal staff are able to keep her comfortable at home." He paused, the thick fingers closing around themselves once more. "You think perhaps that Sapphire's trouble derives from a family trait." He pursed his lips once more. "A genetic component may exist. We don't know for sure." He straightened in his chair and laid his hands flat on his desk.

Meredith read the sign—he wanted to end the interview, but she needed to hear more. She reached over to touch the bronze statue near the end of the desk. "This is a beautiful piece. My granddaughter would absolutely love it."

"A Friesian stallion," he said, his smile becoming brighter. "The breed is quite valuable and originated in Friesland in the Netherlands. It's valued for its ebon coloring and high-stepping gait."

"Beautiful," Meredith said. "You raise horses yourself, don't you?"

"A strong herd—and a few champions among them," he said proudly. He cocked his head. "You ride?" The peppery brows rose in his handsome face.

"Some, but Kinsley—that's my granddaughter—she's the one who's really crazy about horses. She's always cutting out pictures of some specimen or other."

"Ah!" he said vigorously. "Then you must bring her to Riverton Stables." He reached into his desk drawer, drew out a card, and handed it to her. "Just call and arrange it with my man. Tell him I sent you. He'll take good care of you."

My man? Gage Gallagher? His foreman or someone else connected with the ranch? "That's very kind of you," Meredith said. "We may just do that."

The doctor stood. "Not at all. Now as for that other matter..." He cleared his throat. "Your concern for my niece is appreciated, ladies, but I assure you that we have things in hand. I'm sorry for any inconvenience Sapphire may have caused you." He held out a hand as Meredith and Julia got up, his smile once more stretching across his rugged face. "Should we have need for detective services, I'm sure we would be well served by your agency. Magnolia Investigations on Whitaker Street, isn't it?" He gripped Meredith's hand in a strong grasp.

"Yes," she said, surprised at his accuracy. "We appreciate your time, and..." She drew a quick breath. "We wish you all the best with your work here, and with Sapphire."

"Yes," Julia added. "It's our hope and prayer that she'll find the strength and peace she needs."

The partners didn't speak until they reached the car. Meredith climbed in and clasped her purse in her lap. She heard her own deep exhalation.

"Well, that was interesting," Julia said as she put the key in the ignition. "What do you make of Theodore Riverton?"

"He was certainly amiable—friendly even—and anxious to protect his niece," Meredith said, troubled by her own inner confusion. This was hardly a case for them to deal with. Yet she hadn't spoken up about the money stored in their safe. "I wish we could talk to Sapphire, but this probably isn't a good time."

Julia was silent. "Probably," she said finally in a tone marked by uncertainty. "But I didn't like the way he talked down to us—like we didn't know what somnambulism is."

Meredith shrugged, smiling. "Yes," she agreed, "but his invitation opens a way to a possible visit with Sapphire. That's something."

"True, but I bet it'll be on his terms," Julia said.

"She is his patient, after all, and his niece. It's only logical he would protect her." Meredith glanced down at her purse, hearing the *bleep* from her phone announcing that a voice mail was waiting. She reached for her phone and saw the name. The call had come in earlier that morning. "Gage Gallagher," she read aloud, exchanging a glance with Julia. She put the phone on speaker and heard his hesitant baritone drawl:

"Ms. Bellefontaine... I got your message." Five or six seconds of silence, then, "You sound pretty upset with me and I—I don't know why." Another five seconds passed. "Sapphire didn't come home last night. Do you know if she's all right?" The message ended.

"All innocence," Julia grumbled. Meredith had told Julia about the pickup that had followed her and Quin the evening before. She rolled her eyes. "Call him back. See if he answers."

Six rings later he did. "Gallagher," he said, sounding slightly breathless. "Ms. Bellefontaine?"

Meredith had been chewing the inside of her lip. "Where were you last night around nine thirty?" she blurted, even as she chided herself for her quick presumption. But who else would have been following them except this stalker with a cowboy hat?

After a few seconds of strained silence, he said, "I was at home, ma'am. My days start at six every morning. Doesn't leave much time for night life. Have I done something? Has something happened to Sapphire?"

Meredith released a long breath. "You weren't in a dark pickup truck near City Market last night, following me?"

"No, ma'am, I wasn't." Wariness or irritation had crept into his smooth down-home drawl. "Where's Sapphire?"

Meredith considered this, catching the inside of her cheek again. "She's at the clinic. Dr. Riverton says she's fine." She thought she heard a small sigh of relief, which may or may not have been genuine. "We've just come from his office. We weren't allowed to see Sapphire and we didn't mention your name, but if you're really a friend of this troubled girl—"

Gage broke in. "Please, ma'am, could we talk somewhere? That is, if you're still willing to help us?"

Us? Thoughts whirled in Meredith's head. What did this young man know about Sapphire that they should know? Should she and Julia move forward with this case that Sapphire Riverton might forget all about?

She paused, debating with herself. She had a date with Kinsley, beginning at ten in the morning. Sherri Lynn was due to collect her afterward around three o'clock. Between now and five tomorrow— if Gallagher showed up—she'd have Julia and Carmen go over the barn manager's background with a fine-tooth comb. She cleared her throat. "Come to the agency tomorrow," she said into the phone. "I'll be busy until five o'clock. I can see you then."

"I'll be there," he said, and clicked off.

Chapter Eight

"GRAN!" KINSLEY FLUNG HER ARMS around Meredith's waist and buried her face in her soft flannel shirt.

Meredith snuggled her lovingly. She smelled of strawberry shampoo, November air, and the joy of life.

"Mom said I can stay all day at your house!" the little girl exclaimed, bringing her face up for Meredith's kiss. "Can we have chicken fingers and curly fries for lunch?"

"Now, Kinsley, you mind your manners," Sherri Lynn chided without managing to sound very stern. "Don't be asking Gran for everything in the world."

"Not everything, Mom—just chicken fingers and curly fries!" Kinsley's little ski-slope nose wrinkled, and her lips formed a good-natured pout. She had a high forehead like Carter's and fine cheekbones and a petite body like Sherri Lynn's. At four feet, three inches or so, she was just under average height for her age.

"Now, chicken fingers and curly fries are exactly what I've been hankering for," Meredith said, clasping Kinsley's warm cheeks in her hands. "After shopping all those garage sales this morning, we'll need something delicious." It was one of the things they liked to do together, and flush with her allowance, Kinsley would enjoy spending her own money.

"GK!" Kinsley squealed, spying the Russian Blue regarding her from the window seat. She ran toward him then slowed to a stop and knelt to pet his silky fur.

GK rose to his feet, an indulgent expression on his whiskery face, and submitted to Kinsley's fervent attentions. Meredith knew he would put up with it only so long before gracefully prancing out of reach. She smiled, delighted to see no trace of trouble on the little girl's features. Maybe Carter and Sherri Lynn were simply overreacting.

Kinsley seemed to have shot up an inch since Meredith had last seen her, surely not more than four weeks ago! The soft planes of her face appeared slightly more angular, but she was still the compact little package of Kinsley Faith. Meredith laughed at herself. She always marveled at how fast the children were growing and wished she could slow it down. But she couldn't keep them her babies forever.

"Now, you be ready by three," Sherri Lynn said, leveling her gaze on her daughter and kissing the top of her blond head. "Auntie Jean is expecting us for an early dinner." Then, with eyes filled up with thanks, she gave Meredith a wink and a kiss on the cheek. "You two have a happy day!" she called as she exited the front door of Meredith's house.

Kinsley raced into the kitchen and out onto the deck, which was one of the kids' favorite places in her house. They especially liked the soft chaise longue where they could stretch out and read or play on their tablets. They liked to pull books from the shelves kept filled with stories Meredith knew would appeal to them. She always slipped in a new one when they came for a visit.

Meredith brought out two tall glasses of sweet tea—well watered for Kinsley but with a generous slice of lemon and one of lime. "Well now, sweetheart, it's just us girls now. Will you miss your big brother today?"

"He's not so big. He's only one year older than me!" Kinsley touched the tall glass to her lips. "He's staying with Auntie Jean and Mom." She scrunched up her nose. "Probably going to talk about bugs and frogs and stuff. Yuck!"

"Probably," Meredith assented. Kaden was interested in astronomy, but he also found bugs and frogs and all manner of living things fascinating. He excelled in his studies too, though other parts of school life could be a real challenge for him. Like many children with Asperger's, he struggled in social situations because of an inability to connect with other people's emotions. It could cause younger children particularly to become alienated. Meredith knew there had to be times when he was treated unkindly.

To what degree Kinsley understood why Kaden behaved in certain ways, Meredith wasn't sure. But the two had a special bond, and Kinsley was fiercely protective of her brother. Still, Meredith knew it might sometimes be difficult for Kinsley to defend him when curious peers pointed out his behaviors.

"It's okay, I guess," Kinsley said, finishing the last drop of her tea. "But I don't like bugs. Kittens and horses—they're my favorite."

"Well, my little animal lover, we'd better get going before all the good stuff is gone." Meredith had made a list of sales in the area, marking those that had items of interest to young girls. While summer was the biggest season for yard and garage sales, there were plenty in the area in the still-temperate month of November. "Grab your purse and let's go!"

Meredith had given Kinsley a fabric purse in the shape of a cat's head that she'd made, complete with yarn whiskers and emerald-green eyes like GK's. Kinsley picked it up along with her blue corduroy jacket, and after an ardent farewell to GK, she piled into Meredith's SUV.

It was wonderful to see Kinsley so buoyant and cheerful as they drove along together. Kinsley hummed a tune she'd likely learned in Sunday school—one Meredith recognized, which pleased her since she found many of the new songs inscrutable. She hummed along on a few bars, restraining herself from thinking how the "oldies" were much better than modern songs.

They spent at least an hour and a half perusing several sales. There were interesting and practical items, but neither she nor Kinsley found anything that really grabbed them. They exclaimed over things, laughed about them, and made guesses on some odd items that seemed to have no particular purpose. Then they moved on to the next, sometimes having a ten-cent lemonade from children whose mothers ran sales.

"Ah, here's one that looks promising," Meredith said as a rambling clapboard house with charming blue shutters came into view. She parked along the curb next to a short driveway bordered on each side by tables holding colorful items—from cloth to plastics, dolls to dishes—an infinite variety.

Kinsley behaved herself in a dignified ten-year-old way, perusing the items, touching only occasionally, and careful not to break anything. Two women sat at a small table to one side of the garage, one intent on a pad of paper that probably listed items sold and prices paid. The other folded baby clothes. They chatted to each other, eyeing occasionally the few patrons at the tables. They smiled at Meredith and Kinsley and left them to check out their wares.

Meredith watched Kinsley. She was very particular—not grabbing for the first item that merited more than a five-second look. There were several dolls, including one very grown-up one with lovely copper hair and jeweled eyes. Kinsley cocked her head, considered for a long moment, and moved on. Meredith left her for a few moments, turning her attention to a table with china in a particularly pleasing pattern. She chuckled, hearing Julia in her head.

"More china? You've enough to host the queen's retinue now!"

And she would be right. She passed it up, kept perusing, keeping Kinsley in her peripheral sights. A moment or two later, she realized Kinsley's attention had been focused on one table for a considerable time. She moved over to see what had taken her fancy.

"He's beautiful!" Kinsley said in a whisper. The item was a figurine of a gleaming black mare with a foal of the same ebony coat nuzzled alongside. Each had a white star between gentle, soulful eyes. They were mounted on a green platform that resembled a grassy field.

"Totally sweet!" Meredith said. She reached for it and turned it over carefully. She was surprised that the vendor was asking only five dollars for the item, which was in excellent condition without a chip or scratch.

Kinsley's eyes widened, and her lips opened in a delighted gasp as she reached out to hold the figurine. Meredith knew her granddaughter wouldn't hesitate to buy it if it was something she really wanted.

Sherri Lynn and Carter gave her and Kaden each eight dollars and fifty cents a week allowance. Kinsley usually spent hers very wisely, but it was plain that she really wanted this mother and baby pair.

"Go ahead, honey." She nodded to Kinsley's kitty purse slung over her shoulder. "You know you want it." How she loved that look of delight in her granddaughter's eyes.

A shadow crossed Kinsley's face, and her lips pressed together. She set the figurine down carefully and took a step back from the table without meeting Meredith's eye.

"If you don't have quite enough…" Meredith reached into her pocket and pulled out some dollar bills.

"No," Kinsley said, shaking her head. "It's okay. I—I changed my mind." She glanced one more time at the mare and foal figurine and took a few more steps away.

"You've changed your mind?" Meredith asked gently. There was no missing the longing in the little girl eyes. "Really, you should have it. It doesn't cost that much."

"I don't have any money," she said suddenly. "I—I—spent it." Then she darted away to another table.

"Your whole allowance?"

She nodded, her blond curls bouncing. "And Mama says I should only let you pay for lunch."

"I see," Meredith said. But she didn't understand, not really. Kinsley could be very stubborn when she made up her mind about something. And clearly, she was through shopping. She edged away from the tables and headed to the car. Meredith hurried after her. "Okay, honey. I think it's time for some curly fries and chicken fingers anyway. I'm hungry."

At the fast-food restaurant, Kinsley seemed to forget all about the figurine as she enjoyed her favorite lunch. Meredith ordered a small sundae for each of them for dessert.

"We had fun today, didn't we?" Meredith asked, watching Kinsley dive into her sundae with relish.

She nodded vigorously then said with a pretty little angle of her head, "I always have fun with you, Gran."

"Well, I always have fun with you!" Meredith popped the maraschino cherry that topped her sundae into her mouth. "But you haven't told me yet how school is going. What are you learning about now?"

She turned her head to the other side. "Well, we learned how to spell *nonchalant* and *nuance*."

"That's amazing," Meredith said, impressed. She wasn't sure she could spell those words correctly herself. "But you always were a good speller. Good in everything at school." She took the opportunity to introduce Sherri Lynn's worry. "Your mom tells me you haven't been too happy about going to school lately. How come?"

Kinsley shrugged. She studied her ice cream. "Sometimes my tummy hurts," she said, twirling her spoon in the chocolate sauce. She offered nothing more.

After a checkup at the pediatrician, Sherri Lynn had been assured that there was nothing medically wrong with Kinsley. "Honey, did something happen at school?"

She watched the gold-lashed lids that concealed her blue eyes, saw the small negative shake of her head.

"If there's something wrong, you can tell your mom—you can tell me. Maybe we can help."

Another shrug of the small shoulders. Then she said, "I don't think I want any more ice cream. My tummy hurts a little now." She slid out of the booth and shuffled her feet awkwardly. "Thank you for lunch, Gran," she said, as she had no doubt been coached to do. The gesture warmed Meredith's heart. Still, the niggling tug of worry lingered. What was going on in her precious granddaughter's world?

***

Meredith drove toward the agency, her emotions mixed. She'd loved her time with Kinsley, but had learned nothing to allay the concern about school. By the time Sherri Lynn came to collect her daughter, no more had been said about the matter. And if Kinsley regretted passing up the enticing mare and foal figurine, Meredith couldn't tell.

Meredith sighed. She would touch base with her son and daughter-in-law later. But now, she and Julia had a date with the mysterious Gage Gallagher.

"Well, he is who he says he is," Julia told her when they gathered in the conference room some twenty minutes before five o'clock. "He's registered at Texas A&M in a veterinary program. Father is a certified CPA in San Antonio—also owns a small cattle ranch. A few horses too."

"I see," Meredith said. She thought Julia looked weary after a long day's work on the Arbuckle case. Her partner always gave 110 percent in any project she undertook. She smiled as Julia coiled a strand of silver hair behind her ear and sighed.

"Records show the ranch struggles with debt, so he probably couldn't afford the thirty thousand cost of in-state tuition. Hence, our man's need to work his way through." Julia paused, adding sardonically, "In between lurking in the bushes on occasion."

"Well, I guess we can make some judgments of our own after he gets here. *If* he gets here." Meredith had had a long day too, though a far more pleasurable one than Julia's, she was sure. She stifled a yawn.

"I saw that yawn." Julia laughed. "Kinsley tire you out?"

"No, we had a good day," she said, but she had not apparently been able to hide her concern. She met Julia's inquiring gaze. "We're still in the dark about why she doesn't want to go to school sometimes, but it can't be anything too serious. We'll just need to give her some time, I think."

Carmen, who had stayed late, suddenly appeared at the conference door. She ushered Gage Gallagher in with a quick wave of her hand that made her bracelets tinkle. She glanced over her shoulder at the fair-haired cowboy. "They're expecting you, Mr. Gallagher. You can go right in."

Stetson in hand, their visitor nodded, first to Carmen then to Meredith and Julia. Only a hatband crease in his forehead and the light scar over his left eyebrow marred the golden good looks.

Julia stood and was first to address him in a professional, slightly stern tone. "Please take a seat." She was, after all, the one who had scuffed her best flats chasing him through the neighborhood.

He paused at the chair indicated but waited until Julia had resettled in her chair before sitting down.

"Thank you for coming," Meredith said politely. She hadn't risen when he came in. Now she smiled cautiously, sensing his nervousness.

He was wearing a clean shirt rolled up to the elbows above weathered Levi's and the boots with their silver tips. Overhead light gilded the hairs on his forearms, which, she supposed, looked brawny enough to tame a bucking bronco or help a foaling mare give birth.

"Ma'am," he said, leaning slightly forward in his chair, "I appreciate you letting me come." He fiddled with the brim of his hat and briefly averted his serious blue gaze. When he looked up, the square chin was set. "I hope you believe me about last night. I really was home. Mrs. Riverton called me up to chase a bat out of her screened-in porch around nine thirty. None of the men were around. Not even Mr. Riverton."

It was a story too wild to be made up—and they certainly could check such an alibi. Meredith exchanged a glance with Julia. "As you say, we can check. But assuming what you say is true, do you have any idea who was following me and if it has anything to do with Sapphire Riverton?"

Gage shook his head slowly and released a low sigh. "Sapphire says someone's been following *her*—" He paused and shook his head again. "Besides me," he added sheepishly.

"How long have you known Sapphire?" Julia asked.

"About five months. I started at the ranch around the end of June." He furrowed his brow. "I supervise a small crew of wranglers and cowhands. We've all been told to keep our distance from the house." He smiled. "Except when a bat gets in."

"But you've become a friend of Sapphire's," Julia continued, leading him on.

"She likes to ride, comes to fetch Mandolin—her chestnut bay. She loves that stallion. That's how we got to know each other...and sometimes we talk." He fiddled with his hat again before stopping to fold his arms over his chest. He seemed to be testing his words.

"Gage," Meredith said, "you seem to doubt her uncle's assessment that Sapphire is unstable. 'Fragile,' as he puts it. Why?"

"I've gotten to know her. She's sensitive but she's not—" He hesitated. "She doesn't need to be in that place. She's talented and smart. I just wish she could believe in herself instead of letting her uncle run her life. Something has her scared."

His eyes took on a soft glow that Meredith hadn't seen before.

"I know she gets spooked sometimes and kind of goes off the deep end, but..." He stopped and drew in a breath. "They say she used to think her mother was calling her when she was small. I guess it's started up again."

Julia tapped her fingernails on the conference room table, her eyes intent on Gage. "You say the treatment at the clinic hasn't helped her. How often in the five months you've been at Riverton has Sapphire been a patient there?"

"Twice that I know of." He frowned. "She says she hears a voice calling her, and insists that it's her mother." He picked up his hat and thumped it down on his knees. "It's got something to do with what happened when she was a little girl. But she won't talk about it. She says she can't remember and won't even try. And she won't go near the rock garden where her mother died." He cracked his knuckles. "I just can't figure her out."

Meredith stared at him, waiting.

"She saw someone there," he went on. "On that day when her mother died, but she doesn't know who, and every time I try to get her to talk about it, she shuts down."

Meredith released a long breath, recalling Theodore Riverton's account of his niece's trouble. She felt completely out of her element.

Diseases of the psyche were so much harder to heal than those of the body. If they continued looking into affairs at the ranch, might they do Sapphire more harm than good? She frowned at Gage. "Don't you think it's best for her to continue to work with professionals who can really help her rather than get us involved?"

"But she doesn't belong in that place—that clinic, I mean. She's not crazy! She…" He stopped himself with another thump of his hat against his knee. "I've heard—" Once again he didn't complete the sentence. "Look, she's going to be twenty-one in five months. What if someone—maybe even her adored uncle Teddy—doesn't want the truth to come out? Maybe he wants to make sure he still has access to Sapphire's trust fund by saying she's not competent to handle her own affairs."

"Has Sapphire said anything like that to you?" Meredith asked.

He sighed. "No. She's devoted to the man, but I've seen things and heard things—especially from some of the staff who've been at Riverton for a long time."

Meredith stared at the earnest young man. Was it true that Sapphire Riverton was being manipulated somehow? Did someone want her to be declared unfit? "How do you know about this trust fund?"

"She told me. She gets an allowance every month until she's twenty-one. Then the fund is turned over to her. It's no secret. Everyone knows about it." He frowned, looking down at his rough hands.

What was this young Texan's motive in trying so hard to engage their services? Or was it possible he was working in league with Dr. Riverton, pretending to protect Sapphire while reporting her movements to him?

Meredith's phone, which she had set on the table next to her, pinged. She glanced down, planning to ignore it, but caught a familiar name—Wally Parker. NEED TO SEE YOU. ALL RIGHT IF I SWING BY YOUR HOUSE AROUND 7:30? This could be no social call—it had to concern their conversation on Tuesday. Meredith felt her internal antennae rising.

She pulled her eyes back to Gage. "I think we should wait and see if Sapphire contacts us again. When she returns to the ranch, tell her we'd like to speak with her."

Gage stood and turned to go but hesitated at the door, fumbling with his hat. "I'll tell her and—thanks." He strode into the hall and toward the exit.

Meredith tapped in a reply to Wally's text, aware of Julia's quizzical gaze. OKAY. SEE YOU THEN. She looked up, fixing her eyes on Julia. "Wally," she said quietly. "I better get home—he'll be coming by in an hour." She picked up her purse. "I'll call you." And she too left the conference room and headed to the parking lot.

Chapter Nine

Happy to be home, Meredith dropped her purse and keys on the Asian console in the entryway. GK wound himself around her ankles with a husky *mrow* before moving decorously to the end of the couch to regard her with interest. And likely with hunger, though he felt it beneath his dignity to show it.

"Sorry to keep you waiting," she told him, hanging her coat in the hall closet. She had run a few errands before heading home and hadn't yet had supper. She'd grab a sandwich—it was too late to fix anything more substantial, and she didn't feel like eating anyway.

She poured GK's kibble and changed into slacks and a clean blouse. It had been a full day between her adventures—and misadventures—with Kinsley and rushing to the office to meet Gage. She had hoped for a quiet evening and time for a phone visit with Quin, who at that moment she missed acutely.

It had only been two days ago that they'd had dinner together and he'd taken her home after the unnerving episode of being followed—or thinking they had been followed when they left the restaurant. He'd phoned later that same evening to make sure she was all right. And the next night too when they'd talked for nearly an hour. She'd come to depend on his comforting warmth, his strength, his caring.

The house seemed gnawingly empty—GK notwithstanding. In the beginning of her widowhood, she had come home and immediately turned on the television or the stereo, flipped on all the lights, sang, or whistled. Anything to alleviate the silence.

This comfortable house had seldom been silent when Ron was alive. They enjoyed their friends and loved hosting them—including Wally and Emily Parker.

She was surprised how she missed those who, as life went on, became distant. Like Emily with her soft-spoken wit and love of classic literature. Wally and Ron too had shared a close bond born of long years of friendship and similar interests. Neither Wally nor Emily had been in the house since Ron's death. And tonight, it was likely that Wally would come alone.

His cryptic text message was unnerving. Perhaps he had discovered something about the four-day-old appearance of Sapphire Riverton, whose name Meredith had not then known. He'd promised to contact her if anything came up. Still, to text her that he wanted to meet her at her home seemed strange.

She whipped up a batch of cocoa, remembering Wally's love for the treat and his mention of it on Tuesday when she'd come to the precinct. She pulled out the three chocolate cherry bars she had kept back when sending the others home with Carter. Ron's good friend and former partner in the police force had a decided sweet tooth.

She had just placed the treats on the coffee table and turned on the electric fire when Wally arrived. The brisk November wind had whipped his dark hair into disarray and reddened his cheeks. "Wally! Come in!" It seemed so natural to see him here on her doorstep. Shades of the past when Wally and Emily had visited came flooding back.

"Sorry to intrude on your evening," he began.

"Nonsense! I'm just so glad you've come." She gave him a quick hug. "You were right about cocoa weather. I've got some on the stove—just for you."

"I won't keep you long," he said, giving Meredith his jacket. "I don't like to leave Em too long." The lines in his forehead deepened, and he ran a hand across his jaw, giving him that weary look she'd noticed in his office.

"Is she all right, Wally?"

He took the chair by the fireplace. Meredith sat across from him, the coffee table with its cherry bars on a delft blue plate between them. Meredith waited for him to respond and then heard a low sigh that quickly alarmed her. "Wally?"

"I'm afraid she isn't, Meredith." He grasped the arms of the chair and peered into the fireplace for what seemed a long time before continuing. "We got the diagnosis about three months ago."

Meredith held her breath. With Wally and Em it was always "we." Not "she" or "I." Their closeness had always charmed her. Married right out of high school, they'd remained inseparable in a world where fidelity was an anomaly.

"Ovarian cancer," he said in a low voice. "Stage four."

Meredith's heart sank. "Oh, Wally."

"We've been through all the treatments, and there's little more to be done. Em doesn't want any more chemo—any more anything." He swept a hand across his jaw once more and leaned back in the comfortable chair that had been Ron's favorite. "We've left it to the

Almighty," he said with a quick lift of his chin. "And we're taking advantage of the time we have left."

Meredith felt the tears sting her eyes. What could she say? *If there's anything I can do... I'll be praying for you. I'm so, so sorry.* Good, reasonable expressions, but when the heart was broken they seemed as ineffectual as throwing an ice cube at the sun.

"I didn't want to mention it the other day," Wally said, his voice steadier. "And that's not why I wanted to see you tonight." He took a quick breath. "I know you care about Em—and me—and believe me, I'm grateful, but please, let's not talk about it anymore right now."

"I understand, Wally. You know that I'm so desperately sorry, and I will be praying. I'll do anything—" She fought the tears, hoping that anger at the deadly disease would overpower the hurt and keep her tears at bay.

"I know—and that means a lot. Em loves you and Ron—she talks about you so often." He managed a weak smile. "You said something about cocoa?"

Meredith jumped up, glad for something to do with herself. She filled her best delft mugs, which she and Ron used only on special occasions, and carried them to the coffee table.

"Boys doing all right?" Wally asked, obviously tabling the former topic. "How's that history professor getting on?"

"He's busier than ever—especially this semester. It's burgeoning with students." Meredith passed the plate of dessert bars and realized her hands were trembling. "These are Carter's favorite. He's also doing well. When we had dinner the other day, he had the good grace to leave one or two."

"Lucky me," Wally said, grabbing one with relish. Seemingly he was unaware of the irony of his comment.

Meredith cringed. With a dreaded diagnosis looming, Wally and Em were anything but "lucky."

"And this cocoa," he went on. "Nobody makes cocoa like you do. I bet you made it from scratch."

"I did. I like to add cinnamon and cloves. Also, blackstrap molasses. We Southern cooks are terribly particular, you know."

They sipped cocoa and nibbled the confections without words for half a minute or more before Wally set his mug down on the end table. "I came to see you tonight because I wasn't totally honest with you the other day."

Meredith waited as Wally's blue gaze sharpened. His official look. Was another shock coming? "About the surveillance video? Did you see something?" she asked, leaning forward.

"Not exactly. The images were very blurry, as you know, but..." He drew a breath and expelled it slowly. "But I had an idea who the young lady might be. I wasn't sure, but when Riverton phoned yesterday—" He paused briefly. "I didn't talk to him, the chief did, and then the chief sent for me."

Meredith recalled what Dr. Riverton had said about Sapphire's erratic behavior when she was upset and that the police were aware of it. Meredith didn't remember telling him about the captured image from the camera. Perhaps he had simply surmised a private detective might approach the police about the girl's appearance, and he had decided to run damage control.

"You—uh—heard anything more about your young visitor?" Wally asked.

"Well, I've heard a lot but not from her. Turns out the cowboy Julia chased out of the bushes works at Riverton Ranch and is concerned about Sapphire. He says someone is taking advantage of her—her uncle perhaps. Says she doesn't belong in that place her uncle runs." She studied Wally's face, which remained impassive. "I tried to visit her at the clinic but was told she isn't receiving visitors during treatment. But how does this concern the police department?"

"Not really sure. But what I do know is that Theodore Riverton is a powerful man in Savannah. He was largely responsible for the rebuild of the third precinct. The chief wants him handled with kid gloves. Riverton is big money—and he spreads it around lavishly, but…" He took another sip of his cocoa.

Meredith prodded with her eyes.

"I'm not saying the department has done anything underhanded, or that they would. But I am saying that they might look the other way in some matters to stay in Riverton's good graces." He set the mug down once more. "So that's why I was rather evasive the other day. And it's been bothering me."

"I see," she said, though she didn't really understand.

"What's bothering me more is that you and Julia are mixed up in the Riverton family. Has the young lady returned for her money?"

"No. We've talked with both Dr. Riverton and his wife, but I didn't say anything about the large sum of money she gave us. We want to return it but would like to do so in person and make our own judgments about her status."

"I wish you'd let it go, Meredith," he said, frowning.

"Well, there's nothing to let go really," Meredith said. "We haven't accepted her case. We haven't even talked to her—except for that day in the parking lot. And if she's as unstable as her uncle says, Julia and I are not qualified to help her. We…" She let the sentence drop, feeling at sixes and sevens over the entire conversation she was having with Ron's best buddy and former partner.

Wally leaned toward her. "I think you should send the money to Riverton—by registered mail since it involves cash—and let the matter drop."

Meredith was stunned. Clearly, Wally didn't want her delving into matters concerning the wealthy Rivertons. She studied his face, the kindly eyes with their smile lines, the square-set chin and grave mouth. "Well," she said, unsure how to respond, "I appreciate your coming and sharing this information."

"It's just that I don't want you or Julia to get in over your heads."

She nodded to acknowledge his advice, but her heart could not agree. She stood, seeing Wally grip the chair arms, his message delivered.

Wally stood also. "I'm sorry to come barging in so late, and…"

"You didn't barge in, Wally. You know you're always welcome." Meredith felt tears threatening. "Thanks for the information." She bit her lip. "And again, I'm so sorry about Emily. Will it be all right to visit?"

"Of course." He clapped her shoulder gently and retrieved his jacket. "Take care," he said quietly. "God keep you safe." He strode out the door without looking back.

She stared into the fire, rehashing Wally's visit and leaving the remains of their refreshments untouched. He had advised her to forget about Sapphire Riverton. But what if she was a victim of a proud family's hold on wealth and power? What secret lay locked inside this young woman that could break that hold?

She glanced at the clock on the wall. It was getting late but maybe not too late to make a call. Maggie Lu was the best source of information about the people of Savannah. Hadn't she said she knew someone who had moved into the Riverton household?

"I hope I'm not calling too late," Meredith said at the sound of Maggie Lu's voice.

"I was just debating whether it was too late to call you!"

"Really?"

"I've been thinking about the Rivertons," Maggie Lu said. A tinge of wonder had crept into her voice. Meredith imagined her with her old-fashioned landline phone pressed to her ear. "I was going through some old scrapbooks of mine from my teaching days at Spencer Elementary. It's Williams now, of course, but back in the seventies, when I was a young teacher, I knew the mother of that young woman who died nearly two decades ago. She was a hairdresser in the neighborhood, and she had a little girl. After you mentioned the name Sapphire, I got to thinking hard about another gemstone name that was niggling at the back of my mind. And it came to me—Garnet. That was it."

"Yes," Meredith said. "We know that Garnet Georgianna was the name of Sapphire's mother. Details are sparse from what we've learned so far, but she was the daughter of Thelma Chambers, who at one time worked in a beauty shop." A picture of a wild-haired woman holding a doll flashed into her mind. "According to the Rivertons, she suffers from vascular dementia after a stroke."

"Oh," Maggie Lu said softly. After a few seconds of silence, she added, "I'm so sorry. Thelma really was a kindly soul, and she was so proud of that child she dressed up so fancy. Quite different from the other little girls in the neighborhood. Some of them made fun of her, but it didn't seem to faze her. She'd just walk along holding her mama's hand. There was an innocence about her, even as she grew up into her teen years. Almost a naiveté."

"Do you remember anything else about her?" Meredith asked, imagining the scene Maggie Lu had painted.

"That brings me to why I was about to call you. I found a clipping in one of the books. It was from a free local newssheet with the caption, 'Local girl to wed Riverton Estate heir.' It's yellowed and grainy, but it's got her name—Garnet Chambers—under the picture. I'll hold on to it for you."

"Fabulous!" Meredith said. "It's hard to find anything in the press related to the Rivertons."

"I do remember how proud that girl's mama was. She told me she wished I could come to the wedding—she'd even do my hair up free in her shop." Maggie Lu gave a soft laugh. "Imagine that! I've always hoped life would be kinder to Thelma. Working hard to raise that child with people buzzing about her not being married…"

Meredith's mind raced. How much did Sapphire's grandmother know about the day her daughter died? What secrets might lie buried in her now confused mind? Theodore Riverton had described her condition as "vascular dementia." The disease had many unknowns, and each case had to be considered individually. That "imperfect science" he himself had mentioned.

"Do you think Thelma Chambers would remember you?" Meredith asked, an idea hatching itself in her mind.

"It's been many years, honey, and with her dementia…" She hesitated.

Maggie Lu's best friend had suffered from dementia, and she had cared for her for a long time. She certainly knew something about the ravages of the disease, yet she'd been able to break through Delyse Watson's fog more than once.

"Besides, the Riverton place is clear down past Fancy Hall," Maggie Lu mused. "But maybe…maybe I could get Charlene to take a little time off. Lord knows she needs to take a break now and then. That girl's working much too hard."

"The welcome mat will probably not be out for Julia or me given our prior visit and the family's penchant for privacy. But they don't know you, and if you visit with a mind to reconnect with an old friend—kind of an errand of mercy…"

Maggie Lu was a great source of historical information, but she had sometimes proven an effective working sleuth for Magnolia Investigations as well. Meredith could feel, more than hear, Maggie Lu's interest perk up.

"I do have a little hiatus from the library at the present time. I could check with Charlene. What kind of information are you looking for precisely?"

"I can't say exactly," Meredith began, "but there's something about the death of Garnet Riverton that plagues Sapphire's mind. According to both her uncle Theodore and the young barn manager, Gage Gallagher, she feels responsible and can't get over it."

"But she would have been only a child," Maggie Lu said.

"Four years old," Meredith confirmed, recalling the fear in the lovely almond-shaped eyes, the tremor of her voice when she admitted to needing to know. Yet she couldn't bring herself to remember.

"Let the matter drop." Wally's warning echoed in her mind. What had happened that day?

"You know I'll do anything I can to help," Maggie Lu said, her cultured voice reassuring. "I'll connect with Charlene in the morning and call you."

"Thank you, Maggie Lu. I've been advised to leave this alone, but somehow I just can't." Meredith felt suddenly weary. It had been a long day—a long week. And she'd been unable to shake her concern for Em and Wally or to break through Kinsley's problem. She suppressed a sigh.

"You all right, honey?" Maggie Lu, always perceptive, must have heard the angst in her voice.

"I'm fine. Just a lot on my mind, which you have helped to alleviate," Meredith hastened to say.

"Bless you, dear. Just remember what Victor Hugo said long ago: 'Have courage for the great sorrows of life and patience for the small ones; when you have laboriously accomplished your daily tasks, go to sleep in peace. God is awake.'"

Meredith said good night with the benediction echoing in her heart. Could Maggie Lu's visit to the ill and aging grandmother shed light on a dark secret that imprisoned a young woman's mind?

Chapter Ten

"She's here! I just saw the Rolls drive up."

Thelma put her pen down over the appointment book, her heart fluttering. "Gigi!" she exclaimed, unmindful of the turned heads and curious stares in the salon. She hurried to the stylish glass doors etched with her name in flowing script.

The business Thelma now owned was a far cry from the little beauty shop in the depressed neighborhood she had once called home. In all her years she never could have hoped to own her own salon in a genteel area where a cut and style cost five times the amount she used to charge. The shop with its first year's rent paid in advance had been made possible by Garnet Georgianna's wealthy husband, Preston Riverton III.

"You're alone?" Thelma queried, closing the door behind the five stylists she employed. Grabbing her daughter in a hug, she looked beyond her to the smartly dressed chauffeur standing attentively beside an empty luxury auto. "You didn't bring her?" Thelma asked.

"Sapphire cried a lot in the night, so I let her sleep this morning, Mama."

"Oh! What was wrong? Is she all right?"

"She's fine. I think she was just teething. The nanny is watching her." Garnet looked down at her silver-soled sandals. "I'm sorry. I know you were hoping to see her today."

Thelma tempered her quick disappointment, lest Gigi think her visit less welcome without her child. She pulled back to search her daughter's face. There was a haziness about the usually brilliant blue eyes and a slight pallor to her cheeks. "You all right, honey?"

"I'm fine, really."

But she didn't look fine, and Thelma couldn't help but wonder. She and Preston attended so many civic events, and Thelma knew that Preston—ever the garrulous gentleman rancher—imbibed a little too much. She knew too that he sometimes sent his wife home and stayed late at such galas.

Gigi clutched a Vuitton purse and shook back her pale hair, which was long and feathery. She was wearing a petal-pink dress in a swirling paisley pattern with a gold cinch belt clasped around her waist. She'd lost her baby weight after only a few weeks, but she looked even thinner now than she had at Sapphire's first birthday party just a month ago.

It had been a grand affair on the grounds of the beautiful Riverton Ranch. The west lawn of the house had been spread with white tents, and cloth-covered chairs clustered around tables set with flowers and real silver. There were glamorous gifts—including a Welsh pony, which Sapphire could ride *when she was old enough. Thelma had been astonished at the extravagance. And when Preston had insisted on purchasing the storefront and supplies for his mother-in-law's new business, she had been bowled over. Preston Riverton III was known for his over-the-top generosity. Imagine such a gift to his new wife's mother, whom he hardly knew at all. It was as though some lucky star had shone upon her.*

"Sapphire Sue! It's a perfect name for her, isn't it?" Gigi had gushed when she laid the baby in Thelma's arms for the first time. Thelma had been smitten by the tiny heart-shaped face and sweet bow lips like Garnet's. She had the same blue eyes, only deeper, rounder. They seemed to study everyone and everything in her wide new world. "It was Preston's idea," Gigi had said. "He says now he has two jewels in the family."

Thelma had agreed, even if the child wouldn't bear a name with family significance. "Thelma" or "Jean" would have been nice. But she had learned very quickly that Preston took charge of such things. Of most things. Likely all things. And Thelma felt, not for the first time, a gnawing sense of dread.

"I'm just so glad to see you," Thelma said, hooking her arm through her daughter's. "Even if you couldn't bring my beautiful granddaughter this time. Let's have lunch at the new deli across the street. Their sandwiches are wonderful."

Thelma ordered her favorite turkey with asiago cheese on rye bread. "The ham and swiss is nice. You always liked that," she said as her daughter's eyes roved rather listlessly, Thelma thought, over the menu offerings. She'd never been a picky eater. "And how about a strawberry shake to go with it? Remember how you always loved them at Murphy's?"

Murphy's. It seemed a lifetime ago that they'd walked the three blocks from their little apartment above the old beauty shop to the hamburger joint. It had been a treat when business had been good and when the bills were paid up. But most months there was little left for the luxury of eating out.

"Just the sandwich, Mama, and water's fine."

"They do sweet potato fries here," Thelma added, cocking her head at her daughter. "The waffle variety."

"No, thanks." She smiled her soft, wistful smile that had always charmed Thelma. The smile that made her think Gigi was dreaming of unicorns or fairy princesses. Today, she seemed sad, and her voice was flat when she spoke. "I need to watch my weight. Preston has so many engagements to attend—they're important for a man of his position—and he—" She paused, a tic in her left eye manifesting itself. "He needs me with him and looking as fit and trim as possible."

Thelma had never read the society pages in the newspapers before, never been interested in how the rich and famous lived. But since Garnet's marriage, she had become aware of them. She'd seen Preston with his beautiful wife on his arm. She had read the glowing tributes to this board and that charity with which Riverton Ranch was connected. Always there were beautiful people in dashing gowns and tuxedos, brilliant jewels. Surely Garnet was not just another adornment to Preston.

Thelma felt a stab of pain in her left temple. Just that morning, Kathleen had shown her a news clipping before

starting a perm for a customer. "Isn't that your girl's husband?"
she had asked. Preston with his glossy black hair and white
teeth smiling into the camera, extending a glass as though to
toast the photographer. His face was flushed, the eyes a bit too
glittery. Was she imagining that he was not quite sober?

She knew the look well enough—whether on the face of a well-
dressed gentleman rancher or a down-on-his-luck dock worker
like her father. She had shielded Gigi from that seamier side of life
and raised her to hold her head high, to know she was someone.

"Were you out again last night?" Thelma asked with a
nonchalance she didn't feel.

"Yes, but I left early. Teddy brought Preston home later
when—when the party was over." Garnet nibbled at her
sandwich, averting her gaze.

Teddy. Theodore Riverton, Preston's business partner.
Also his half brother, Thelma had learned. Medium build,
sturdy—not quite the dashing figure that Preston was. But
obviously the steady one who kept the ranch going. How often
did he have to cover Preston's excesses?

Gigi hadn't mentioned that Teddy had a wife. She had
told her there were several hands at the ranch, some of whom
occupied the bunkhouse. Others lived off the grounds. There
was a nanny and a full-time cook.

"The cook's name is Glady," Gigi said, wrinkling her
nose. "But Grumpy might be a better name. She gets very cross
sometimes. She mumbles a lot while she works and shucks
everyone out of the way, but I like her."

"Is Preston's half brother married?" Thelma asked.

"No. I think he might have been once, but he's very smart—graduated from some famous college. Preston needs him." She hesitated. "Sometimes..." Gigi bit her lip before continuing. "Well, there's an awful lot to running the ranch and all, and Teddy..." Her words dwindled once more.

Thelma sipped her iced tea and felt the condensation dripping down her arm. The air-conditioning was too high, but the shiver she felt had little to do with the temperature in the café. Had they made a mistake? Had she been wrong to encourage Gigi's friendship with the handsome Preston Riverton? She had always been able to intuit her daughter's moods, to know when something was wrong. But now... Thelma bit her lip again and tasted the blood.

Suddenly, she longed for the tiny beauty shop and the timeworn street she once knew. She yearned for the neighborhood school where she walked Garnet Georgianna Chambers each morning with the sun smiling down like a benediction. Friends waved as they passed, calling cheery "good mornings." Kind neighbors like the tall, dark-skinned teacher who would stop to chat before moving on down LeGrand Street, always with a parting "God bless you."

Thelma searched the down-turned eyes of her lovely daughter. Had God blessed her and tiny Sapphire Sue? Would they be all right, or did she have reason to fear the days ahead?

And she, who had never learned to pray, could only plead in her fearful uncertainty for a loving God's help.

It was late on Saturday afternoon when Meredith and Julia slid into the smooth vinyl booth at the Downhome Diner to wait for Maggie Lu. After they ordered their meals, Meredith leaned back and heaved a sigh. She had crammed a month's worth of housekeeping duties into one morning, and it felt good to sit still in the cozy atmosphere of the diner and simply chill.

"It's depressing to realize how much dust and clutter one lone woman can generate," she said wearily.

"Well, don't be too hard on yourself," Julia replied with a knowing wink. "It's been a busy week."

"It has at that," Meredith concurred with mild chagrin, knowing she'd procrastinated. While the results were satisfying, housework was not nearly as enjoyable as running an investigation agency. "It's been a busy several weeks."

"Yep, and before we know it the holidays will be here. Then we'll really have to pull up our socks," Julia said. "Thanksgiving, Christmas shopping, church bazaars, baking cookies, parties, and wrapping..."

"Stop!" Meredith groaned, laughing at the same time. "You're killing me." The approaching season would be challenging, but it never failed to release a joyful enthusiasm, a sense of renewal that filled up every corner of her spirit.

Julia lifted a steaming cup to her lips. "Beau says we might need to buy a bigger dining room table for Thanksgiving this year. I think he's invited every shirttail relative on the planet."

Meredith shook her head in mock sympathy but knew Beau wasn't the only one looking forward to sharing the holidays—especially Thanksgiving, which brought out Julia's natural generosity and goodwill. Meredith loved the season too and had wonderful memories of the family table with Ron at the head, carving the turkey with the precision of a surgeon and always lamenting the result: operation successful; patient died.

Carter had taken over the job to the praise of Sherri Lynn and the giggles of the children, who watched with undisguised misgiving. A little stab of sadness threatened. Thanksgiving wasn't the same without Ron. *Let it go*, she told herself. There was plenty to recall with a glad heart and much to be thankful for in the here and now.

"I can't wait to hear about Maggie Lu's visit to the Riverton place," Julia said.

Meredith nodded. "Maggie Lu's a trouper. Interesting that she knew Thelma Chambers back in the seventies."

Julia, Meredith realized, was as intrigued as she was by the case of Sapphire Riverton. The case that wasn't really a case, at least not one confirmed by the young woman in question. "Here comes Maggie Lu now," Meredith said, waving to the tall woman pushing through the door.

She came toward them in a brown midcalf dress and a dark green jacket to which she had pinned a yellow daisy mum. "I hope you weren't waiting too long. I just got back."

"No, just a few minutes," Meredith said as Julia moved farther into the booth to give Maggie Lu room beside her. She looked across the table at the sage woman on whom the years lay gently. Her dark eyes, simultaneously soft and canny, punctuated her still unlined face. "We've decided what we want already, and we're eager to hear about your visit to Thelma Chambers. But why don't you order first."

Julia, who had asked the waitress for an extra cup, poured coffee into it as Maggie Lu quickly scanned the menu.

After ordering, Maggie Lu settled her handbag in her lap. She picked up her coffee and glanced over the rim of her cup at Meredith. "It was quite an excursion," she began. "That house may not be as grand as the old mansion, but it's a sight to behold. I never saw so many trees and gardens so perfectly placed—like jewels in a field of gold."

"We were pretty impressed too," Julia said.

"When no one came to the door, I walked around to the back," Maggie Lu continued. "I saw the pool—a palette-shaped, turquoise glory, all glistening in the sun. The young woman sunning in her red bikini wasn't exactly glad to see me though."

Meredith's ears perked up. "Sapphire?"

"No. She didn't look anything like the young lady you described. This one had dark eyes and hair she must have streaked with a red dye."

Sounded to Meredith a lot like the maid who had answered the door for her and Julia. She hadn't been thrilled with their visit either. Lara Somebody probably had the day off.

"I interrupted something between her and a young man in a cowboy hat," Maggie Lu continued. "They didn't see me standing there. She was cozying up big-time to him, but he wasn't having any of it. When she kept hanging on, he gave her a not-so-friendly push and told her to leave him alone." Maggie Lu's eyebrows rose. "She had some words for him and for the rival who apparently had moved in on her territory. Referred to her as an addlebrained idiot."

Lara obviously had other interests on the ranch besides cleaning and serving. Nor would her companion spend all his time tending the livestock. She hesitated, fearing who the cowboy might be. "Tall, clean-cut, curly light hair? Sea-blue eyes?"

"No. This one had a week's growth of stubbly black hair and eyes dark as mudholes. The woman asked if I was looking for Glady. Their cook, apparently." Maggie Lu shrugged. "According to the young lady in the bathing suit, the lady of the house was away. I insisted that I was an old friend of Thelma's, so she took me up a grand staircase to the second floor."

"One wonders who was taking care of 'Granny T' while Mrs. Riverton was away and the maid was doing—well, whatever she was doing," Julia said, exchanging a glance with Meredith.

Maggie Lu pursed her lips, frowning. After a few quiet seconds she continued. "I found Thelma sitting in a rocking chair by a window, a Raggedy Ann doll in her lap. She didn't look much like the woman I used to know. She just stared at me blankly for the longest time, not saying anything."

"Vascular dementia takes a rather harsh toll on a person," Meredith said.

"I sat down on the end of the bed and kept talking," Maggie Lu said. "I asked her if she remembered me and tried to help her recall those long years past when Garnet was a little girl—how she'd walk hand in hand with her all dressed up in frills. Such a pretty child but so quiet, so dreamy-like. You wondered if she was from some other world." Maggie Lu shook her head sadly. "I don't know whether Thelma understood me or not. I just sat across from her, recalling the little beauty shop and the old days."

"Did the maid leave you alone to talk?" Meredith asked, recalling how Lara had been listening from a hidden corner when she and Julia had been at the house.

"Not at first, but then I think she got tired of waiting around in her bathing suit." Maggie Lu pursed her lips again thoughtfully. "I asked Thelma about the doll in her arms, and she surprised me by asking if I wanted to hold her. She handed that doll to me with such tenderness it made me want to cry. 'Gigi's cold,' she told me. 'You have to keep her warm.' And then I remembered that she called her little girl 'Gigi.' That's why I couldn't remember her real name before."

"From her middle name, I guess," Meredith said. "Garnet Georgianna."

Maggie Lu nodded. "I asked her why Gigi was cold. I thought it might bring her into the real world and get her to talk about her daughter's death. But nothing she said made sense at all. She asked me to say 'God bless you' to the doll." Maggie Lu's brow knitted. "I always said that when we parted on the street corner, like I do most folks. Imagine her remembering that!"

"Sometimes it's the small things that touch a person's heart, that can stir something long forgotten," Meredith said. "When we ask God to bless someone, He takes it seriously, like any other request."

"Of course He does," Maggie Lu said, her face taking on a glow. "Even when it doesn't seem like He's blessing, we have faith that He is working to bring about something good."

"Do you think she really believes the doll is her little girl?" Julia asked, leaning forward earnestly.

"It could be," Maggie Lu said. "Dementia can take a person along strange and unproven roads with lots of twists and turns. But

I kept feeling like Thelma wanted to tell me something. She stared at me for the longest time. Sometimes her lips would move but no sound came."

"Do you think it might have something to do with how Garnet died?" Meredith asked. She thought about how the death would affect others in the household. Who would benefit from it? Was it possible the death wasn't an accident? Gage suspected Theodore's life and business could change radically if Sapphire were to inherit. Meredith didn't feel entirely comfortable with Theodore. Julia had distrusted him too. She inclined her head toward Maggie Lu, who hadn't quite finished her tale.

"I was praying hard as we talked, and I did ask God to bless little Garnet. Thelma started humming again and rocking with the rhythm. But then suddenly she got real upset and started yelling, 'Give her to me. Don't hurt her.' Scared me proper, I can tell you. I gave the doll back, and Thelma didn't look at me again. Just cradled the doll and rocked back and forth. I might as well have been a bed-stead or a chest of drawers."

Meredith pictured the scene, her senses jumping.

"And then the young woman—that maid or whatever—popped in. She was still in her bathing suit but she'd added a cover-up. She told me I better go." Maggie Lu sighed deeply. "Of course, I left. I hurried down the stairs and out to Charlene's car."

"That must have been very upsetting, Maggie Lu," Meredith said, reaching across to touch the older woman's hand, which rested on the table.

"I'm sorry. I don't think I accomplished anything, and I—I feel so sorry for my old friend and for little Gigi, or the poor grown-up

Garnet Georgianna, who is beyond our reach now." Maggie Lu grew quiet. After a few seconds she opened her purse and drew out something wrapped in a handkerchief. "Before Thelma got upset and started yelling, she gave me this."

Maggie Lu placed a small bluish stone the size of a silver dollar in Meredith's palm. Possibly quartz or a mix of sedimentary rock, Meredith supposed. "Thelma told me that Garnet was found in the Riverton rock garden," she said.

"Maybe this stone came from that garden," Meredith said, feeling her nerves tingle. But what was Thelma doing with it, and why had she given it to Maggie Lu?

Chapter Eleven

"WHAT DO YOU MAKE OF it?" Meredith asked Julia after Maggie Lu left the restaurant.

"It was just a rock. Maybe Granny T collected them. Rock hounds aren't all that rare." She paused. "But Sapphire's mother died in Riverton's rock garden. And didn't Gage say that Sapphire was apparently traumatized to the point of refusing to go near it again?"

Meredith had studied the bluish stone as though it could speak to them before returning it to Maggie Lu. "I think Thelma might very well think of the Raggedy Ann doll as her lost daughter. It happens with dementia patients."

"She might imagine all sorts of things, given her state of mind," Julia said. She twined a strand of hair around her ear. "Thelma didn't move into Riverton Ranch until years after Garnet's death. Maybe she took some strange comfort in keeping a rock from the garden."

"Maybe Granny T knows a lot more than anyone thinks. Maybe we should look again at newspaper or broadcast reports from 2005. We could have missed something," Meredith said.

"I'd get right on it tonight if Beau hadn't arranged a barbecue," Julia said. "I'll be up to my ears in prepping for that committee, the folks who served with him on the hospital wing."

"We'll ask Carmen to work her magic on Monday morning. I'll be tied up tomorrow with Carter and Sherri Lynn and the kids. They're coming for a late lunch. More like an early supper. Should get here around three if they have a quick snack and leave right after church."

Of course, Kinsley would be coming too. Meredith recalled her unsuccessful attempt to get her to confide in her grandma when they had their playdate yesterday. What did that strange reaction mean? And how could she have already spent her whole allowance in four days? "Oh, I'm sorry. What was that?"

"You zoned out on me," Julia said. She gave her partner a discerning glance. "Still no headway on Kinsley's sudden avoidance of school?"

Meredith shook her head. "No, but I'm holding out hope for Sunday afternoon." Another chance to draw her favorite granddaughter out. "As Scarlet O'Hara always said, 'Tomorrow is another day.'"

"I'm pulling for you, Mere," Julia said. "Pulling—and better yet, praying."

***

Meredith was up early on Sunday and after breakfast prepared the roast and the potatoes that would later brown along with it. She'd come home quickly after services at Wesley Chapel, taking time only for a hasty greeting or a wave. Fellowship was an important part of worship, but there was much to do to get ready for her family's visit.

She set the table with her best china—softly hued stargazer lilies in pink and gold centered on the plate with a half-inch rim of gold.

The twelve-place setting was special to her because Ron, knowing how much she loved them, had always brought her stargazer lilies. She set the plates gently on the white linen tablecloth. About to add the fifth, she suddenly remembered. Kaden wouldn't be with the family today.

Sherri Lynn had apologized on the phone, explaining that her sister Bella and her husband, Cal, were able to get three tickets to a special exhibit at the science museum and wanted to take Kaden. She had tried to get her sister to understand that they had plans in place that included Kaden, but Bella had insisted that Kaden shouldn't be denied this experience.

Meredith had told Sherri Lynn she would miss Kaden but assured her that he would love the exhibit. She had tried to lighten her daughter-in-law's mood. "He'll be over the moon, no pun intended."

Meredith took a deep breath. She would miss her beloved grandson today, but perhaps it would allow her more time to focus on Kinsley, who was obviously troubled about something.

She was just steaming the vegetables when they arrived. Carter had given her his usual heads-up by phoning when they were five minutes away. "Come on in," she called. "Door's open."

Kinsley came rushing into the kitchen, her blond curls bobbing, eyes merry. "Look, Gran!" She thrust a Sunday school paper under Meredith's nose. "We learned about Queen Esther today and the festival called Purim that Jewish people still celebrate. That awful man Haman tried to get all the Jewish people killed. He built a gallows and was going to hang Esther's uncle and—" She drew a quick breath before adding with unabated enthusiasm. "And Esther got the king to listen to her and saved the people."

Meredith bent to hug Kinsley, exclaiming at her granddaughter's recital of the amazing story. Maybe whatever was troubling her had resolved itself. She certainly seemed like her usual gregarious self.

"We acted out the story, and I got to be Esther!" Kinsley gave a little toss of her head to underscore her achievement. Meredith sent her to wash her hands, and Kinsley took off, nearly bumping into Sherri Lynn.

"Whoa there!" she said as Kinsley rushed past her. Sherri Lynn draped a tan cardigan over the back of a kitchen chair. "She was so anxious to tell you what she learned today. That girl!" She shook her head, her honey-colored hair flowing straight and fine to the shoulders of her tailored blouse. She had added a rakish autumn scarf pinned with a gold oak leaf brooch and looked her usual elegant, unwrinkled self, even after hours riding in the car.

"These are from my garden," she said, setting a bouquet of purple asters and yellow mums on the end of Meredith's long counter. "I wrapped the stems in a wet towel. I think they weathered the trip all right." Her soft brown eyes were warm as she kissed Meredith's cheek.

"They are absolutely perfect!" Meredith said, wiping her hands and hugging Sherri Lynn.

"Hi, Mom," Carter said, joining Sherri Lynn in the kitchen and giving Meredith a kiss on the cheek. "Something smells terrific. We grabbed some McDonald's fries on the way, but we saved big appetites for the feast you've got cooking."

"Make yourself comfortable, hon," she told him. "Grab a drink from the fridge if you want. We'll be ready soon."

"Now, what can I do to help?" Sherri Lynn asked.

Meredith pointed to the five small plates waiting on the counter. "You can serve up the salads if you like. Dressing is already in it. I whipped it up with that raspberry vinaigrette you liked last time."

"Yum!" Sherri Lynn said. She glanced down. Her voice grew softer, her expression perplexed. "Sorry about Kaden. Bella will bring him here around six. Which means we'll be late when we get back to Charleston, especially since there's school next morning, but..." She pressed her lips together and thrust back a stray lock of hair. "Bella can be so stubborn sometimes."

"Don't worry," Meredith said, wincing inwardly. She knew that Bella sometimes pitted herself against her, as though it were a contest to see which family was more important to the children. "I'll miss Kaden, but it's important for Bella to stay close." She cocked her head, wanting to restore Sherri Lynn's earlier buoyancy. "Kinsley seems happy today. Plumb proud of herself over her Sunday school class."

Sherri Lynn responded with a smile, but anxiety was etched in her eyes.

"She doing better?" Meredith asked.

But there was no time for a reply. Kinsley came bouncing in, shaking her hands and scattering drops of water. "I washed my hands twice because I petted GK."

Soon they were gathered around the table. Carter led grace and the food was passed to hearty compliments. After a few moments with each intent on attacking their plates, they launched into their usual lighthearted conversation rehashing the week's events.

"We sealed a significant loan to a major conglomerate this week," Carter said after washing down a roasted potato with sweet tea.

"If he keeps it up," Sherri Lynn said proudly, "they'll give him a bonus."

"The chickens you're counting haven't even begun to roost," Carter said in mock reproof. But Meredith could tell he was pleased.

"Well, I think those chickens will be hatching before you know it!" Sherri Lynn pushed the basket of bread toward him. "Have another roll. A growing boy needs his nourishment."

Meredith laughed at their good-natured banter. If Chase could make a match as compatible to him as Sherri Lynn was to Carter, she'd be happy. Chase was an outgoing people person, but he was cautious about making important decisions.

She smiled as she looked at the faces around her table. She was blessed indeed. It saddened her that Ron couldn't be with them, but she knew he would want her to keep the family close. She would not allow time or circumstance or anything else to distance the members of the Bellefontaine family from one another.

Kinsley asked to be excused and went in search of GK, who was last seen camouflaged on the ledge in the screened-in deck. "Check out the book rack," Meredith called after her. "I found a couple I know you're going to love."

"So what's new in the life of our favorite investigator?" Carter asked. He leaned back in the chair with a satisfied groan and patted his stomach.

"A whole lot of the usual," Meredith responded. "References to check for wary employers, schools, insurance agencies, and such.

We solved that breach of contract dispute, and Julia's closing in on the Arbuckle jewelry claim." She drew a deep breath, full and satisfied.

"Heard any more about that young woman? The one with the money she got dealing drugs?" Carter gave her a shrewd glance. "I trust that case was put to rest."

"Uh, no. And the money didn't come from drugs. Turns out she's the niece of Theodore Riverton. A wealthy young woman, but she has problems." She paused, avoiding her son's skeptical gaze. "She was traumatized by her mother's death and claims to hear her calling from the rock garden where she died. Thinks someone's following her too."

"Sounds like a case for Riverton's clinic." Carter leaned back even farther and stuck his hands into the pockets of his trousers. "Hardly a case for Magnolia Investigations, is it?"

Meredith shrugged, pursed her lips, and looked away as Sherri Lynn began to collect the dishes.

"And what became of that guy who was following her? Is he another potential Riverton patient?"

"No. As it happens, he's the barn manager at the Riverton Ranch. Handles the horses and riding stable. He's the one urging Julia and me to look out for Sapphire's interests. He thinks someone might be tampering with her inheritance." Meredith met her son's inquiring gaze, heard the keys jingling in his pocket. "That's the name of the young woman. Sapphire."

"Sounds pretty involved. The Riverton name is big in these parts. He's got his hand in a lot of investments. I wouldn't mind handling his portfolio." That shadow of worry she'd come to recognize crossed his handsome features. "I just hope you're not getting in over your head."

Useless to tell Carter not to worry. She didn't want to discuss the perplexing details that had arisen so far. They would only add to Carter's discomfort. She got up and began helping Sherri Lynn clear things away. "Go on and relax. You too," she added as Sherri Lynn came back into the dining room. "Just leave those dishes. I'm going to see what Kinsley's up to on the deck, and then I'll join you in the living room."

Carter disappeared, but Sherri Lynn crossed her arms over her chest. "I can finish..." She glanced toward the deck with its brass lanterns and comfortable outdoor furniture, and the worry in her gentle brown eyes deepened.

Meredith paused. "Okay, stack them up, but don't wash them. You go relax. It's a long trip back to Charleston."

Sherri Lynn bit her lip. "Yes, and tomorrow's a school day." She sighed. "I'm glad the kids can sleep in the car." No doubt her daughter-in-law was thinking about the struggle to get Kinsley up and moving on a Monday morning.

"I'll go see how my favorite granddaughter is getting on," Meredith said. "She's been quiet out there. Most likely engrossed in those new books I got for her." She heard Sherri Lynn sigh and patted her arm. "Don't worry. We'll find out what's bothering her."

Meredith loved the deck with its magnificent view of Troupe Square. It was the ideal place to keep her many potted plants that lined the window ledges. She enjoyed the ritual of watering them and occasionally talking to them. It was something she wouldn't admit, especially to Julia, who would probably ask her, with an exaggerated eye roll, what the plants said in response.

She surveyed the plants quickly as she went toward the deck. They were still happy! No need to speak.

"Kinsley?" She had expected to find her granddaughter lounging on the floor by the bookshelves, her back to the sun, which was still warm and golden as the day waned. But she wasn't there. Nor was she tucked into one of the comfortable chairs or the chaise. The new books were still on the shelves. "Kinsley?" she called again.

Silence. GK peered down from his perch along the ledge, green eyes secretive. Meredith felt an unreasonable sense of alarm. Obviously, Kinsley had gone back into the house, perhaps to the bathroom or to explore her grandma's bedroom with all the photographs of her and Kaden from infancy to the present.

"Did Kinsley come through?" she asked Carter and Sherri Lynn, who were poring over the Sunday papers, their cups of coffee cooling on the table near the couch.

"Nope," Carter said.

"I thought she was on the deck," Sherri Lynn said congenially and returned to the newspaper she was reading.

Meredith shrugged. "She must be checking out my 'rogue's gallery.'"

But there was no sign of her and no answer to Meredith's call. She spread her hands when she passed into the living room again and headed for the deck. "Maybe I missed her. She come by you in the last few seconds?"

Both parents shook their heads but abandoned their newspapers and got up to join Meredith in the search.

"You don't suppose she went out, do you?" Meredith asked, knowing that the kids were never allowed to leave her house without asking and almost never unaccompanied unless to step out into the garden so they could wave at the adults inside.

"She wouldn't," Sherri Lynn said, flushing. She ran from room to room calling and returned to the deck, where Carter and Meredith stood watching.

"I'll just go outside and see," Carter said, his frown belying his calm voice. "I'm sure she's fine."

Suddenly a small voice chirped from behind them. "Here I am." Kinsley scooted out from under the round table in the corner, peeping through the flowered floor-length chintz cloth that covered it. A vase of roses Meredith kept on the table wobbled in the movement but righted itself.

"What in the world?" Sherri Lynn exploded. "We've been looking all over for you." She stood with hands on hips as Kinsley crawled out, holding a book.

Carter, who'd come scrambling back inside, scowled. "Didn't you hear your grandmother? Didn't you hear your mother and me calling you?"

Kinsley dropped her eyes to her feet and clasped the book against her chest. "I'm sorry," she said quietly. "I was hiding..." Her voice trailed off. "And reading. I—"

Meredith went to her, stooped, and hugged her granddaughter, who began crying. "I'm sorry."

"We were worried about you, sweetheart," she said. "You don't usually hide from us."

"And you are not to do it again," Carter said severely, his relief palpable.

Meredith looked over the top of Kinsley's head, appealing with her eyes to let her talk to her granddaughter alone. When they complied, Meredith took Kinsley's hand and led her to the glider couch.

"I'm sorry, Gran," Kinsley said again, sniffling. "But I didn't want to go home. I was pretending I could stay here with you so I wouldn't have to—" Her small lips trembled.

"So you wouldn't have to go to school?" she finished for her. "Darling, you've always loved school. And besides, if you stayed here, your mommy and daddy would be miserable without you. Don't you know how much they love you? How much we all love you?"

Kinsley leaned into Meredith's chest. Her small fingers trembled against the book she held.

Meredith pressed her gently back to look her in the eye. "Now, it's time to tell me what this is all about," she said firmly.

Kinsley stared down at the book, which was a retelling of the story of the tortoise and the hare. The story had long been one of her favorites. The animal characters were humanized with names and speech. The turtle's name was Maud, and the hare's was Murphy.

"Maud looks like Shelly," Kinsley said as she touched the shell of the happy-looking tortoise on the page. "They're both girl turtles."

"Your class pet," Meredith confirmed. Kinsley had talked about the small painted turtle with the beautiful shell that lived in a terrarium in her fourth-grade classroom. It occurred to her now that Kinsley hadn't mentioned Shelly in a while. Novelties wore off, she supposed.

"Shelly's gone," Kinsley said quietly as she inched closer to Meredith so that her golden head rested on her grandmother's shoulder.

Meredith smoothed her hair. "Where did Shelly go?"

Several seconds passed before Kinsley said, "I took her."

"You took the turtle? I don't understand, Kinsley."

Kinsley became agitated, jiggling her feet. "Emma Colette and some of the kids were poking Shelly when Miss Javers was out of the room. They were being so mean, and Shelly was scared!" Kinsley wiped her nose with the back of her hand. "Emma and some of the boys said that Shelly would make really great turtle soup. And they kept nudging her with a pencil." She scrunched up her lips angrily. "So when it was time to go home, I picked her up and put her in my backpack and took her home. I put her in an old aquarium Daddy keeps in the garage." She sniffled again. "I cleaned it first, and then I put her in." Big tears formed in her eyes. "I just wanted her to be safe."

"Oh," Meredith breathed.

"Miss Javers asked us what we knew about it, but I didn't tell," Kinsley said. "And I didn't think anybody saw me." Her lips quivered. "But that mean Emma Colette was watching. She saw me take Shelly. She said she was going to tell." Kinsley's feet jiggled faster.

Meredith waited for her to continue.

"She said I would get in trouble, big trouble, and might even get expelled." She took a breath jagged with sobs. "She said if I didn't hand over my allowance every week she was going to tell."

"Oh, Kinsley," Meredith said, holding the little girl tightly in her arms. "So that's why you haven't wanted to go to school. Oh, sweetheart, why didn't you tell your mom or dad?"

Meredith was aghast with indignation. That a child would bully another like that! Of course, she knew that bullying was only too rampant, both on the internet and in daily interaction. There were always people who used blackmail and intimidation to get what they wanted. *Dear Lord*, she prayed silently, *my sweet Kinsley couldn't bear to see the turtle hurt.*

"It's all right, honey," she whispered into the little girl's ear. "Nothing like that is going to happen. I promise. It's going to be all right."

Sherri Lynn and Carter would iron things out. She had no doubt. Amelia Javers was an intelligent teacher who understood children. She would handle the matter sensitively.

Meredith looked her granddaughter squarely in her beautiful blue eyes. "I'm so sorry this happened to you, but it's going to stop. You are not going to give away your allowance to Emma Colette or anyone else anymore."

Kinsley sniffled, her sobs subsiding.

"I'm so glad you told me," she whispered, smoothing Kinsley's hair. "You don't have to be afraid anymore now that you've found the courage to face this problem. Oh, sweetheart, don't worry. Now, let's go talk to your mom and dad, shall we?"

A half hour later, just as Bella was arriving with Kaden, a much-relieved Carter and Sherri Lynn had heard the whole story. Meredith knew they would sort out the best way to handle the situation with the school and their daughter and ensure that she would no longer be bullied over the class turtle incident.

Meredith's cell phone began chiming as she stood waving good-bye to her family after hugs all around. Still tender with the loving sense of family, she pulled it from her pocket without checking the caller.

"Mrs. Bellefontaine," drawled a now familiar voice. "I hope you'll pardon me for calling on a Sunday, but I need to tell you. Something went down at the house yesterday, and I'm worried about Sapphire."

Chapter Twelve

SUDDENLY THRUST INTO ANOTHER WORLD, Meredith struggled to switch gears. "What happened? Where is Sapphire?"

"At the clinic," Gage said, anxiety in his tone. "At least, I think that's where her uncle took her. Mrs. Bellefontaine, she was doing so well. When she came to ride Mandolin on Friday, she was calm, and happier than I've seen her in a long time. We talked for a while, and I told her what my parents always believed—that God could help us to be strong when we're in a position of weakness...." His voice trailed off as though he were testing his own belief in the promise.

Meredith remembered the scripture: *"My grace is all you need. My power works best in weakness."*

"My folks taught us to have faith," Gage said. "But sometimes I lose track. I know it would make a big difference for Sapphire too, but right now, she's having a tough time. I'm really worried about her."

"What happened, Gage?" she urged.

"Glady says they took Granny T away. They wheeled her right out of the house on a gurney."

Meredith swallowed. *Glady?* She searched her mind for connection. "Do you mean the cook who works for Theodore? She told you this?"

"Yeah. And she says Sapphire went running after her, crying and carrying on." Gage drew a quick breath. "She's very close to her granny, who's been like a mother to her since her own mama died—well, until her illness. Anyway, Glady says Elena got Sapphire calmed down. The next thing she knew, Theodore was taking Sapphire away. Just sat her in his big BMW and took off."

Meredith said nothing, trying to absorb what Gage was telling her. Had Granny T's dementia worsened? What was it all about? "When did all this happen, Gage?"

"Yesterday afternoon, I guess. But I just found out a little while ago. I came to the ranch to take a group of women on a trail ride—some friends of Elena's. I ran into Glady when I was putting away the tack. Sometimes she brings apple peelings for the horses. She seemed upset, and I asked her if I could help. At first she just glowered at me, but then she told me about Sapphire going off with her uncle."

"Does Glady live there at the ranch?" Meredith asked, thinking she'd like to have a good long talk with the cook.

"She has a room at the back of the house during roundups and harvest, but otherwise she has a place near Fancy Hall. Only comes two or three days a week now when the boss needs her." Gage sighed. "I don't know what to do," he said. "This is going to hit Sapphie hard."

"You sit tight," Meredith said, hardly knowing what to make of this news. "Keep your eyes and ears open. I'll find out what's going on. That's what investigators do. So hang in there, okay? We'll be in touch."

Meredith mulled over the startling conversation while she cleaned up from supper and put away the leftovers. Had Granny T suffered some kind of breakdown? Had she tried to harm herself and needed hospitalization? Meredith shook her head. This case was proving more and more convoluted. They had a retainer, but it was hardly a formal agreement between parties. She had yet to speak with her "client." She and Julia were acting on the word of a self-proclaimed friend. Yet Meredith was aware of an overpowering sense she couldn't shake. Sapphire Riverton needed their help.

For now, however, Sapphire was cloistered at her uncle's clinic and her grandmother was receiving professional care. *What I need,* Meredith told herself, *is a good night's rest.* She should make it all a matter of prayer and start fresh tomorrow.

But where had they taken Thelma Chambers? St. Joseph's Candler Hospital was less than thirty minutes from Fancy Hall via US 17. Besides being the closest, it was the first that came to her mind. Julia's mom had been treated there after a fall not long ago.

Meredith tucked the last of the dishes into the dishwasher and went into her study. GK, watching, stretched. Ever the dignified feline, he'd trotted along after her when she wasn't looking. "Maybe we can find where Granny T is," she told him with a knowing wink. "Let's give it a shot."

She dialed the number to the hospital. "I'm looking for a Thelma Chambers, who may have been admitted there yesterday," she said when the hospital service had routed her through several choices on their telephone menu. "Yes, probably afternoon or early evening."

But admissions had no record of a Thelma Chambers at Candler's. Meredith googled the list of hospitals in the Savannah region. Landmark on 68th was a possible choice, as were Memorial and

Georgia Regional. All were clustered in the same area. With the list prominent on her screen, she punched in the telephone listings for each, starting with the most logical from a standpoint of proximity as well as care.

Her pulse raced when a "Chambers" was noted at Memorial Health University Hospital, but the first name and the age were off. Long moments later, she closed the page of listings. Sunday evening was a terrible time to get information. Best to let it wait until morning. There was nothing she could do at this point, even if she found where Thelma had been taken. Besides, it had been a long day. As for pending trouble, worry would not relieve it.

The words of scripture filtered through her mind: *"Don't worry about anything; instead, pray about everything."* It was good advice, and so was the last part of the verse: *"Tell God what you need and thank Him for all He has done."*

November was the perfect month for Thanksgiving and every day a reason for gratitude. This day especially. Kinsley had found the courage that frees the spirit. If Sapphire needed that kind of courage, would she be able to find it?

***

Meredith made her way to Magnolia Investigations on Monday morning after a surprisingly restful sleep. She was grateful. She would need it to decide, with Julia's help, the next steps to take. Seven days had passed since Sapphire Riverton had run toward them in the parking lot asking for help. They'd learned some interesting things about the Riverton family, but a great cloud of unknowns still hung over them. She shivered in the fifty-plus chill.

The sun would need to break through those clouds if they were to reach the promised seventy degrees today.

Julia was heading toward the building as Meredith pulled into the parking lot. Her burgundy car coat flagged open to reveal a silky blouse over black slacks. She was wearing stylish low-heeled boots with petite silver buckles. "Morning, Mere," she called.

"Well, you don't look like you cooked dinner for twelve," Meredith said when she caught up to her. Somehow, Julia always managed to look like a page out of *Vogue* or *Harper's Bazaar*. "Did you decide to cater instead?"

"I'll take that as a compliment, but Beau wouldn't let me get away with that. It was a full-course Cajun delight…minus the delight!"

Meredith laughed, putting her arm through Julia's. "Just what your husband would expect from his 'Julie-bean.'"

"Actually, it went very well, and everyone was pleased."

"But of course," Meredith said. Julia claimed she was only a passable cook, but she always came through in grand style.

"I have to admit I fell asleep the minute my head hit the pillow. Didn't even hear Beau's snoring. And how was your family dinner with Carter and his crew?"

"Eventful," Meredith said. "And I do mean eventful."

"You didn't burn the roast—"

"No, but we thought we'd lost Kinsley." She met Julia's quick stare. "Only for a few minutes. She was hiding under the skirt of my deck table. Almost knocked over a full vase of roses. She said she wanted to stay at my house instead of going home." Meredith couldn't hold back a smile.

"And?" Julia prodded.

"Poor girl," Meredith said. "She was being blackmailed. Can you believe it? Blackmailed in the fourth grade! Seems one of the enterprising girls in class saw her take the class turtle from its enclosure. Kinsley took it home."

Julia waited, wide-eyed.

"Some kids had been taunting it, and Kinsley felt she had to rescue it. She found an old aquarium in the garage and fixed it up. But the little blackmailer saw her and threatened to tell the teacher. She told Kinsley that she would get in big trouble—not just when her parents found out—but that she might get expelled from school. Kinsley was terrified. She believed the girl's threats and has been giving away her allowance every week to keep her quiet."

"That's terrible!" Julia exploded. "I'd throw the book at her!"

Meredith laughed. "Your Irish is showing!" Julia's ethnic background was a mix of English and Irish, but her temperament leaned more toward Irish. Judge Julia was no one to fool around with. "Carter and Sherri Lynn will handle it," she said, sobering. "I'm just glad my sweet girl had the courage to face her fear and say something."

"She takes after her grandmother," Julia said as she pushed through the door. "Let's have a double mocha to celebrate!"

"Well, you two sound happy for a Monday morning." Carmen gave her mouse a click with red-tipped fingernails and pushed back from the computer screen. "I think I've found something that might make you even happier. *¡Un momento!* I'll show you."

Meredith shrugged out of her bulky knit sweater and peered over Carmen's shoulder. Julia leaned in too, though she gave the coffee cart in the hallway a yearning glance. The coffee would have to wait.

"You know I had that appointment with Harmony the other day, right? Well, while I was waiting for her, I picked up a newspaper. It was turned to the society pages—which I don't read. Never read—if I can help it. So pretentious!" She wrinkled her nose, but her eyes quickly widened. "I was going to toss it aside when something caught my eye. It's that guy Riverton you went to see."

Meredith peered down at the page as she and Julia leaned over Carmen's shoulder. A smiling Theodore Riverton, dressed in a tux, stood at the podium. A distinguished elderly gentleman was shaking his hand. The caption beneath the photo read, "SAVANNAH'S OWN THEODORE RIVERTON RECEIVES BENEFACTOR'S AWARD FROM LOCAL CHARITY." A column of print followed that began with the organization's particular brand and a description of its good works in the community.

"That's Theodore, all right," Julia said. "He does get around." She pressed even closer. "There are some people behind him."

Meredith squinted to see a small group of well-dressed people in the background who appeared to be applauding. Two were men and one was a young woman in a formal purple gown—not clapping, and appearing somewhat bored with the whole affair. Pendant earrings highlighted dark hair with strategically placed streaks of red. "I'm looking," Meredith said with a gasp. "But I don't quite believe what I'm seeing."

Julia, parsing the article with her finger, read, "'We are honored at the presence of Dr. Theodore Riverton, whose generous gift kicks off our long-planned and much-needed fundraiser. Accompanying him is his stepdaughter, Miss Lara Franco.'"

"That name popped out at me when I was reading it," Carmen said, tapping it with the eraser end of her pencil, "because I saw it on the whiteboard. Lara's not a name you hear every day. I never knew a Lara. Well, except in the movie *Dr. Zhivago*. The interesting thing is what you just read," Carmen said, clearing her throat and giving her dark hair a toss. "She's not the maid. She's Elena Riverton's daughter, and her real name is Mary Ellen Franco. Her father's name is Ricardo Franco. He and Elena are divorced, of course. Elena married Theodore five years ago—in Reno, but Elena's name at the time of the marriage was Elena Crossley Franco Weems. So that means she had another husband in between the rich Mr. Franco and Riverton. Also very wealthy."

As is husband number three. Meredith drew in her breath. They had only guessed Lara was the maid. She'd behaved like one, had a dish towel slung over her shoulder, and Elena had issued her an order when Thelma appeared on the landing. But Lara was in fact a step-cousin to Sapphire.

"*¿Interesante, no?*" Carmen remarked slyly.

"Interesting, yes." Meredith flung an arm around Carmen's shoulder.

"Good work," Julia added. "Obviously, we need to learn more about Miss Lara Franco, or to be more correct, Mary Ellen Franco."

"I have some news too," Meredith said, crossing her arms. "Gage phoned last night as I was cleaning up after dinner. Something happened out at the ranch and Granny T was taken away. Sapphire's gone too. Back to the clinic, according to Gage."

Julia and Carmen fixed their eyes on Meredith.

"There was some trouble apparently, and Gage is worried about Sapphire," Meredith continued. "I checked out hospitals in the area, searching for Thelma Chambers, but no luck."

"Did Gage say anything else?" Julia's brows drew together.

"He said he heard about it from the cook, who came to the stable to bring apple peelings for the horses. A crochety lady with tight lips, so he says, but I bet she could tell us a lot. I told Gage to sit tight and keep his eyes and ears open."

Julia pursed her lips and released them, her brows rising even higher. "So...time for a second visit?"

"My thoughts exactly," Meredith said. "Of course, we're not supposed to know about Granny T, so we'll have to be careful what we say."

Julia had already pushed her arms through the sleeves of her coat. "Sapphire is our client. We have a right to confer with her and anyone else with a connection. So let's do it, girlfriend."

***

Meredith and Julia drove up the narrow road bordered by thick foliage toward the impressive house on the rise. With the Monday commute over, they had made good time, planning as they rode how they might approach the Riverton Ranch. The house stood in abandoned elegance with no evidence of anyone nearby. The surrounding fields too lay in gilded solemnity, the harvest having already ended but for late apples and root vegetables. Horses grazed in the meadows, their sleek bodies glinting beneath a gradually warming sun.

Somewhere on the ranch, along with other hands, was Gage, hopefully keeping his eyes and ears open to what was going on.

They would guard his "cover," knowing Theodore's hands-off policy about his family and private affairs.

What exactly was Theodore Riverton hiding? Meredith wondered. Or was he simply guarding his family's privacy, especially where his "fragile" niece was concerned?

"Quiet for a Monday morning down on the farm," Julia quipped as they rounded a curve to enter the circular driveway.

Meredith was startled by the sound of an engine approaching from behind. A shiny black Ram truck came to a stop several yards from the house by a long garage with many bays, which likely housed the fleet of vehicles used at the ranch. A man in a broad Stetson climbed out and walked toward them as Meredith parked the car close to the house. She had a sudden flashback to the night with Quin when they had been followed from the restaurant. The person in the truck had worn a cowboy hat and driven a dark vehicle. *Could be the same man*, Meredith thought, or else her imagination was working overtime.

Swarthy and formidable, with muscles visible even through his denim jacket, the man studied them through dark eyes that held curiosity as well as warning. "Help you ladies?" he asked, tipping his hat in acknowledgment. A developing beard shadowed his square jaw.

Meredith met his gaze with surprise that kept her from responding readily. She remembered Maggie Lu speaking of a cowboy with "stubbly black hair and eyes dark as mudholes," the cowboy who had appeared to resist Lara's advances near the swimming pool.

"We're here on business, Mister—" Julia paused, her chin resolute.

"Cameron Wiley," he supplied. "I'm the foreman here." He shifted a sack from his right shoulder to his left and shrugged. "Not sure the lady of the house is up yet, but you can try."

"Thank you," Meredith said. She headed up the walk with Julia but in her peripheral vision saw Cameron Wiley half turn and peer after them from beneath his Stetson. "The watchdog?" she whispered to Julia, feeling a shiver.

"Or something," Julia whispered back.

As they approached the door, raised voices carried from inside. Women's voices. Meredith recognized Elena Riverton's cultured alto and remembered her stern command to Lara to take Granny T back to her room. Her voice resounded now with controlled anger. "If you are going to stay in this house, you will do as I say! You will not sit around playing with that phone all day and flirting with Cam Wiley!"

A younger, petulant voice whined something in response, and suddenly the door burst open. A decidedly peeved Lara took one look at the visitors and fled back inside the house, slamming the door shut. Or trying to. Elena stopped it with a quick action of her wrist. The maid who was not a maid disappeared, strands of hair straying from a hasty ponytail.

Meredith faced a blushing Elena, who stood in the doorway in a turquoise tunic with wide, flaring sleeves. Her olive skin had reddened, and dark eyes glinted in her handsome face.

"It's you again!" She glanced from Julia to Meredith, her hands on her hips. Her wide purple skirt swirled like a Spanish dancer's as she stepped back in surprise and undoubtedly embarrassment at being caught in the midst of a domestic disturbance. "I must apologize. This isn't a good time." She bit her lip. "And Sapphire is not here."

"I see," Meredith said evenly. She smiled, hoping to ease the tension. "No problem. But I wonder if we could talk. Just for a few minutes," she clarified. "It would help us to understand Sapphire's situation. As we mentioned before, Sapphire is our client."

The grand lady seemed to struggle to pull herself together. "Of course." She gestured for them to come in with one elegant sweep of her hand. As though knowing some explanation was necessary, she added, "My daughter and I had a small disagreement. It is nothing really."

Meredith and Julia were directed to a luxurious sunroom off the entryway—a kind of reception area—and seated in one of two white leather loveseats that flanked a coffee table on which purple chrysanthemums bloomed in a glass bowl.

Elena did not sit but looked from Julia to Meredith, clearly at a loss. "I do not know what more I can tell you. I thought you understood about Sapphire."

"We know she has emotional problems, but she feels threatened in some way. If we can come alongside her and put her fears to rest, we may be able to help her." Meredith smiled, meeting Elena's dark gaze steadily. She didn't mention Gage's further concern, namely that Sapphire heard the voice of her mother calling and that something about her mother's death frightened her.

"Really, I don't see why you are involving yourselves in our affairs. Sapphire is under the care of her uncle, who is well qualified to treat Sapphire's problem." She paused with a look clearly intended to question what qualifications Meredith or Julia could possibly offer. "He is with her at the clinic now. He will know how to treat her. She has been upset since Granny T's breakdown."

"I'm so sorry," Meredith exclaimed. Then, with studied innocence, she asked, "Sapphire's grandmother is ill?"

Elena cleared her throat. "She has been ill for some time," she said, releasing a sigh. "Theodore has been very generous to give her a home here, but it is no longer possible—" She broke off, as though measuring her words. "I am afraid it rather upset Sapphire. She takes such things hard, you understand. It has been so since her mother died."

"Sapphire was what? Four or five years old when it happened?" Julia asked.

"Yes." Elena cleared her throat. "As I understand it, after her mother's accident, her father was rather ill-equipped to care for this huge ranch and for Sapphire at the same time. It was his brother, my Theodore, who stepped in." Elena lifted her chin, flaring her nostrils slightly.

Clearly, Elena was proud of her husband. *A proud woman overall*, Meredith thought. She waited for Elena to continue.

"My husband took care of her. He saw that she received a good education and every consideration. And then when her grandmother had the stroke, he brought her here to the ranch. He took care of them both, though he had no familial obligation." She clasped her hands over her waist like a diva about to deliver an aria. "Theodore is a very generous man. Also, a very private man."

Meredith absorbed the information while not missing the veiled rebuke. "Yes," she responded meditatively. "It must have been difficult for him, at least until you and Lara came along."

"Actually, my daughter hasn't been with us long. She was living with her father in Atlanta before she decided she wanted to study acting." She drew a slow breath, as though the topic wearied her. "She is in between jobs and planning her next move toward her career—" She turned at a scraping sound from an adjoining room.

Was Lara listening in on their conversation as she had been on their prior visit to the house?

"She has been helping out here," Elena went on. "Especially during harvest and when Glady is away. It is not exactly her idea of a job, but it is better than waiting tables in Atlanta."

"I imagine she's been helpful in seeing to Sapphire's grandmother too," Meredith said casually. "How is she, by the way?"

Elena cleared her throat once more and twined her fingers with their silver and turquoise rings. "Unfortunately, she needs more medical and emotional care than we can give her here now. We arranged some time ago for her care at Good Haven Health Center when it should become necessary." Elena, still standing behind her chair, lifted her chin in a decided gesture. "Good Haven has one of the finest facilities for long-term dementia care. She will be well looked after."

Julia exchanged a quick glance with Meredith before giving Elena a direct look. "That must have been hard on Sapphire."

"Sadly, yes. Theodore took her to the clinic for some rest…" She paused in midsentence and grasped the chair back more firmly. Not dropping her eyes from Meredith's face, she said in a raised voice, "You might as well come in, Lara!"

The young woman stepped around the corner into the room wearing, as she had before, a butcher-style apron that appeared hastily flung over her peasant blouse. Her close-set eyes were lighter than Elena's, golden brown and heavily mascaraed, giving them a dramatic flair. "Hello," she said with demure sweetness in contrast to her previous haughty demeanor. She turned to her mother. "Sorry to intrude, but was it the stewing chicken or the rib roast you wanted out of the freezer?"

"The roast, dear." Elena smiled but put a hand on Lara's arm, deterring her from a quick exit. "Never mind now. These ladies are here about Sapphire."

"Meredith Bellefontaine," Meredith said. "And my business partner, Julia Foley."

"Pleased to meet you," Lara said, looking anything but pleased. The amber eyes met Meredith's and quickly dropped.

"Actually, Sapphire is our client," Julia put in.

At Lara's frown, Elena explained. "Sapphire hired these investigators to look into some personal concerns."

A kind of exasperated sigh accompanied Lara's quick eye roll and pursed lips. "That girl doesn't need private investigators. She needs a shrink—"

"Lara!" Elena scolded.

"Another shrink, that is, since Teddy dear hasn't been able to fix her yet." She clasped her arms defiantly over her chest. "I'm sorry, Mother! But it's true. She's as nutty as Granny T. Maybe she'll start throwing rocks too!" She pushed up the sleeve of her blouse to reveal a reddish bruise. Then she turned, her shoes making a squeaking sound on the marble tile. And abruptly she left the room.

"I am sorry," Elena said. "My daughter is upset. I am afraid she has learned some rather bad manners from my former husband."

"Rocks?" Julia exclaimed.

"Granny T always liked walking in the garden," Elena said. "I suppose because of what happened. Losing her daughter like that, but I had no idea she was collecting stones and keeping them in her drawer." Her face darkened, the carefully drawn eyebrows raised high. "Throwing that rock could have given my daughter a concussion! You can see that we had to do something. It is why we had to take Granny T away—for her own protection and ours."

Chapter Thirteen

"You have to see the rock garden, Mama!" Gigi's eyes shone. She grasped Thelma's hand to lead her away from the party. "It's so beautiful. It's like a paradise!"

"But shouldn't we stay with the others? We won't be able to see Sapphire from there."

"Just for a moment. I want to get away from all that noise. Sapphire and the children will be riding Patsy, now that they've had lunch. And besides, Teddy will be there."

Patsy was the pony Preston had bought for Sapphire's first birthday. Teddy, or as Thelma knew him, Theodore, was the psychologist turned rancher and indispensable keeper of his brother. It occurred to Thelma that she saw more of him than Preston when she was at the ranch.

Sapphire was three years old today, and the grand party taking place on the extravagant front lawn of Riverton Ranch was a display of fabulous color and luxury. Huge balloons in pink and purple filled the air, and great urns of flowers in matching hues were interspersed among meticulously trimmed hedges and decorative trees.

Crystal decanters of lemonade and endless plates of food adorned the festooned tables. Sandwiches were cut in enticing shapes—owls and dogs and kittens and monkeys. A few yards from a colorful bounce house, a popcorn machine turned out great fluffy balls that were scooped into bags to the delighted whoops of children. Clowns made balloon animals and pulled magical bouquets of flowers from behind their backs. Endless silk streamers flowed from their pockets.

Sapphire, in a yellow dress that matched her golden curls, looked awed and delighted as she took it all in. The party included adults as well as children, all come to celebrate Sapphire Sue Riverton's special day. All bearing extravagant gifts.

"Let's go to the rock garden," Gigi said, tugging at Thelma's hand. "It's such a beautiful place."

The lush space had been built years before by the first Preston Riverton. Though less grand in scope and cut out of a hill behind the ranch house, it was said to rival the famed Rock Garden of Chandigarh in India. Although Gigi insisted it was her special place to find a sense of peace, Thelma found it bleak and lonely.

Thelma looked back at her small granddaughter and saw that she was in her father's arms. He was holding her aloft, his white jacket flapping as he danced with her, cheering loudly and whirling her around. How tiny and fragile she appeared, her blue eyes dark with wonder and maybe fear.

Preston's face was florid, as it often was lately. Perhaps he'd been drinking already at three in the afternoon. Thelma's heart flailed. It was a normal reaction. However able the daddy, a grandmother shudders to see a tiny child tossed into the air.

"He drinks too much, Gigi. You know he does." She had told her daughter so on more than one occasion.

Gigi's hand tightened on Thelma's as she too took in the scene. She hesitated, as though she would turn back, but suddenly Teddy appeared before his brother could bounce the child up in the air again. Theodore Riverton was shorter than Preston, younger and brawnier, with red hair and thick sideburns. He wore a western shirt dressed up with a fancy vest and bolo tie.

"That's probably enough excitement for now," he said, taking a firm hold on Sapphire. "Jeanie can get her some lemonade, and she can sit in the shade until Patsy is brought out." Then he leaned close and said something into Preston's ear.

A matronly woman in an oversized tunic over a long skirt emerged from the milling crowd. Theodore handed the child over to her. But his eyes spanned the distance to Gigi, and he gave her a smile of reassurance.

They walked away to the back of the massive house and up the shrouded trail to the rock garden that stretched beyond and beneath Thelma's gaze. It had been built in tiers with a dazzling display of rock and flora, stone, and sculpture. It began high on the hill and descended downward. Huge boulders rose in the air. Some loomed tall and pointed, others rounded and smooth. Water from some upper source trickled over them, dancing down among ornamental trees, multi-colored flowers, and rocks. On wider ledges were benches where one could sit and contemplate from a safe position.

It was beautiful, but Thelma felt an odd sense of awe or dread or some emotion she couldn't name. She'd lived her whole life in the city. She had never been surrounded by so much wild beauty. She felt somehow detached, transported to a kind of alternate universe she didn't understand.

Gigi lifted the latch on the gate that enclosed the upper part of the garden and kept curious children at bay. She stepped inside, moved in a kind of rapture to a stone bench, and sat down. She stared for a long time at the panorama spread out beneath them before turning to Thelma.

"Could heaven be as beautiful, Mama?" she asked, blue eyes dreamy. Not knights-in-castles dreamy or queens-in-gorgeous-dresses dreamy, but an otherworldly vacuum Thelma couldn't quite reach.

Thelma drew in her breath. Her daughter had always been different, often unique in her expressions, but this remark unnerved Thelma. "I don't know, but I'm sure heaven is quite beautiful. More beautiful than even this garden you like so much."

Gigi tossed her hair over the shoulder of her pale blue dress and breathed in the heady air that wasn't quite warm enough for comfort. "Someday I'll see it, Mama, and I think it will have a beautiful garden."

"Here, put this on," Thelma said, wrapping her own shawl over her daughter's thin shoulders. "Are you all right, Gigi?"

"*Mm,*" *she mumbled under her breath, as though she hadn't heard or considered the question of any importance.*

"*Has it been all right? I mean with you and Preston?*"

She said nothing right away. Presently, she shrugged and bent to pick up a small stone from among the blades of blue fescue grass near the bench. "*I especially love this one, Mama. It's almost the same color as the grass, isn't it?*"

"*And very much like your eyes, honey,*" *Thelma said gently.*

Gigi tucked the stone into her mother's hand. "*This one's for you,*" *she said.* "*Keep it always to remember me.*"

Why did she say things like that? As though Thelma needed anything to remember her by! They were separated by only a few miles and could see each other whenever they wished. Thelma put the bluish stone into her shoulder bag, wishing she could tuck her daughter inside too and take her home. Take her away from this place. But she was a married woman now with a daughter. For better or for worse, Garnet had chosen her life. "*It's a bit chilly up here so high,*" *Thelma said, shivering.* "*Besides, Sapphire will be looking for you, honey.*"

"*Mm,*" *she mumbled again with a sigh. But she let Thelma lift her to her feet and turn her reluctantly away from the captivating vista.*

After leaving Elena and Lara Riverton, Meredith and Julia stopped at a favorite coffee shop. They reflected on what they had learned, first from the newspaper article, which was then confirmed by Elena herself. Lara was not the maid but her own daughter.

"Guess we know what Lara thinks of Sapphire—'crazy as Granny T,'" Julia said.

"It's hard to believe that an old woman like Thelma would have a stash of rocks in her bedside table." Meredith toyed with the pastry she had ordered, burdened by the tragedy that Thelma had experienced.

"And that she would pitch one at Lara, though in her place I might have been tempted."

"Lara's quite the character," Meredith said. It had to be difficult to deal with broken relationships and ever-changing homes and lifestyles. Divorce had terrible consequences, and almost always it was the children who suffered. Elena had mentioned that the argument between herself and Lara involved some work Lara was supposed to do but hadn't wanted to. Apparently, "helping out" at the ranch wasn't something Lara enjoyed. She recalled the oversweet remark to Elena about roast beef or chicken. Yes, acting would be more her line.

Julia raised an eyebrow. "Guess she has to keep things on an even keel with her mother and stepfather if she wants a place to hang her hat while she's 'in between' things."

"We'll have to do some more checking," Meredith said. "There must have been some friction between her and Granny T. I'd like to be a fly on the wall in that house and see how they all really get along."

"I feel bad about Thelma, though," Julia said. "Even a place like Good Haven—however good it may be—isn't anything like home."

"Mm," Meredith affirmed. The whole story was terribly tragic. Garnet Georgianna Riverton with so much to live for and a small child left feeling responsible for her death. Why? What had really happened in that garden? What did Thelma Chambers know? "Let's stop at the library and tell Maggie Lu about Thelma. I'm sure she'll want to send her a card or something."

Julia whipped her cell phone from her purse. "I've got that four o'clock appointment, remember?"

"Oh yes, I do remember," Meredith said. She too had an appointment. Dinner with Quin. They had kept in touch the last few days by phone, but nothing took the place of being together. As always, her feelings for Quin came mixed with doubt. What would Ron have thought of him? How would he feel about their friendship? She sighed and shook away the questions. "As it happens, I have a date with Quin tonight, so we'll both have to make it a quick visit at Carnegie."

Julia smiled and gave her friend a knowing glance. "Absolutely, Mere. Make sure you have time to change into something special. You don't want to keep that charming man waiting!"

Carnegie Library came into view. Meredith veered sharply around the corner and gave Julia a mock scowl. Julia liked to tease her about Quin, but she thought him a good catch.

Julia gave an innocent shrug. "Just sayin'."

"As it happens, I asked Quin to keep his ears open at the courthouse. Sometimes he learns things from his colleagues that can be helpful. We don't know the terms of Sapphire's trust fund. I'm hoping that Quin might be able to glean something from his rambles through jurisprudence these days."

"Of course," Julia said, still grinning. She nudged her playfully. "But don't spend all evening talking about the case."

They found Maggie Lu clearing the reference desk in preparation to leave. The area was empty of visitors, and Maggie Lu's jacket and purse lay at the ready on her chair. She looked up with surprise and a quick smile.

"Didn't expect to see you today." Maggie Lu crossed her arms loosely over her navy dress. "Something up?" As always, her perceptiveness was spot-on.

"We've just come from the Riverton place," Julia said.

"We don't want you to miss your bus," Meredith said, seeing that Maggie Lu had been about to leave for the day.

"No worries. Charlene is picking me up, but she probably won't get here for another fifteen minutes." Maggie Lu nodded to the clock on the wall. She moved her jacket and purse off her chair and sat down, motioning for them to sit also.

"We knew you'd want to know," Meredith began after they were settled. "Thelma Chambers was taken to Good Haven. I guess it was an arrangement they knew would be necessary if she got worse, so when things spiraled out of control, they took her there."

"Oh, I am sorry," Maggie Lu said, dark eyes registering concern.

"Elena said there was a flare-up between her and Lara—she's Elena's daughter. Her real name is Mary Ellen. She chose Lara as a stage name."

Maggie Lu's grave expression deepened. "I didn't know Elena had a daughter. Theodore's too?"

"No," Meredith replied. "She's from a previous marriage and hasn't been at the ranch long."

"Long enough to cause some friction, apparently," Julia put in. "But in any case, Thelma threw a rock at Lara." Julia grimaced. "We saw the bruise on her arm."

Maggie Lu listened until Meredith and Julia had related all they knew about the incident. She remained still, her brows knit together, and after a few seconds opened her purse. She drew out the stone that Thelma had given her.

"I've been studying up on rocks and minerals," she began thoughtfully. "Haven't done that since I taught sixth grade science." She turned the lumpy blue stone over in her fingers. "I think it's a moonstone—aluminum silicate, part of the mineral family of feldspars. I read it can be found in many colors, including pink, green, and brown or blue like this one. There could be deposits in the rock garden on the ranch, but this one is a particularly fine specimen." Maggie Lu held it up to the light, and its blue luster shone.

"It's lovely," Meredith agreed.

"Could be Thelma's favorite because of the color. Blue, like sapphire," Julia suggested.

"She must have held on to it for a long time, since she couldn't have been in the rock garden for years," Maggie Lu said. "No one has tended it, and they've fenced it off for safety."

Meredith met Maggie Lu's discerning gaze. Whatever the significance of that stone, it clearly meant something to Thelma.

Meredith mulled it over all the way back to the office, where she dropped Julia off for her appointment.

***

Meredith had barely finished applying her blush when three quick rings of the doorbell announced Quin's arrival.

He was seldom late but thankfully, never early. She passed the hall mirror, reasonably satisfied with the burgundy knit dress she'd chosen. It had a subtle flare to the skirt, three-quarter sleeves, and a round neckline to show off her favorite gold-leaf necklace. She shook her head at herself, wondering that she could still feel like a college coed about to welcome her homecoming date.

But the man standing in the doorway in a gray Donegal tweed jacket was no collegiate. The passing years had marked him pleasantly, leaving the shine of gentility on his handsome features. His smile never failed to stir something in her—something that said the world was better because he was in it.

"I'm not late, am I?" he asked with the assurance of a man who knew he wasn't.

"Right on time," she said, taking the bouquet of red and gold chrysanthemums he held toward her. "They're lovely, Quin. Thank you." The quilled variety of mums with their pointed petals and starburst centers were her favorite.

"The street vendor said it was the flower of the month," he said, admiring her with his amazing eyes. Disarming at first but not disturbing, they seemed to absorb the whole of life with its infinite variety.

"Perfect," she declared, ushering him into her comfortable sitting room. "Long day?" He didn't look in the least weary, however, despite having traveled many miles and just returned that afternoon.

"Actually, I got back earlier than I expected," he said. "I checked on our dinner reservation, and we're good. There's no hurry."

"I'll put these in water," Meredith said, heading toward the kitchen. "Can I bring you something to drink? Cider? Cheerwine? Ginger ale?" She kept the fridge stocked with Diet Dr Pepper for Julia and Cheerwine for Beau, a cherry-flavored soft drink manufactured in North Carolina. Ginger ale was usually Quin's first choice, and she enjoyed it too.

"Ginger ale would be great."

When she returned with two glasses, Quin looked pensive, his head tipped back slightly, hands folded. "Those thoughts are worth more than a penny—and more than one ginger ale," she said, setting the drinks on the coffee table and joining him on the couch.

"I was thinking about what you told me about the Riverton case you're working on." He frowned. "You've turned up quite a few interesting aspects. By the way, have you seen any other strange vehicles around?"

"We don't know that someone was really following *us*," Meredith said. "Gage Gallagher insists he wasn't, and we haven't seen anyone tailing us since then...."

But she was remembering something else. The foreman—Cameron Somebody—had driven up behind them in a big black Ram when they called at the Riverton Ranch that morning. He'd seemed amiable enough, but who knew what he was up to besides fending off Lara Franco's advances? Maybe he had been the one tailing them from the restaurant. Maybe he was the eyes and ears of Theodore Riverton.

"You've yet to actually talk with your client, right?"

"That's right," Meredith said with a sigh. "Gage says she was ready to talk to us, but now with what's happened, I'm not sure what to think. I'm told she was quite upset when they took her grandmother away. She's back at the clinic and in a nervous state, so I understand."

"But you're thinking something is going on, maybe something to do with her inheritance," Quin said quietly.

"Well, we understand that Riverton Ranch is being held in trust for her. Gage says it's common knowledge."

Quin was quiet for several moments, a frown perched on his forehead. Then he said slowly, "Courthouse gossip is often just that, gossip. But the word is that the ranch is bleeding money right now. Theodore might need to keep Sapphire's trust fund as it is to keep things afloat. There's also the possibility that Preston could have revised his will. Someone else might have a motive."

Meredith bit her lower lip reflectively. Theodore had cared for Sapphire since she was a child. *I couldn't love her more if she was my own flesh and blood.* But if he needed money from her trust fund, he might have a reason to keep her dependent on him. And how did Elena figure into the estate? Could she be working against Sapphire somehow? "Oh, Quin, it's so sad. There's always someone ready to take advantage of a weaker party. But somehow I think this has less to do with money and more with Garnet Riverton's death."

"Whatever you do, tread carefully," he said. Then he reached for her hands. "If what you uncover proves to be a threat to Theodore or someone else, you could be in danger, and I—" He broke off, releasing a quick breath. "I just want you to be safe."

The earnestness in his manner touched her. In the past she'd quashed his protests about putting herself in harm's way. She'd told him she could take care of herself, much as she did with Carter. Now, the warm pressure of his hands filled her with tenderness. It was almost too much to contain. "I promise to be careful," she said. Then she rose from the couch abruptly and pulled him up with her. "But right now, I'm hungry, and you promised me dinner."

Chapter Fourteen

THE SENTIENT BEAN, FRAGRANT WITH the aromas of coffee and caramel, buzzed with early-morning activity. It was a familiar haunt, and Meredith had agreed to meet Julia for breakfast. Meredith slid in across from her. "You beat me. And I thought I was early."

"And still glowing, I see," Julia remarked dryly. She fluttered her eyelashes coyly. "How was dinner last night?"

"Dinner was perfect," she answered. "Chicken Marsala, asparagus with goat cheese, and Southern peach upside-down cake for dessert. But I don't suppose you were inquiring about the cuisine."

Julia laughed. "Touché."

"Quin was good too," Meredith said. "We had a very enjoyable evening…candlelight, silver, and he even brought me flowers. Gold and crimson mums, perfect for this autumn month."

"Uh-oh, you better watch it. Sounds like he's circling the wagon and closing in."

"It was just dinner!" Meredith said. "Besides, last night wasn't just about a date. He had some news about Theodore Riverton."

Julia set her cup down and raised an eyebrow. "Want to order first?" she asked as they were interrupted by the waitress setting a blueberry Danish in front of her.

"That looks good," Meredith said, pointing to Julia's pastry. "I'll have one of those, please."

"Coming right up." The dark-haired waitress darted away with a quick smile.

Meredith groaned. "But after last night, I should be fasting for the entire week!"

"So, tell me about Quin's news," Julia pressed.

"It's not really news. Quin was careful to say that what he heard was simply courtroom gossip."

"Well, I know all about that." Julia frowned. "There was a lot of that going around back in my tenure as judge. Still, sometimes gossip can be useful."

"The word is that Riverton Ranch has been losing money. Could give Theodore a motive to keep Sapphire dependent on him."

"Really," Julia said. "The ranch still looks like a frontier Taj Mahal, but these are difficult financial times." She studied Meredith's serious eyes. "Are you thinking that Theodore might borrow funds, say, funds held in trust in order to tide him over?"

Meredith shrugged. "It would be a desperate move. And illegal, of course. But it does give him a motive to keep Sapphire dependent on him. We know that she has to be twenty-one and able to handle her own affairs to take over the trust."

"So do you think it would be in his best interest if she's not well enough to be on her own?"

Meredith sighed. "He's pompous and domineering but says he cares about Sapphire. He has been taking care of her for years. For Thelma too since her stroke. A lot of people view him as a philanthropist, and as for Sapphire, according to Gage, she adores him."

Julia pursed her lips and said nothing for a few seconds. "I haven't been a fan of Theodore Riverton, but there's a whole lot more we'll need to know before we suggest that he might be tampering with Sapphire's inheritance. Do you suppose she hears a real voice under her window at night? Could someone be acting with sinister intent?"

"Maybe," Meredith said. "Quin also reminded me that Elena might have a motive to keep Sapphire from taking over her own trust fund. I think we need to talk to someone who can fill in some gaps."

"Who would that be?"

"Gage says the cook has been around for a long time and knows a lot about the family's affairs," Meredith said. "She's the one who told Gage that Thelma was removed from the ranch. Her name is Glady Livingston, and she's not staying at Riverton right now since the roundup is over and most of the harvesting is done. She has a place south of Fancy Hall and goes in to work when she's needed. We were planning on paying her a visit. I think we ought to take a run over now—or as soon as possible. Could you be ready to go this afternoon?"

"I was born ready," Julia said, pressing her plate away and straightening to her full height.

**

"Glady Livingston has worked at Riverton for more than twenty years," Meredith said as they drove onto the street directed by the GPS. "She's got to have a wealth of information."

Julia frowned. "But what will she be willing to share? That's the question."

"I think we're about to find out," Meredith said. "I'm told she's a crochety old lady, but according to Gage, Sapphire is fond of her. Oh, there's Magnolia Lane." She navigated the turn onto a shaded street and almost immediately heard the automated voice tell her, "You have reached your destination. Your destination is on the right."

"Miss Velva always sounds so smug, doesn't she?" Julia quipped. Miss Velva was Meredith's name for her GPS. Julia enjoyed mimicking her fractured pronunciation.

"That's it—217," Meredith said. She pulled up along the curb. The street was attractive—old Southern streets attractive—with tasteful, well-kept cottages. Bushes and late flowers bloomed beneath windows that sparkled with cleanliness.

"Look at those kids playing," Julia said, pointing. "Neighbor kids, or does Glady the cook have grandchildren?"

Two small girls were jumping rope, and a boy of seven or eight threw a tennis ball at the door, which opened abruptly.

A stout woman clambered onto the porch. "What do you kids think you're doing with all this ruckus?" She clamped her hands onto wide hips and stared down at them through stormy eyes overhung with bushy brows.

The kids continued their play, including the boy with the ball that ricocheted from the lady's door back to his waiting hand. "Ah, Miss Glady, we thought you were up by now." There was not the slightest hint of fear or shame in his voice and a twinkle of mischief danced in his eyes. The boy tossed the ball into the air two or three times and caught it deftly each time.

"I suppose you think I'm made of money, you motley bunch of hooligans!" The lady of 217 Magnolia shook her head and stomped back inside. *To call the police*, Meredith thought. Confused and mesmerized, she stood with Julia watching. But the door didn't slam shut.

The woman reappeared, holding a large plastic bowl, which she plunked down on the stoop of her cottage. "Here! Stuff your grubby little mouths with these and let an old woman get her rest!"

Cookies! Grumpy Glady Livingstone had brought them cookies, likely just as they had anticipated, for they leaped chattering and laughing to help themselves from the bowl.

Glady cast her stormy eyes at the two women standing a few feet from her house. "And what do you two want?" she demanded in a voice that would have wakened the whole neighborhood if its occupants were sleeping at eleven o'clock in the morning.

The children danced off with their sweet prizes, leaving their ferocious benefactor glowering at the partners, her hand braced against the doorframe.

"Mrs. Livingstone?" Meredith inquired tentatively, stepping closer to the porch.

"You presume!" she said testily but with a little gleam of humor at her joke.

"I'm Meredith Bellefontaine, and this is my partner, Julia Foley. We're from Magnolia Investigations and were hoping to talk to you about Sapphire Riverton."

The truculent expression morphed into avid curiosity and then a forced return to severity. "I suppose you want to come in," she said, moving slightly to one side. "Hope you aren't expecting hospitality. Those brats ate all the cookies."

"Just some conversation," Julia said as she took a step nearer.

"I got no time for chitchat," she said grumpily. "But you might as well come in. And wipe your feet! I just cleaned this floor! And don't let that mangy bunch of kids in!"

Meredith nodded with a smile. Glady Livingstone protested too much. The woman was nearly as wide as she was tall and sinewy despite her bulk. Meredith guessed that one might underestimate her strength at their peril. Dressed in a housedress that had likely seen many years of wear, she had a paisley scarf wrapped around wiry gray hair.

"I'm sure you're busy," Meredith began. "We're sorry to disturb you."

"If you were sorry, you wouldn't be here bothering me!" she said. "Sit there, if you've a mind to." And she herself plopped down in a straight chair by a window across from them. The sun shone on her mahogany skin and highlighted its abundant wrinkles.

The living room was tidy with old but well-cared-for furniture of good quality. A plaid slipcover draped the sofa, and a few photos in oval frames hung on the wall of the living area. There were blinds at the window but no curtains. Nothing feminine or fluffy, except for a few flowered china cups in a cabinet near the sofa. The room, it seemed, was as severe as the woman herself.

"Who'd you say is calling?" she demanded.

"Meredith and Julia," Meredith said. "We are partners at Magnolia Investigations."

Glady's eyes flickered briefly but her lips remained fixed.

"We know that you are employed at the Riverton Ranch, Mrs. Livingstone, and we wanted to ask you a few questions about Miss Sapphire Riverton."

Glady pursed her lips but said nothing.

"Sapphire has asked us to help her. She expresses a fear that someone has been watching her." Meredith paused briefly. "Also, that she hears her mother's voice calling. We know about her mental and emotional history and that she is often a patient at her uncle's clinic. But she has asked us for help, and so we are trying to understand if her complaints are valid. We thought someone who has worked at Riverton Ranch as long as you have might know something about all this."

Glady regarded them quietly through hooded eyes, silent so long that Meredith wondered if she intended to reply at all. "You've been employed there for more than twenty years, haven't you?" she urged mildly.

"That's true," she responded, scrutinizing her interrogator. "But I don't get involved in my employer's affairs. It's none of my business and it's hardly healthy."

"We don't want to compromise your position at Riverton, but a young woman's future is at stake here. Not to mention her happiness."

"You been talking with young Gallagher," she said with a sidelong glance.

"As a matter of fact, he's concerned too. He believes Sapphire could succeed on her own but that someone might be holding her back for reasons that aren't clear at all."

Something hard glittered in the cook's eye momentarily. "That child has had a hard row to hoe from the time she first saw the light of day."

"What do you mean?" Meredith urged.

"Oh, she had everything a child needs…perhaps." Glady drew her bushy brows together. "But Sapphire's mother was like a child herself. And the two of them—she and Mr. Preston—always off to some party, flouncing around town, leaving that child with one nanny after another." She shook her head. "Sometimes, money is nothin' but a curse."

Meredith nodded. She had always had the close attention and love of her parents. Had those things been lacking for Sapphire?

"When did you come to Riverton, Ms. Livingstone?" Julia interjected.

"Ever since Mr. Preston brought Miss Garnet to the ranch. They got married there. Biggest society wedding folks around ever heard of."

"So you were there when Sapphire was born—some twenty years ago?" Julia crossed her legs and leaned in closer.

"Prettiest little thing she was. All yellow hair and eyes like the jewel she was named for. Looked like her mama, she did. They were so proud—gave that child everything." Glady's wrinkled fingers gripped the arms of her chair. Her eyes took on a faraway mistiness.

"Please go on," Meredith said quietly.

Glady leaned forward, pursed her lips, and rocked a little in the overstuffed chair. "There was always one party after another. I was running from morning till night cooking for them and for the farm-hands. Had to get extra help in. But when Sapphire's mama died, things changed. Mr. Preston took to drinking more and more—sometimes late into the night in that big office of his. Little Sapphire cried and cried for her mama."

"The newspapers said she died in an accident at home, in that rock garden behind the house," Meredith said. "They said she was alone, that it was a terrible accident." She studied the face across from her, looked for clues in her body language.

Glady sighed deeply. "Miss Garnet was always running off to that garden. She sat there for hours. Lonely place it is, all shadowy trees and old statues. Always gave me the heebie-jeebies." She paused, her dark eyes narrowing. "It was terrible what happened, and Mr. Preston never got over it. If it hadn't been for Mr. Theodore, everything would have fallen apart, including that little child who kept crying for her mama."

"Mr. Theodore? Preston's brother?" Meredith asked.

"They'd have lost the ranch without him," she said. "Mind you, Mr. Preston was a kind man and generous to just about everybody, but he started drinking more and more after the tragedy. Didn't surprise anyone when he wrapped his car around a tree one night. Sapphire was still a child in school. Losing both parents…" Glady's frown deepened, and she shook her wiry gray head more vigorously. "Well, that's a hard pill for any child to take."

From available records, Meredith had learned that Sapphire had attended an elite private school. She had made average to good grades and completed her studies. "So," she murmured after several seconds of silence, "her uncle took care of her as well as the ranch after Preston's death?"

"He did," she said. "It's what Mr. Preston wanted."

Julia looked up sharply.

"You must have known Mr. Preston well," Meredith said quietly, her pulse picking up. How did Glady Livingstone know what Preston Riverton III had wanted?

"I was witness to his will," she said with a shrug. "They needed someone outside the family. Somebody impartial, I suppose. I just happened to be handy the day it was drawn up. Me and Studs Wiley, Mr. Preston's foreman. Mr. Preston was odd that way. Had to do things his way and just when he wanted them done. Wasn't twenty-four hours later he set off in that big black car of his and crashed into a tree on old Highway 17."

Meredith shivered involuntarily. Did Sapphire's father have a premonition about his death and want to get his affairs in order? Or, in his anguish over the loss of Garnet had he...? She closed her mind to the dreadful possibility. Altogether too much tragedy in the Riverton family without adding suicide.

"So you and this Mr. Wiley are the only ones who witnessed the will aside from Theodore?"

"Yes. It was no secret though. Miss Sapphire gets it all, and Mr. Theodore holds it in trust for her until she's twenty-one."

Twenty-one and of sound mind. It was the provision in almost every such document. As trustee, Theodore held Sapphire's future in his hands. Was he behind her fear? She remembered Quin's suggestion that Riverton's financial holdings and disbursements could have changed after the will Glady had witnessed.

Meredith stared at Glady's solid form across from her. Neither she nor Mr. Wiley would have knowledge about that. The name Wiley suddenly resonated. They'd met a Wiley. The foreman with stubbly black hair and shadowy eyes who had introduced himself.

Glady crossed her arms over her stomach. A nostalgic look floated over her features. "Studs was foreman back then. Sylvester was his name, but everybody called him Studs. He had a special liking for Miss Sapphire. Watched out for her, you know. His nephew Cameron's the right-hand man now that Studs is laid up." She made a face like something tasted bad. "He's not half the man his uncle was. The young now don't have the gumption the good Lord gave 'em." She made a harumphing sound. "Present company excepted."

Meredith smiled at Glady Livingstone's view of sixty-something women as young.

"Maybe you got gumption." The dark eyes narrowed. "Reckon you'd need it to take on the rich folk at Riverton." She rocked a little in her chair as though mentally chewing on something. "Mr. Theodore doesn't like folks getting in his business, and he's mighty protective of Miss Sapphire."

Meredith studied the elderly woman's face. There was no truculence in it that she could see. Her eyes had held disdain for Stud Wiley's nephew, but as she spoke of Dr. Riverton something proud and tender colored them. Or was she simply being careful or loyal to an employer?

"Been taking care of her all these years, he has," Glady said. "Thelma too, once she moved to the ranch. Mind you, she's been bad for some time. Had a stroke nearly six years ago. She could have ended up in a nursing home except for Mr. Theodore. Reckon he knew Miss Sapphire didn't need to lose someone else." She turned to look out the window, squinted at the brightness, and turned back, seemingly distracted. "But I guess she lost her granny too—to the dementia, you know. Poor child loves her granny, she does."

"Wasn't it you who told Gage Gallagher about the trouble when you went out to the barn with apple peelings?" Meredith asked.

Glady scrutinized the two women on the sofa, frowning. "You ask a lot of questions."

"We're private investigators," Julia put in. "That's what we do."

Meredith pulled out a business card and added her cell number to it. "Sapphire is the one who contacted us," she said, handing the card to Glady. "Our only interest is to help her."

Wordlessly and without a glance at it, Glady deposited the card on the table beside her chair.

"You were working at Riverton Ranch when Sapphire's mother died, right?" Julia asked. At Glady's nod, Julia continued. "Where was Sapphire when it happened?"

Glady sighed. "It was all a mighty long time ago. She was just a little thing. Far as any of us knows, she was in the house." The dark eyes narrowed. "I recall the nanny saying she'd been difficult that day, didn't want to eat her supper or take her nap. She could be a handful, that one."

"It was Garnet's husband who found her, wasn't it?" Julia asked. "In the rock garden?"

Glady nodded. "And Mr. Preston took it bad. Spent whole days in his room alone." She pursed her lips and seemed to change course suddenly. The dark brows furrowed. "How is Miss Thelma?"

"We haven't seen her since before she was taken to Good Haven on Sunday," Meredith said. "Apparently she threw a rock at Elena's daughter Lara. Has she ever been violent before?"

"Couldn't say, really," Glady pursed her lips once more and peered through the window. "But if she did throw one of those pretty stones she liked to collect, that Lara Franco must have deserved it."

"Why do you say that?" Meredith asked.

"That girl's only been at the ranch a few months, but she's prickly as a hedgehog...rubs just about everybody the wrong way—except Elena, of course, who coddles her and lets her get away with lazing about the place like she's a queen or something." Glady shook her head. "I couldn't believe it when Elena—the girl's *own mother*—let herself be bullied into calling that girl 'Lara'—like she didn't have a perfectly good name already."

Meredith replayed in her mind their recent visit and the argument they had overheard at the door. "Elena says Lara has an eye for the young foreman at the ranch."

"I suspect she has an eye for a lot of young men, but Cam hasn't got time for the likes of her." She leaned forward in her chair suddenly and looked at Meredith and Julia with searing directness. "You just gathering gossip to pass the day? Or you gonna help that girl?"

"As I said, our only interest is to help Sapphire."

Glady blew out her breath. "Then find out what's scaring her so bad she runs off and hides."

"You think she really hears her mother's voice? That someone is watching her?"

Glady mumbled something in anger or frustration and glared through the window again. "She had some trouble in the past, especially after her mama died, but she was doing so much better. I'd hoped it was over. We all did. We hoped she could get on with her life, get her own shop maybe and make those flowery table pieces she's so good at. Maybe even go to college or find herself a good man."

"Does she ever confide in Elena?"

"That'd be like cozying up to a broomstick!" Glady said. "Don't know what Mr. Theodore ever saw in her. Reckon he needed help after Mr. Preston died, but seems to me she's done nothin' to help that poor child." Glady rocked a little in her chair that wasn't built for rocking.

"How so? What do you mean?" Julia asked.

"The bad dreams starting up again and Miss Sapphire running off by herself. 'Course, I suppose fifteen is a troubling age for a girl." She stood up suddenly and pushed aside the blinds that clacked noisily then dropped back in place. Glady turned to Meredith with a knowing gleam in her eye. "You should have asked your other detective to come in too."

"What?"

"You have him on lookout or something? I suppose two women alone stirring up the dust need a bodyguard when they're investigatin'!"

Meredith rushed to the window with Julia right behind her. She flicked the blinds back and stared out onto the quiet block. A shapeless figure in dark clothes darted around the corner at the end of the street and disappeared.

Chapter Fifteen

Was it a man? A woman? It was impossible to tell. It was just a shadowy figure neither short nor tall that had flashed past Glady's window. There was no one to be seen along the quiet street now. Even the children who had been playing on the sidewalk and begged cookies from Glady Livingstone were gone.

"What now?" Julia asked as she and Meredith sat glumly in the car and gazed out at the quiet neighborhood. "Someone was definitely out there. But I suppose it could just be a coincidence and have nothing to do with us."

"Imagine Glady thinking we had a fellow sleuth out there—just in case we needed masculine help," Meredith said. "Well, this is the second time I thought someone was watching us. Quin and I weren't sure the first time, but now…"

"That figure was too big to be one of Glady's neighbor kids," Julia said, still scanning the empty streets. She frowned at Meredith and set her chin. "You know what I think?"

"Probably the same thing I'm thinking." Meredith pulled in a deep breath. Someone didn't want them getting too close to whatever was going on at the Riverton Ranch. Was it only four days ago that a man in a Ram truck had tailed her and Quin from the restaurant? Could today's visitor have been that man?

They drove toward the office without talking for the next few minutes as Meredith mentally rehearsed their conversation with the puzzling Glady Livingstone. She had witnessed Preston Riverton's will and clearly had a soft spot for Sapphire. *She gets it all, and Theodore Riverton is holding it in trust for her.*

"Interesting lady, Glady Livingstone," Julia said, breaking the silence. "Imagine working on the same ranch for two decades. Seems to be quite loyal to the Rivertons."

Meredith let her breath out slowly. "Loyal, yes, but I discovered something when I checked on the property. 217 Magnolia Street in Fancy Hall is deeded to Theodore Riverton. Glady is hardly going to say anything negative about the man who's not only her employer but also her landlord."

Julia straightened in surprise. After a few seconds of silence, she said merely, "Fancy that." Then a few seconds later, she added, "It's interesting that Glady says Sapphire's trouble started up again after Teddy's marriage to Elena."

"'Cozying up to a broomstick,'" Meredith said, repeating Glady's words. "Guess she doesn't think too much of Elena or Miss Lara either."

"There's more to the story, for sure, and I'm itching to dig it out," Julia said. "Sadly, I'm expecting a conference call on that Arbuckle case this afternoon. I have to get back to the office and prep."

Meredith nodded. "Well, I think I'll drop you there and head over to the library. Maggie Lu's off today, but I hope Rebecca is in. I'd like another look through accounts of the death of Garnet Chambers Riverton." After all, Sapphire hadn't expressed a concern for any money that might accrue to her. Her fears seemed to center around her mother's death.

"Has anyone suggested that it might not have been accidental?" Julia asked.

"Not in so many words, but if that's when Sapphire's trouble began—as has been suggested—there must be something more about that event, something we're missing." Meredith shrugged. "It's worth a try, in any event."

"Tell Becca hi for me, and that handsome husband of hers too." Julia reached for the door handle as Meredith pulled up along the curb outside Magnolia Investigations. "And be careful. If you see any more shadowy characters tailing you, you know who to call."

"Ghostbusters?" Meredith suggested with a grin.

"Maybe we need to bust a few ghosts." Julia rolled her eyes. "Just take care of yourself."

***

Meredith never entered the Carnegie Library without a profound sense of history and progress. With each of the fourteen steps leading to the front entrance, she thought of the men and women who had preserved the lessons they had learned for future generations.

Established by eleven Black business owners from the Colored Library Association of Savannah, Carnegie was one of the most prestigious branches in the Live Oak Library System. Here famous Americans studied, including James Alan McPherson, the first African American writer to win a Pulitzer Prize. Maggie Lu always said she felt honored to volunteer there, privileged just to walk on its hallowed grounds.

She found the librarian, Rebecca Thompson, at her desk. She was smiling as she handed a young man a slip of paper, no doubt containing a reference he had requested. Sixtyish with silvering fair hair, she was extremely knowledgeable and loved her job. "Becca! So glad you're in," Meredith said, drawing up to her desk.

Rebecca pushed back her chair and got up to give Meredith a brief hug. "Me too! How are you? And Julia?"

"We're fine. It's so good to see you. And Julia sends her best to you and Kevin too." Meredith glanced over her shoulder to see if the librarian had anyone waiting for her. "If you have a few minutes, I need you to point me in the right direction. I'm looking for local newspapers from 2000 to 2005."

"Ah," she said with her customary twinkle where history was concerned. "You're on a case, of course. I hope it's going well."

"We could use a break, which I'm hoping the record can provide." Surely even the Riverton wealth couldn't hide everything.

Meredith settled in for what was likely a long afternoon, but who knew? She might get lucky. She decided to begin with the year 2005, which was the death year registered for Garnet Georgianna Chambers. Major events dominated the news: Iraqi prisoners abused at Abu Ghraib that had sparked outrage, the World War II Memorial dedicated in Washington DC, the reopening of the Statue of Liberty to the public. In the same year, George W. Bush was reelected president, defeating John Kerry, and Ronald Reagan died at age ninety-three. Economic news reported the Gross National Product at $12,740.51 billion.

She skipped through sports news in her march toward local matters, specifically society features, though economic reports might have a bearing on the Riverton fortune at the time. She searched pertinent sections for "Riverton" through a plethora of newspapers: *The Daily Telegraph, Savannah Morning News, Georgia Gazette* among a host of others. Preston Riverton had shown up in prior searches during what were probably the "fat years" for the ranch, which had appeared to grow leaner after the eighties. Nothing pertained to the death of Garnet aside from the obituary listing.

She paused in her searches to revisit the account of Preston's death in 2015. The brief and unsatisfactory account simply listed his death from an automobile accident and included a photo of a darkly handsome rancher in a tasteful suit and bolo who was heralded as "Gentleman Rancher and Philanthropist."

Meredith sighed and returned to yet another journal that tended to feature grassroots stories. She found mention of various organizations being awarded a grant or receiving recognition for cultural advancement and the like. Preston Riverton was among the wealthy Southerners lauded. Meredith made notes of each mention, quickly filling the first page, headed in bold letters RIVERTON. She was about to turn over the leaf in her notepad when she became aware of someone standing off to her left, someone who hadn't moved in what seemed a long time.

Lifting her eyes, she was startled to see a familiar face. Sherri Lynn's sister Bella Conrad stood looking at her, an odd expression highlighting her features. She had Sherri Lynn's rounded eyes and light hair, which she wore in a smooth modern style that touched her sharp collarbone. She was proud of her hair, and every time

Meredith had seen her she appeared to have just come from a salon. "Her one extravagance," Sherri Lynn had told her. "Since we were teenagers."

For as long as Meredith had known her, Bella seemed all angles and edges. Her real name was Belladonna, "beautiful lady," which was also the name of a poisonous plant known sometimes as night-shade. Meredith wondered that her parents would give such a name to their daughter, but maybe they hadn't known its more sinister connotation.

"Bella?" Meredith heard the surprise and confusion in her own syllables.

"Hello, Meredith." The woman took a hesitant step toward her. "I didn't mean to disturb you. I—" She faltered and drew her jacket closer around her thin frame. She lifted her chin in what seemed resolve. "I thought it was you sitting there. How are you?"

"Just fine, Bella." The night Bella had brought Kaden to Meredith's house after their visit to the science museum, she had barely acknowledged Meredith. Again, she felt the sadness of two families connected by marriage but disconnected in spirit. "You and Cal okay?"

"Very well. Thanks." Sherri Lynn's thirty-five-year-old sister had lived on the outskirts of Savannah all her life and had been devastated by her hardworking parents' passing before they'd had time to enjoy retirement. The family farm had to be sold—another arrow in Bella's arsenal of regrets. Then her little sister and family had moved lock, stock, and barrel to Charleston. She'd taken it as a personal insult to the family's solidarity.

"I'm glad," Meredith said, at a loss as to how to proceed. Bella simply stood there, shifting her feet in low-heeled pumps. "I didn't know you frequented the Carnegie. I'm here a lot, mostly doing research." She paused, not sure how to continue.

"I was passing through and thought I'd pick up some books on winter gardening." Bella pushed a pair of dark-rimmed glasses higher on her sharp nose. "Might be able to keep my hibiscus happy indoors this year...."

Her voice trailed off, and Meredith stood, pulling back the chair next to her at the table. "Can you sit for a minute?" She gestured to the chair.

Bella shifted, as though considering. Her hazel eyes blinked uncomfortably. "Actually, I didn't come for books." She looked down at her feet. "I—uh—spotted you as I was driving east on Henry. I—followed you because...because I wanted to see you. Actually, I've been meaning to come to your house—maybe your office, but I kept putting it off. Then when I saw you at the stoplight, I thought it was like kismet, you know? So I followed you." Bella pushed up her glasses again.

"Oh," Meredith said, taken aback. She resettled in her chair. "Please, sit down a minute. It's good to see you. We didn't have a chance to talk when you brought Kaden to my house." She gestured again to the chair. "I heard he was absolutely fascinated by the science museum."

Bella balanced herself on the edge of the chair, clearly uncomfortable. Still, a new expression softened her features. "I came in because I wanted to say—well—to apologize for some things, like pulling Kaden away from your family the other day. I—uh—know I've been hard to get along with. I've been unfair at times, I'm afraid." She paused again and pulled at an imaginary thread on her jacket. "I—well—I just couldn't...I mean, you have such a great relationship with my sister and with the kids. They love going to your house...."

"Bella," Meredith said, impulsively patting the younger woman's arm. "You hold an important place in Sherri Lynn's life and Kinsley's and Kaden's. We're all part of the same family with lots of love to go around."

Tears leaped to Bella's round hazel eyes. Meredith had never seen Bella appear vulnerable since she'd met Carter's in-laws a dozen years before. What had come over the unbending Bella Conrad?

Bella sniffled and straightened in her chair. "I want you to know that I admire you. Sherri Lynn has always said you're every woman's dream for a mother-in-law. I've always wished that I—well, that I could look at life the way you do. Sherri Lynn has told me that you pray for me. Well…" A broad smile appeared on her face. "Maybe it's working—the prayers, I mean." She sniffled again. "I just want to say I'm sorry and that I hope we can be friends."

"We're more than friends. We're family," Meredith said, touched by Bella's unusual overture of friendship. It would make Sherri Lynn so happy and by extension Carter, who felt the Conrad coolness more deeply than he acknowledged. "I'm so glad you stopped in." Bella started to rise but Meredith detained her with a hand on her arm. "I was just finishing up here." When she saw Bella follow her gaze to the opened notebook, she closed it. "Can you take time for coffee? There's a nice shop just around the corner."

"I—well—" she stammered again.

"Please," Meredith urged.

The smile that softened Bella's angular face appeared again. "Well, yes. I'd like that."

When they were seated and had ordered coffee and an assortment of small pastries, the silence descended until Bella said, "I noticed that you were researching the Riverton family." She reddened slightly. "I don't mean to pry."

"Of course you don't," Meredith said quickly to put her at ease.

"But I was surprised because—well, it was such a long time ago that I heard the Riverton name." She frowned as she met Meredith's puzzled glance. "I never met any of the Rivertons, but I've often passed the clinic. It's truly amazing." She took a bite of her strawberry Danish.

"Yes, it's a stunning facility, and the ranch is beautiful too. The Rivertons have had a long and prosperous history in Savannah down to the present generation. If the mansion hadn't burned and been replaced by a modern house, it might have made the registry of historic homes." Meredith was aware that Bella appeared distracted.

"I knew someone connected to the family. My hairdresser. Well, she used to be before she went to live with her granddaughter. Must have been, oh, five years ago or more."

Meredith nearly choked on her hazelnut coffee. "Her granddaughter? Sapphire Riverton?"

Bella's mouth tightened—as though she'd said something she shouldn't. "I don't know. I mean, I didn't know Thelma's granddaughter by name, but I know her mother died. Such a tragedy." She cocked her well-coiffed head. "I haven't thought about the Rivertons since Thelma left the shop." Her eyes clouded, and the pale brows drew together. "I think Thelma was worried about her granddaughter. That's why I suggested she talk to your husband."

Meredith swallowed. "You what?"

Bella's features remained perplexed. "Maybe nothing came of it, but when she said she was afraid something was wrong and wanted to make sure of her daughter's future, I suggested Bellefontaine Investigations. I told her I knew Ron because he was my brother-in-law's father."

"I know who you are," Sapphire had said that first day they'd met in the parking lot, and then something about her grandmother. Meredith struggled to absorb what she was being told. So Thelma had contacted Ron on the recommendation of Bella Conrad to investigate Sapphire's status in the Riverton household. But they had found nothing in the files that remained after the office fire. The case had not gone cold but up in flames.

Bella was looking at her with perplexed eyes. "Have you taken over the case now that Ron's...?" She looked away. "I'm sorry—"

"No, it's quite all right." Meredith reached over to pat Bella's hand. "I'm just really surprised. I didn't know that Thelma had contacted my husband with her concern. It was Sapphire herself who came to see me just last week."

"Is she all right?" Bella asked, frowning.

"Well, I don't know. Julia and I are still working on it."

Bella was silent for a long time. "Well, I know you'll be able to help. I think about Thelma and wonder how she is. She was my hairdresser for a long time. I was sad when she left. And surprised that she sold that beautiful shop. She told me she used to work in a pretty dingy place across town until she got her new salon, where I met her." Bella tipped her glasses up once more. "Do you know how she is?"

"Thelma had a stroke and now suffers from dementia. She's a patient at Good Haven."

"Oh, I'm sorry. I liked her."

"You say it was about five years ago when you told Thelma about Bellefontaine Investigations?"

She nodded.

Meredith ran the timeline of events through her mind. Sapphire's father had died six years ago in an automobile accident, and a year later his half brother Theodore had brought Thelma to Riverton Ranch to live. It was also about that time that Elena became his wife. And only a few months since the advent of Lara…and of course, Gage Gallagher. How did all these people figure into Sapphire's current trouble?

"You've been very helpful, Bella," Meredith said. "Until today, I didn't know why Sapphire reached out to us at Magnolia Investigations."

Bella looked across at Meredith with an energetic nod. "If any-one can help her, you can," she said quietly.

Meredith met the gaze that had once been filled with cold regard. "Bella, I want to thank you for coming today. It means a lot to me— and to the whole family."

"Well, goodbye, Meredith," she said with a shy smile that made her seem younger and trimmed off several of her rough edges.

Immersed in thought, Meredith watched her go. She was so engrossed that she only slowly became aware of a distant buzzing. Uh-oh. Not so distant. Her phone, which she had placed on vibrate during her library foray, was humming inside her purse like a fretful bee.

"Hello," she responded as soon as she could pull it from the depths of her bag.

No answer. Meredith repeated her hello and waited. She took the phone from her ear to check the identity of the caller. Unknown but the same area code as hers. She should know better—she never answered a call from an unidentified person. If they really wanted to talk to her, they'd leave a message.

Puzzled, she waited, hearing in the background something like a bell ringing faintly. Unmusical, mechanical. Clearly, Mr. or Ms. Nobody had not ended the call. After a few more seconds of listening to the odd sounds unaccompanied by a voice, Meredith clicked off. She was surprised by an odd shiver of foreboding.

Chapter Sixteen

"...Happy birthday to you, happy birthday, dear Sapphire. Happy birthday to you!"

A summer evening barbecue was in full swing on the green lawn where pink balloons and yellow streamers were hung from filigreed poles. Steaks and chicken sizzled on a huge outdoor grill. A long table covered with red-and-white cloths groaned under the weight of a feast fit for a queen. There was enough to feed the whole of Georgia, but as it was, fewer than twenty guests gathered around the tables—family and ranch staff, along with two or three friends from the private school the birthday girl attended.

The guest of honor sat before an enormous layer cake with thirteen candles. Surrounding the candles on the frothy white icing was an eruption of sugary flowers—pink and yellow roses and blue forget-me-nots. So perfect for the girl who loved flowers and all things beautiful, whose hands could create something lovely out of seemingly nothing.

Sapphire Riverton, thirteen years old and so like Garnet. The same pale blond hair swirled like fairy floss to the shoulders of her pink peasant blouse over jeans, which her friends seated on her right also wore. The girls were giddy—as junior high girls should be at a party. On Sapphire's left, Thelma put her arm around Sapphire, pulling her in toward her. "Happy birthday, sweetheart," she whispered.

"Thanks, Grandma." Sapphire's startling eyes—dark as an ocean at dusk—touched Thelma's then roved over the beautiful mansion behind them, the turquoise pool, the horses grazing in the distance as the guests ate and chattered. Her eyes searched—ever moving, ever watchful, never settling.

Another birthday, the ninth since her mother died, but it seemed Sapphire still looked for her, still marked her dreadful absence. Thelma could read it in her gaze, especially when her eyes fluttered in the direction of the rock garden hidden now from view, the garden the girl refused to go near. Thelma always searched for a lovely stone to save in Garnet's memory whenever she visited the ranch. She would invite Sapphire to go with her to the place where her daughter had loved to go, but the answer was always the same.

"No, Grandma." Sapphire's cobalt gaze would widen with unnamed terror then fall away as some memory took hold, harsh, haunting. If only she could face whatever troubled her, Thelma thought, Sapphire would know that she wasn't to blame for what happened....

"But it was my fault, Grandma. I was hiding. I was angry and wouldn't answer. She called and called for me, and I stayed under the bed because I had been bad. She looked for me. If I had only answered…"

Thelma tried to soothe Sapphire whenever the memory gripped her. She tried now to hush her fierce reprisal, but Sapphire couldn't let it go.

On that awful day, the child had gone to the rock garden—she had seen her mother fallen among the sharp stones. So still, a small pool of blood forming on a wide, jagged rock. They found the tiny girl sitting in front of the gate, which she was too small to unlock, crying and staring into the place where her mother had died.

Four years old—not old enough for kindergarten—but the day had left scars that now, as Sapphire celebrated the beginning of her teen years, yet remained.

Cheering erupted as the guests, swallowing the last of the beautiful cake, clapped their hands. The ensemble Teddy had arranged for the party began to tune up their instruments. Preston would have only the best for his little girl, but as always it was Teddy who arranged the parties, who made sure the invitations were sent and that the bills were paid when it was all over.

Thelma recollected that through the years since Garnet's death, it was Teddy who kept the ranch going. Teddy who came to the rescue when Preston's melancholy led to possible disastrous decisions. Teddy who saw to his niece's education and who wielded his considerable influence to silence gossipmongers.

Thelma felt Sapphire's nervous glance when Preston rose from the far end of the table. Her father had grown

*thinner—much thinner than Thelma had seen him before—
but he was still startlingly handsome, dark eyes bold and ruddy
face gleaming in the afternoon sun.*

*He lifted a glass and strode toward the place where
Thelma and Sapphire sat. He swayed slightly in his lithe
dancing gait. His face was merry…too merry from whatever
was in his glass. "A toast to my beautiful Sapphire," he said in
a loud voice and descended upon his daughter with kisses.
"Happy birthday, my darling."*

*"Oh, Daddy!" Sapphire said uncertainly as he stumbled,
overturning a water glass on the table. Thelma could see the
perspiration on the man's face and the tears forming in his
eyes. Was he going to fall apart and make a fool of himself on
his daughter's birthday?*

*Suddenly Teddy appeared and took a firm hold on his
brother's arm. His voice was cool and very calm. "Come on,
Pres, let her have her cake in peace." And miraculously,
Preston let himself be spirited away toward the magnificent
house—away from curious onlookers.*

*Over his shoulder, Teddy called to the little band of musi-
cians. "Strike up the music!" And after a few more steps,
"Choose your partners and get those feet dancing."*

*Thelma patted her granddaughter's arm. "He'll be all
right," she said softly without conviction. Preston, like his
child, hadn't been all right since Garnet's death. Thank God
he had his half brother to keep the ranch going and later the
clinic. Did Dr. Theodore Riverton resent pouring years into
his brother's ranch? Working for something that would never*

be his? Was his stipend as executor of Sapphire's estate enough for him? There was no time to dwell on these thoughts, for she saw a young man heading toward their table and felt quick apprehension.

"Well, young miss. How are you liking your birthday party so far?" Studs Wiley's nephew, lanky and tan at nearly eighteen, tipped his hat back on a head of unruly black hair and flashed brilliant white teeth.

Cameron Wiley was as unruly as his hair. Had been since Thelma had met the foreman's smiling, insolent nephew who fluttered around Sapphire like a moth to a flame. Studs took him in after his much younger brother was killed in a hunting accident. He taught the boy everything there was to know about working a backhoe and handling livestock, but he was growing old and unable to keep up his former pace. By contrast, Cameron could clear a field in a fraction of the time it took his uncle. Likely he would eventually take his uncle's place as foreman.

"How about a birthday dance?" Cameron smiled at Sapphire and held out a sinewy arm, the calloused fingers appealing.

A frown wrinkled Sapphire's pale forehead. Thelma's antennae rose as they always did when Cameron was around. How many times had she warned Sapphire to watch out for him? He was too suave by half, and Thelma had heard his uncle had to intervene in a few skirmishes with the law. Besides, he was far too old for Sapphire. She was a child! Thelma laid a restraining hand on Sapphire's knee. Cameron Wiley *clearly had an eye for her granddaughter. Thelma had seen it and worried.*

"The first one's reserved for her uncle Teddy. Right, princess?"

Thelma hadn't seen Theodore return from the house where he'd taken Preston. But here he was, a sudden unexpected knight, gently lifting Sapphire to her feet as a scowling Cameron Wiley took a step back.

Thelma watched as her granddaughter was led out to the open area ringed by decorated barrels and streamers. She recognized the tune the bluegrass group played: "Virginia's Reel" from the '70s: "Gents to the middle said a young girl's fiddle, and you ain't got nothin' to lose." Soon the small group of revelers joined in.

But the girl who had already lost so much and held her secrets behind those enigmatic blue eyes had a great deal yet to lose. A fortune perhaps, but most especially her heart.

Of course, it wouldn't be that simple, Meredith mused. Why should finding a simple cell phone number be any easier than this whole case had been from the beginning?

She clicked out of the white pages' directory, which had yielded no match for the number of the silent caller. A more intensive search, which required purchase, could be accomplished at the office, but for tonight Meredith was tired. This single day felt more like three. Besides, the call that came through after she and Bella talked together at the coffee shop could likely have just been one more robocall.

GK regarded her from his bowl, which she had guiltily filled as soon as she'd gotten in the door. "You've had to wait a long time for your supper," she said, casting him a fond look before returning to the mail she'd brought in and tossed on the kitchen counter.

Speaking of supper, it had been a considerable span of hours since she'd eaten. She mulled over the events of the day: the visit to Glady the cook. "Grumpy Glady" who revealed a kind heart by handing out cookies to raucous neighbor children and worrying about her employer's troubled niece.

And who was the unexpected voyeur, whom Glady had wrongly thought an operative of Magnolia Investigations? Someone possessed of considerable agility and speed had apparently been watching their movements. And why? It couldn't be anything else—she hadn't bought the notion of neighborhood youth hanging around Glady's house. Not for a minute. Nor had Julia.

As though Meredith's thought of Julia had wafted through the airwaves, her phone rang. "You home yet?" The lilting voice was marked by energy to burn.

"Just got in a few minutes ago. How about you?"

"Me too. Got the Arbuckle case sewed up. The lady was so grateful she gave me a gift card to the Olde Pink House for dinner. In addition to a bonus! Things are looking up." Julia should bottle her unique brand of enthusiasm. "So how did it go at the Carnegie?"

"I didn't come up with much from the newspaper archives, but I had a surprising visitor midway into my research." Briefly, Meredith relayed the highlights of her conversation with Sherri Lynn's sister.

"Who would have thought Belladonna had it in her?" Julia asked.

"No poison in her words today," Meredith said, reliving the warm rise in her spirit. She had few secrets from her best friend and had from time to time shared her concern over Bella and the other Conrad relatives. "This will mean a great deal to Sherri Lynn and Carter, especially to Carter. He's often felt like an outsider."

"That's great, Mere." Julia's voice softened. "I know you've been praying for this."

"But the real surprise is that Bella knew Thelma Chambers, our Granny T. Apparently, Bella had her hair done in Thelma's salon some years back. She knew that Thelma had moved to the ranch after her stroke."

"Did she shed any light on what happened to Garnet Riverton?"

"No, she read the same obits and news stories as everyone else, but here's the real kicker." Meredith paused, for her heart had leaped to a bittersweet ache that was never far away. "Thelma apparently shared her concern about Sapphire while styling Bella's hair. This would have been five years ago. Bella recommended the only private investigator she knew."

Julia was silent for several seconds before whispering, "Ron."

"Yes."

"So that's what Sapphire meant when she said she knew who you were. Her grandmother had appealed to Ron."

"Yes." Meredith drew in her breath. She'd been reduced to monosyllables, thinking of Ron mulling over the Riverton case. She could almost see his handsome head bent over his desk, perceptive eyes searching a page, hands with their clean blunt nails folded on the desk. Almost she could reach out and touch them. Had Ron also visited the Riverton Ranch and spoken to the same people she had talked with that very day? Had he too been troubled over a pair of frightened blue eyes and the secret that hovered behind them? Meredith was glad when Julia spoke again.

"But we searched everywhere at the office and didn't find anything useful. Any notes about the Rivertons must have perished in the fire."

They were both quiet for a long moment. Then Meredith said, "It won't hurt to take another look at the office tomorrow, but I doubt we'll uncover anything. We have some other knotty problems to work out."

"You mean like who was creeping around while we were talking to Glady."

"Mm," Meredith mumbled, thinking again of the odd call, the sense of someone breathing on the other end but saying nothing. *Okay*, she told herself, *so you know it was no telemarketer. The call meant something.*

"Mere?"

"Yes. That and other things." The urge to connect with Wally reasserted itself. "I'm going to see if there's anything official on Lara

Franco and that young foreman Cameron Wiley. Could have been one of them snooping into Sapphire's business and ours."

"I sure wish we knew what was in Thelma's head when she lobbed a rock at Lara," Julia said.

"It was just a small one," Meredith amended. "And it didn't make much of a bruise on Lara's arm."

"Yup." Julia laughed. "But remember, David knocked down Goliath with a single stone and a slingshot."

"Poor Thelma. What do you think was on her mind when she asked Ron to investigate the Rivertons? Will we ever know, I wonder?"

"Well, not tonight, anyway," Julia said. "Get some sleep. I'll see you in the morning. And lock your doors!"

"Julia…" Meredith paused and looked down at the numerals she had written on a tablet by the phone. The number of the silent caller.

"What?"

"If you have a minute, maybe you can trace this number." She listed the digits slowly, repeating them for clarity.

"Sure." Julia was clearly curious.

"Don't bother with the white pages, I tried that."

Julia was quiet, waiting.

"No big hurry. Probably a robocall anyway. It came while I was in the coffee shop. We'll talk in the morning." She hung up, eager to put an end to a long twenty-four hours. Tomorrow was another day.

***

"I hope you don't mind my dropping in," Meredith said, stepping into Wally's cubicle office in the Central Precinct building. She'd rested surprisingly well and decided to stop by the police station before going to the office.

It was her second visit in a little more than a week, and five days since Wally had come to her house. Was it possible he was even thinner? And there was no mistaking the shadows beneath his eyes.

"Mind?" Wally repeated, rising quickly. "A visit from you is always a welcome treat. And at the top of the morning, at that!" He reached for her hands and squeezed them warmly. "Please, sit down."

"I have a favor to ask, but first, tell me how Emily is."

He settled himself in his chair and pressed some papers aside with deliberate motions before responding. "She's about the same," he said, sounding weary, then looking up with a smile. "She loved the flowers you sent, by the way. That was very thoughtful."

"I remember daisies are her favorite." Meredith brushed an imaginary speck from her navy jacket. Daisies were so like Emily— clean and fresh with sprightly stems and sunny faces. The debilitating illness she suffered would challenge her resiliency and optimism. "I'm praying for her, Wally, and for you. I know these days are hard for you."

He nodded his thanks and said slowly, "It's good to have work to do. Mind you, taking care of Emily comes first, but having a corner here at the precinct helps, even if what I do is pretty much behind the scenes these days."

Ron and Wally had been a good team, on the job and off. It hurt to see how age and caregiving had taken their toll on the once vigorous and energetic law officer.

"There's no shortage of crime, unfortunately," he went on. "But you said something about a favor. You—uh—still working on the Riverton case?"

"We're not sure if we can help Sapphire, given her history of emotional trouble, but she might have concrete reasons for the kind of distress she's experiencing. We've been checking on the background of family members and some of the staff at the ranch."

"I see." Wally's concerned expression carried a note of anxiety.

She recalled his earlier caution that the chief wanted Riverton treated with kid gloves. "We're looking into the background of the young foreman at Riverton," she continued. "Name's Cameron Wiley."

"Studs Wiley's nephew," Wally said thoughtfully, leaning back in his chair. "He's foreman now?"

"Yes, quite a responsibility for a young man not yet thirty." Meredith studied the earnest face of Ron's old friend.

"I expect he'd be about twenty-six or twenty-seven now. Grown up." Wally seemed to peer into some long-ago window. "Studs had that place running shipshape in his day. He could outwork most men, even in his later years. I was sorry to learn he's so ill. He's been at Groverton Manor for a while now."

Meredith knew of the extended care facility. She waited, for he seemed to still be looking out that invisible window.

"The boy could learn a lot from him. Probably did if Theodore made him foreman in his uncle's place." He gave Meredith a searching look. "I hope he isn't up to any of his old shenanigans."

"Shenanigans?"

"Well, a kid is bound to sow some wild oats," Wally answered tentatively. "A few drunk and disorderly charges way back in his teens, petty theft investigations, but nothing drastic, and he didn't have to serve any time that I know of."

"I see." Meredith pictured the brawny young man who was reportedly connected with Lara Franco, recalling his sudden appearance on their second visit to the ranch. Wally's information wasn't incriminatory, but it did say something about Wiley's character, at least his past character. Clearly, Gage was wary of him. Could he be the one who followed her on at least two occasions? Was he the watchdog for Theodore?

She pulled herself back to the moment. "Well, thanks, Wally. Just trying to get a better understanding of the players involved."

"Sure. I'm glad if it helps."

"It does. But I won't keep you any longer. I'm on my way to the office." She heard her phone buzz inside her purse. "That's probably Julia. Gotta go," she said with a laugh.

Wally stood when she did. "Always good to see you."

"And you. Please give my love to Emily." Outside, she put the still buzzing phone to her ear. "Is this the National Guard?"

"Nope, just me," Julia said. "Sorry if I interrupted something, but I thought you'd like to know as soon as we did."

Meredith halted in her steps. "Know what?"

"That number you asked us to look up? It's registered to Sylvester Wiley."

Chapter Seventeen

"That's really interesting," Meredith said when she arrived back at Magnolia Investigations and had joined Julia in her office. "Wally and I were just talking about him."

"Really?" Julia's eyebrows rose. "Wally knew Riverton's old foreman?"

"He did. He does. He knew he's ill and that he's at the Groverton Care Home." Meredith looked at Julia, mystified. "How do you suppose Sylvester Wiley got my cell number?"

"I would have expected him to phone the agency," Julia said. "It would have been easy enough to look up."

"But my cell?" Meredith pushed back a lock of hair that humidity had dislodged.

Carmen suddenly appeared, waving a sheet of notepaper. "Here it is, ladies! It's not far. Twenty minutes or so." She stood in the doorway of Julia's office, one hand on her hip, a pencil stuck in the labyrinth of her dark hair. After identifying the caller, she had gathered the necessary information with her usual efficiency. "Does that mean you're heading out again, boss ladies?"

Meredith exchanged glances with Julia.

"Oh, by the way," Carmen added. "I checked. Patients at Groverton get lunch at twelve. They're probably through with dressing and the rest of their morning routine by now." Carmen placed the note on Julia's desk. "Drive carefully."

"Thanks, Mom," Julia said with a roll of her eyes.

"*No es nada.*" Wiggling her fingers, Carmen slipped into the hallway.

"She's a gem, our Carmen," Meredith said when they had climbed into the car, which hadn't had time to cool down after her return from the precinct.

"She's that," Julia said as they headed away from the agency. "And you know, if she plies her usual persuasiveness with a certain young man, you could be her mother-in-law."

"When Chase makes up his mind to end his long affair with history, I'd be proud to become a mother-in-law again."

The care home where Sylvester Wiley lived was situated in an old Starland District neighborhood. The area had changed dramatically in the last twenty years. Once an area where low-income families lived, it had shifted into a cultural district with small boutiques and cafés. Some neighborhood owners renovated their houses to rent out to young professionals. Groverton was no posh "home away from home" like Good Haven, where Thelma was, but it was a respectable brick building with forest-green awnings and carefully trimmed hedges.

What could the aging former employee of Riverton Ranch want to see them about—or see her? It was, after all, her cell number he had called. Meredith's mind still whirled with what Glady Livingstone had told them the day before and with the sudden knowledge that someone had been watching them outside the cook's house.

They signed the register at the reception desk, adhered VISITOR badges to their lapels, and followed the directions to Room 17.

Most of the doors were open as they passed through the halls. Patients lay in their beds or sat in wheelchairs with cards or flowers or small trinkets on tray tables beside them. From some doors, sounds of need or discomfort emanated. Nurses and aides went about their tasks with brisk efficiency, only a few noting the presence of visitors.

Meredith struggled with her sense of unease. Since her mother's illness and death, she had found it difficult to be around those who suffered or were incapacitated. She admired people who were able to overcome an innate distaste. After all, who enjoyed such places as these? But those who lived there needed the light and energy visitors brought. And many who visited to give comfort found themselves strangely comforted. She would like to be among that number.

Still, when they stopped at the door of Room 17, she was immediately repelled by the gaunt man immobile on a bed, a curtain partially drawn around him. An adjacent bed in the ample space was empty, the covers drawn tight. A spare dresser near the bed held a single browning photo, a box of tissues, and a dark figurine of a bronc rider.

Meredith looked away from the inert figure on the bed to consult the nameplates to the left of the door. Beside the letter *A*, signifying the first bed, was HUGO TURNER, and next to the letter *B* was the name they were looking for—SYLVESTER WILEY. He of the made-up bed and spare dresser.

The sound of wheels broke Meredith's concentration. She turned, as did Julia, to see a man propelling his wheelchair toward them. He had a thick, curly head of gray hair and a broad upper body dressed in a weathered plaid shirt. He pressed forward as though to command attention, stopping the chair a few feet from them and peering from craggy brows that hung over his eyes like eaves.

"You Bellefontaine?" The voice was strong, edgy, the eyes dark and slightly rheumy in a face that must have once been tanned and rugged but now appeared drawn and age spotted. He eyed them warily. His hands, poised over the wheels, were thick and brown, decidedly muscular, especially when compared with his atrophied legs in faded trousers.

"I'm Meredith Bellefontaine," she said, returning the stern gaze. "And my partner, Julia Foley. Are you Mr. Wiley?"

"Studs Wiley," he pronounced from beneath a gray mustache that Meredith hadn't noticed at first, so commanding were his dark eyes. Eyes not unlike those of Riverton's current foreman.

"We understand that you were looking for—" Meredith was quickly cut off.

"Not here." The chin rose, the dark eyes narrowed. "Can't hear a word in this confounded hall, and ain't no place to sit in there." He gestured to Room 17. "Besides, my roommate needs his beauty sleep." He spun his wheelchair around with amazing agility. "Follow me."

He led them to a room at the far end of the hall and pushed himself in. They entered a conference area of sorts with several tables around which chairs were placed. One table held a jigsaw puzzle in midsolve. Wiley wheeled past these to a table at the far corner of the room, turned himself around, and waited, hands tight on the wheels of his chair. He said nothing as he waited for Meredith and Julia to sit down in the two available chairs. He studied them with an inscrutable expression.

"So, you found me," he said.

"You did call, didn't you, Mr. Wiley?" Meredith asked, pressing her hands together in her lap.

He pushed his lips out, and the mustache quivered slightly in the movement. "Studs," he said emphatically. "Folks call me Studs around here." He grimaced again and added with a twitch of his broad nose, "Sylvester is a cartoon cat."

"Or a famous macho actor," Julia said in her unabashed fashion, which brought a quirky smile that quickly settled into a grimace.

Wiley's eyes scanned left and right and returned to his guests. "This is where we old horses go to pasture when we can't kick up our heels anymore," he said in a wry tone. "But I reckon there's worse places. Leastwise, it ain't no glue factory."

"Mr. Wiley—" Meredith began again. "Studs...we know you placed a call to my cell phone. I'm wondering...well, two things. One, how you knew my personal number and two, why you called." In truth there was one more: why he hadn't spoken, just breathed heavily for a few seconds, and hung up.

Wiley's mouth pursed once more under the bushy mustache as he continued taking their measure. Then, apparently satisfied to some degree, he said, "Glady told me you two were all right."

Ah, that's where he had gotten her cell phone number. She had added it to the business card she had left with Glady. Meredith waited, matching his scrutiny.

"She says you two are trying to help young Sapphire." He fumbled with some mechanism on his chair then leaned back again. The dark eyes took on a faraway expression. "She don't deserve the hand life dealt her. Me and Cora didn't have children. That's my wife. Well, we kind of adopted Sapphie. Don't like hearing she's still troubled about something. She's always been a good girl—used to love the horses and took to riding like she was born to it." The eyebrows dipped heavily like storm clouds falling.

"Sapphire came to us quite unexpectedly," Meredith said after a few seconds of silence in which Studs appeared to be corralling his thoughts. "She wanted to know what really happened to her mother."

"That woman bowled Preston over from the minute he met her and brought her to the ranch." He shook his craggy head. As though to compensate for his wasted body, his hair had remained vigorous. "Sweet, innocent kind of girl. He'd have roped the stars for her, lassoed the moon. But she wasn't cut out for the kind of high-society life Preston lived. She preferred to stay home, pick flowers and such. But we all liked her—tried to look out for her. Especially Teddy."

"Preston's half brother," Julia affirmed.

Studs released a weary breath. "Came after the child was born—ended up being more father to her than Preston was. Tried to make things work between him and Garnet. You know, took her places when Preston was busy. Saw that Sapphire got what she needed. Ain't no wonder she looked to him from the time she was a toddler, 'specially after her mama died."

"You were foreman there when she died, weren't you?" Meredith asked, feeling a shiver thinking of the accident in the rock garden.

"Worked for Preston and Preston's daddy before him. They were fair-minded people—treated me right. Mr. Theodore done right by Preston, worked hard to keep the ranch running. And saw that the little girl got good schooling and all." Suddenly the old man reached an unsteady hand to his chest as though startled. He raked in his breath.

Meredith pressed toward him. "Are you all right, Mr. Wiley?"

Julia scanned the area for available staff. "I'll get some water."

"No! Ain't nothin'," he said, putting his hand back on the arms of his wheelchair. He cleared his throat and scowled at them, apparently frustrated by his own weakness. "Ticker just letting me know it's still workin'." He jutted his chin forward like a determined bulldog. "Now Sapphire's no child anymore. She gets it all, you know. The ranch, everything."

Meredith studied him. Glady had said the same, had said she and Wiley were witnesses to the will Preston had made.

"Belongs to her," he said somewhat fiercely. "Now with what's going on…" He stopped. "Don't like to think someone's trying to cheat her out of it."

"Do you think someone is?" Meredith asked quietly.

The old man shrugged. His hands moved awkwardly on his legs. His lips seemed to move beneath his mustache, but no words came right away. He shrugged again. "I don't know. I just… Well—" His dark eyes flashed. "I just know she ain't crazy. And she did see someone."

"You mean when her mother died?" Meredith felt a lump forming in her throat. "How can you know that?"

"Because I saw someone too." The words came out in a wheezy rush. "I was up high on the ridge across from the garden—working the back forty. I couldn't see Mrs. Riverton, but I saw someone—a man—just a flash. Running—" He brushed a knobby hand over his eyes.

"Who?" Meredith heard her own voice as though from far away.

Wiley shook his head, lips still moving silently.

"Did you tell the police?"

He shook his head again. "Said I saw someone, but I couldn't tell who. Could have been any one of the hands or—"

"Or Preston?" Julia broke in. "Or Theodore?"

"You were afraid it was," Meredith said. Was Theodore Riverton buying Studs's loyalty? It might be useful to find out who covered the high cost of nursing home care.

Wiley shook his head again and squeezed his eyes shut. "Couldn't be. They wouldn't. Not Preston. And sure as you're born not Dr. Theodore. He adored—"

"But you aren't sure," Meredith said insistently. "You were afraid for your job—"

"It wasn't like that!" he sputtered. "My wife was ill—she needed care—expensive care. If I lost my job, she—" He dropped his head in his hands and remained that way for several seconds before looking up. "But it's the truth. I don't know who was there. Even after fifteen years I still don't know."

Meredith and Julia exchanged anxious glances. Sylvester Wiley was not a well man—he had been showing signs of heart distress. What if bringing up all this brought on a full attack? Meredith got up, glanced around for a staff person.

"I'm all right!" Wiley stretched out his hands to restrain them from calling for a nurse. "I'm not going to keel over. At least not right now." He took a raspy breath, seeming to relax a bit when his visitors were once again seated. "But there are some things I want to settle in my mind before my time's up."

"What things?" Meredith asked as calmly as she could.

He studied his own hands, rested now over the blanket covering his knees. "My nephew, for one."

Meredith waited for a long moment. Fifteen years ago, his nephew would have been a boy—not the mystery man he'd seen in a rock garden.

"He ain't a bad kid. He got into some foolishness, but he straightened up for the most part. Only he don't think straight when it comes to Sapphire." He took a long breath before going on. "Had it bad for her, he did. Since he was a kid, but she wasn't for the likes of him, and I told him so. Besides, she didn't cotton to him. Not like that. Crazy kid should have left that place long ago, got himself a college education—gone up in the world. It was her that kept him there."

"Has he told you that?" Julia wanted to know.

Wiley grimaced. "Don't tell me anything. Hasn't been to see me since last spring." He shook his head. "He's bitter—bitter about his ma, about me losing the use of these confounded gams." He curled his gnarled hands over his knees. "And bitter about *her*. Wants to give her the moon like Preston and Theodore did for her poor mama. I swear, it's like history repeatin' itself."

Maggie Lu had witnessed the young foreman spurning the attentions of Lara Franco. Because it was Sapphire he wanted? And what history was being repeated? Studs was adamant about defending Preston and Theodore.

Studs's voice rose in agitation. "Now that daughter of Elena's cozying up to him and making him crazy!"

She'd only been around a few months. What did Studs know about her? "You mean Lara Franco?"

"That's what she's calling herself, Glady says, but she's a troublemaker, sure as you're born, and got no love for Sapphire. Glady and me, we worry about Preston's girl. Why Teddy ever got mixed up with Elena and that daughter who thinks she's a movie star is more than I can figure. And I sure don't want my nephew caught in the middle. That high-toned Lara's been after him. Glady saw it."

Meredith remembered Lara's outburst when they had gone to the ranch in search of Sapphire: "*That girl doesn't need private investigators. She needs a shrink…. Nutty as Granny T. Maybe she'll start throwing rocks too.*" Meredith exchanged a look with Julia.

"Mr. Wiley," Julia began, half rising. "Just what is it you want from us? Why have you contacted our agency?"

"I just told you. Sapphire ain't crazy. She saw someone that day. Whoever it was, it's been bearin' down on her like a two-ton bale. Someone needs to find out the truth for all our sakes. Most especially hers."

Meredith exchanged a look with Julia and rose to her feet. "I hope this hasn't been too hard on you, Mr.—that is, Studs," she said. She heard herself sigh. "We want very much to help Sapphire, but we haven't even been able to talk with her yet."

"She's back at that clinic, isn't she?" he asked gloomily.

"Glady keeps you well informed," Julia said with irony and pushed the chair she'd vacated under the table.

"She's got faith in you," he said. Then he released the brake on his wheelchair and pushed himself toward the door. He paused before reaching it and made a quarter turn. "Sorry about the phone call. I just wasn't sure how to tell you what needed to be said." And then he disappeared, leaving Meredith and Julia to stare after him.

"Anything clearer in your mind?" Julia asked in the wake of the old man's absence. She sounded weary, on the edge of sarcasm.

Meredith studied her partner's discerning gray eyes as though the answer to the mystery lay in their depths. Sapphire wasn't the only one to believe her mother hadn't been alone when she died. Whatever happened continued to trouble more than one life, even after fifteen years. "Come on, let's get out of here and talk in the car."

As Meredith drove away from the nursing home, the old man's sadness clung to her like the odor she'd always connected with sickness and disability. Wiley had once been a strong worker upon whom people relied. Now his wife was gone, his health was failing, and there were no children to look after him in his old age. Not even his nephew, who Studs said hadn't visited since spring.

"Quite a revelation, isn't it?" Julia said. "That poor woman wasn't alone in the garden. If Sapphire knew that someone else believed her about that, it might make a real difference."

"Might," Meredith said, still trying to sort out what Studs had told them. "But without knowing who he saw, it wouldn't do much good in the long run. There was no indication of foul play. Authorities would need more to prove it wasn't an accident."

"Besides," Julia noted, "Garnet didn't inherit. Only Sapphire. Unless—"

Meredith negotiated a busy intersection in the historic district. "Yes, the will could have changed from its original form, but Sapphire seems concerned about her mother's death and her own guilt, not the money."

"But Studs suggested someone might use her emotional disturbance for personal gain," Julia said. "Her uncle? Elena? Lara? Even his own nephew. By the way, any word from Gage Gallagher?"

"Not since he called about Thelma being taken away. Would have been Sunday night." She paused. It had been longer than she'd realized. "Let's give him a call," she said, decisively.

Julia shrugged, tapped something into her phone, and put it on speaker.

Meredith listened to the rings—ten in all before Julia clicked off. Nearly noon. Maybe he'd gone for lunch or was out on the trail with a group of riders. Very odd not to get voice mail though. They'd left messages for him before that were answered. "I'd like to get his take on Cameron Wiley," she murmured, recalling what Studs had told them. "Imagine that foreman being obsessed with Sapphire since his teens and staying at Riverton to be close to her."

"No wonder Gage hasn't been on the best of terms with his supervisor. Cameron would not like to see Gage getting close to Sapphire."

They drove through three more intersections before Meredith had a sudden thought. "Jules, how do you feel about horseback riding?"

"Ambivalent, at best," she retorted. "But I say, giddyap, if you will."

"Good. Call the stable number and set it up with Gage."

"I'll have to look it up. We've always contacted Gage by cell." Julia made a series of taps on her phone and then said, "Here it is," and dialed. "I'll put it on speaker."

The answering male voice was not one Meredith recognized.

"I'd like to speak to Gage—Gage Gallagher," Julia said.

"Sorry. Gallagher doesn't work at Riverton Riding Stables anymore."

Before a blinking Julia could reply, the connection ended.

Chapter Eighteen

"WELL, FOR LAND'S SAKE!" JULIA exclaimed.

Meredith bit her lip. "It's got to be a mistake."

"I knew there was something too good to be true about that cowboy!" Julia said, her face reddening.

"But he wouldn't—" Meredith began. "He wouldn't just take off without saying anything. Besides, he cares about Sapphire."

"Well, he says he does, but the proof is in the pudding, my mama always said."

Meredith sped on, feeling her fingers tense on the wheel. It didn't feel right. Not at all. She turned off Whitaker and headed for the parking lot behind the agency. Turning in, she spotted an unfamiliar vehicle near her space and a white-haired man in a charcoal-gray suit pacing a few feet away.

He jerked around at the sound of her car, and Meredith recognized him instantly. Dr. Theodore Riverton stopped his pacing and returned to the black Mercedes adjacent to her space.

"Good grief," Julia said. "Look who's come calling."

Meredith stilled the engine and emerged to confront the rancher-psychologist. His face, which in their previous encounter had emitted a glow of good health and success, appeared blanched of color.

His hair was ruffled as though by anguished fingers, and there were gray shadows beneath his dark eyes.

"Dr. Riverton," Meredith said politely. "Is there something—?"

"Where is she?" He seemed to be making a grand effort at control.

"I'm sorry," Meredith said as Julia came around to stand next to her. "Who—?"

"My niece," he said through clenched teeth. He drew in his breath and brought himself up to his full height. "Sapphire is gone. I have good reason to believe you know something about it."

Stunned, Meredith found herself groping for a response.

Julia, using her height to good advantage, looked Theodore square in the face. "Excuse us, Dr. Riverton, but exactly what are you implying here?"

"I'm saying my niece has disappeared—with her luggage—from her bungalow. She did not check out, and no one knows what has happened except that she was seen earlier with that former stable hand friend of yours."

"Do you mean Mr. Gallagher?" Meredith broke in.

"I give the kid a job, and this is how he repays me for taking him on. My foreman warned me about him. I also know you have been conspiring with him, putting my niece in jeopardy."

"Excuse me," Meredith said. "We learned only moments ago that Mr. Gallagher was no longer employed at your ranch and—"

"Of course, you are familiar with my affairs," he said with considerable irony. "Running around, asking questions of my wife and staff, butting into matters that don't concern you. I know all about your...activities!" Color heightened his drawn features.

He knew where they went and to whom they spoke. Obviously, he had been trailing them or having them followed. Meredith held his gaze. "The fact is, Doctor, your niece asked for our help. You seem to forget that."

"And I explained to you the way things are with Sapphire. She— she—" He ran a hand through his disarrayed hair. "She has suffered severe blows in her young life. She needs to be looked after, handled carefully." Something in him seemed to crumple. "She wouldn't just go off on her own without telling me. She had a bad night. She heard the voice again. I thought that had ended." He rummaged through his hair again. "I had the nurse on call give Sapphire something to help her sleep. I stayed the night at the clinic in case she might need me, but when I went to her bungalow after breakfast, she was gone."

"Please, Dr. Riverton," Meredith said. "I assure you that we were not aware that Sapphire left the clinic, and we don't know where she is now. We need to discuss this properly. Let's go inside and sit down." Gingerly, she touched his arm. "Maybe we can help."

"This way, Doctor," Julia said, pushing ahead.

Stiffly, he allowed himself to be directed to the back door that led into the bright, airy kitchen.

"There's coffee on," Meredith said, glad they had avoided the front door of the agency. The kitchen would afford some privacy. "Please, sit down."

Julia found three mugs, poured the coffee, and set it down quietly. She sat at one end of the table, leaving Theodore and Meredith facing each other across it.

"I assume you've checked at your house to see if Sapphire went there," Meredith began.

"Of course I did," he scoffed. Then settling himself down, he went on. "Elena hasn't seen her. She's not in her room. She's gone, I tell you. And if that worthless cowboy—" He left off in apparent frustration.

"Why do you assume she's gone off with Gage?" Meredith asked as Theodore once again plowed a path through his curly hair.

"I know what he's been doing. Taking her on trail rides, sitting out there under the trees, talking." He let his breath out in a quick puff. "At first I thought it might be good for Sapphie. I told Cam that sometimes it's easier to talk to strangers. I thought maybe—well, maybe he could help her work through her depression and guilt. But he's stirred up things that shouldn't be stirred. And now, he's taken her—gone off somewhere doing who knows what..."

Stirred things that shouldn't be stirred. Meredith flinched. "If you believe she's in danger, why haven't you called the police?"

"I don't want the police involved in our family affairs. You can understand how bad that would be for business." He swallowed. "And for Sapphire. I've come here to ask for your help." His arms went rigid at his sides. "I want you to find her."

"You have refused to allow us to speak with her at the clinic. Your wife doesn't let us see her. You have had us followed as though we were engaged in some devious undertaking, and now you want us to help you?" Julia snapped.

"I had my foreman keep an eye on you," Theodore sputtered. "I admit that, but only because..."

"You had my friend and me tailed on a simple dinner date that had nothing to do with you!" Meredith said, her own ire rising.

"And someone was following us all the way to Fancy Hall," Julia added.

He neither confirmed nor denied the allegations but pulled out his buzzing cell phone. "My secretary. I asked her to call me," he said gruffly. His voice when he spoke into the phone was ragged. "Have you seen her? Is she there?"

Theodore's face paled, and following that a shattered grimace appeared on his face. "Lara was there? To see Sapphire?"

As his voice rose, the secretary's urgent soprano also rose and grew loud enough that Meredith could hear from across the narrow table. "Last night, she said she came to visit. I thought she must have had your permission."

Theodore's mouth clamped shut for a long moment. Then he said in a dull voice, "Check the surveillance footage and call me." He clicked off. The wrinkles in his forehead deepened, anger and confusion sparking his dark eyes. "Elena said…," he muttered to no one in particular and didn't finish his sentence.

"Perhaps you ought to go back to the house," Meredith suggested. "We can meet you there. Your office can keep you apprised if she shows up back at her bungalow." Meredith was seeing Lara in her mind's eye, hearing the sarcastic comments about Theodore. *"That girl doesn't need private investigators. She needs a shrink. Another shrink, that is, since Teddy dear hasn't been able to fix her yet."*

Teddy dear. It was hard to believe that Lara had paid a friendly visit to Sapphire, whom she described as "nutty as Granny T," someone likely to lob a stone at her. "Does Lara often visit your niece when she's at the clinic?" Meredith asked.

He shook his head, saying nothing as his brow furrowed even more deeply. He picked up his cell phone once more. "Put Lara on," he said. After several seconds, he spoke again. "Never mind. I'm coming home." After a few seconds, he added, "I'm bringing the Magnolia ladies." He stood, replaced his cell phone in his pocket, and looked at Meredith and Julia in turn without saying anything. The request, the ambivalence, the fear—all were reflected in his dark eyes.

"We'll be right behind you," Meredith said, rising. All three left cooling coffee on the table and moved to the parking lot.

***

A late November stillness lay over the land as Meredith and Julia approached the Riverton Ranch. Beneath a smoky sky, browning fields stretched wearily, spent after a long year of growing and gleaning. Horses grazing on dry leftovers didn't bother to lift their heads.

Following Theodore's BMW, the partners navigated the winding driveway past a thick grove of pines that shielded the ranch from casual view. All but three of the bays in the long garage were closed. The largest of the opened bays contained a huge tractor. A Ram truck filled a second, and the third housed a red Nissan Rogue with the license plate containing the letters ER. *Elena's car*, Meredith surmised and wondered what other vehicles might be parked behind outbuildings or shrouded by trees on the vast property.

They followed the agitated man to the door. Once he'd reached it in a few quick strides, Theodore held it open, tacitly inviting them to follow him inside.

Elena appeared at the top of the grand staircase where they had seen Thelma stand with her rag doll in her arms. Elena's black hair, unbound today, fell over a crimson tunic blouse with embossed flowers in a riot of color. She cast fleeting glances at Meredith and

Julia from restive, almond-shaped eyes, fixing finally on Theodore. "Teddy?" Apparently, she didn't need to ask if Sapphire had been found. She had read it in her husband's anxious face.

"Her things are not in her room," she said, eyes still trained on Theodore. "Could she have gone to see her grandmother? You know how she misses her."

He shook his head impatiently. "No. We checked there. Elena, where is Lara?"

Elena hurried down the stairs toward him, elegant even in her haste. "I do not know. I think maybe she is sleeping late, but she must have gone out." Her accent thickened, perhaps due to nerves.

"Was your daughter home last night, Elena?" Theodore asked once she had joined them in the broad front hall.

"I—I retired early. I am not sure. I—"

"You're not aware that she went to see Sapphire last night?" His voice was tight with emotion simmering beneath the surface.

Elena wrapped her arms at her waist. Her elegant head dipped. "She—she did not say where she goes. She—"

"I'll tell you where she was," Theodore said. "She was at the clinic terrifying Sapphire!" His voice thundered. "It's all on the sur-veillance footage—calling Sapphire's name while she slept."

Meredith caught her breath. Lara had been behind the voice Sapphire heard! How could she cause such anguish for the troubled young woman who had lost her mother in such a devastating way? Physically, Lara could carry it off. She was training as an actress and from all appearances had no love for Sapphire. But why had she done it? Out of meanness, or had she something to gain?

Lara, apparently unaware of what was going on, walked into the house. She gaped at the little group clustered there, and if a person could wilt, she did.

Theodore pierced her with his nearly black eyes. "What were you doing at the clinic last night? Why were you outside Sapphire's bungalow?"

No words came from the young woman's lips. Only the amber eyes, shadowed by dark eyeliner, admitted guilt.

Elena pulled her into the foyer by the elbow. "What have you done?" she demanded in an angry tone.

"What have *I* done?" Lara mimicked.

Meredith stepped toward the little group. "What's important now is that we find Sapphire. Do either of you have an idea where she might be?"

Mother and daughter shook their heads. Elena said something in Spanish, worried eyes intent on her husband's face. Lara stared down at her feet.

"This is the time for truth!" Theodore said. When both continued to profess no knowledge of Sapphire's whereabouts, he turned to Elena with controlled anger. "We will talk later, and I trust you will not leave the house. Either of you!"

"We need to check her room," Meredith said sternly into the charged atmosphere.

Elena snapped her head toward her husband, a challenge in her eyes.

He said nothing but jerked his chin, indicating that they should head upstairs.

The spacious bedroom at the far end of the hall had old-fashioned flowered wallpaper and a bed with a white eyelet comforter and shams. Two bookcases sported more than a dozen shelves of books and many pictures of flowers. Vases of silk arrangements adorned the room.

"Lots of clothes in the closet," Meredith said. "If she didn't plan to return, would she leave all of this behind, along with her personal items—books and mementos?"

"She may be terribly frightened after what happened last night," Julia said.

"I'll check the bathroom." Theodore went back out into the hall.

Meredith searched around the bed and dressers for a note but found none. "But look at this," she exclaimed in a whisper.

Julia leaned in. "It's one of those blue stones from the rock garden—like Thelma gave Maggie Lu. I've never seen that place, but I've heard it's quite magnificent—or used to be anyway."

Meredith turned the stone over in her hand, watching the facets shimmer in a surprising palette of blue. She looked up at Julia. "We've asked Gage to try to get Sapphire to revisit the day her mother died, to recall everything that happened. Do you think maybe he's convinced her to go to the rock garden?"

Julia drew in a sharp breath. "That's a definite possibility."

Meredith pocketed the stone and turned in to the hall, where they nearly bumped into Theodore. "We're going to search the grounds," she said, and motioning to Julia, climbed down the winding staircase. As they left the house, they could hear Elena and Lara, the voices alternately strained and pleading.

"Look, isn't that Gage's Jeep?" Julia asked when she and Meredith had rounded the stable situated some hundred yards from the mansion. "In that grove of trees?"

Meredith saw the vehicle, partially hidden because of its olive camouflage exterior. "It sure looks like it," she agreed. The narrow path just beyond the thick foliage was densely overgrown and wound upward. "I wish I had my walking shoes," she said, panting from the climb. It was no surprise that Theodore was following them, and she wondered again what really drove this man—concern for Sapphire or something else?

The sun had lowered in the bank of clouds and filtered sparsely through overhanging trees. A heaviness in the air teased at something waiting. Behind them Theodore had picked up his pace, as though aware of the same urgency. Meredith felt a shiver pass through her. Were they crazy to be out here in this lonely place? The place of that long-ago tragedy that might very well involve Theodore. Were they in danger from him? Yet an odd steadiness held her.

They rounded the next curve, and Meredith grasped Julia's arm. They both had seen, and time seemed to stop. Not more than thirty yards ahead and leaning over the railing of an iron gate was a slender figure in pale blue, a cloud of blond hair tumbling around her shoulders. Leaning toward her was Gage Gallagher, not touching but saying something in a posture of earnest appeal.

The figure, unmoving, could be none other than Sapphire Riverton gazing out on a vista of rock and tree and statuary made eerie in the dim afternoon. As one, Meredith and Julia stepped soundlessly forward until they could hear Gage's voice.

"When you finally came out from under your bed, you went to look for her, to tell her you were sorry."

"Yes," came the whispery voice of the young woman they had talked to in person only once.

"And you saw her there." Gage gestured slowly with one hand to indicate the garden beyond the gate. "What happened, Sapphie? What did you see?"

Theodore, having reached Meredith and Julia, now made to move past them toward his niece. Meredith put up her hands, challenging him to stay back. He must not interfere with this moment.

The two at the gate seemed oblivious to the presence of anyone but themselves. Gage continued to speak quietly, but his voice carried easily in the stillness. "It's all right. What did you see?"

"She was running. So fast. I wanted to go to her, to say I was sorry. Oh, Mama! Please stop! Please wait! And he was running after her. Running so fast!"

"Who?" Gage urged. "Who is running, Sapphie?"

In the long silence that followed Gage's urging, Meredith held her breath. Nothing moved for what seemed an eternity, and then Sapphire appeared to bend over as though stricken by unexpected pain.

Gage reached for her, put his arms around her. And seconds later, both straightened and moved suddenly apart, obviously realizing they were not alone.

"Uncle Teddy!" Sapphire's anguished voice pierced the air as she stared at him through astonished eyes. "You! It was you!"

Theodore ran toward her, arms outstretched.

"Oh, Uncle Teddy!" Sapphire dropped to her knees. Her eyes remained fixed on him. "You were with her. You—"

"Yes," came a voice almost unrecognizable in its grief. "I was there." He dropped down beside her. "I only wanted her to stop before she got hurt." Theodore seemed oblivious to the audience clustered now around him, eyes intent on Sapphire alone.

"She fell! Oh, Uncle Teddy! She was running—crying and running. And you—you were running too! I wanted to go to her, but I couldn't open the gate to help her."

"I am so sorry," Theodore said, his eyes wet. "I didn't see you."

"I never got to tell her… I never saw her again." Sapphire rose to her feet at the same moment Theodore did. She shook her head, stared into her uncle's face. "Why? Why, Uncle Teddy?" she wailed.

"Sounds like a reasonable question to me," Gage said, stepping close to Theodore. He stood with hands on his hips. "I think she deserves an answer."

"Of course she does," Meredith said, coming between the two men. She could see that Sapphire was trembling and tried to comfort her with her eyes. She gave Riverton a piercing stare. "I suggest we go back to the house. It's cold on this bleak hill, and Sapphire has had a shock."

"Yes, of course," Theodore said. Tentatively he reached for his niece, but Sapphire grasped Gage's hand and began moving away from the gated pinnacle with Meredith and Julia. Theodore, ashen faced, stumbled along after her as thunder rumbled low in the distance.

Chapter Nineteen

"IT'S NOT AN EASY STORY to tell." Theodore clutched his hands in his lap. He sat in a chair set apart from the two leather sofas in the luxurious reception area where Meredith and Julia had been directed on an earlier visit to the grand house.

Meredith assumed control, seating them like guests in the absence of Elena. Sapphire, with eyes wide as moonstones, sat next to Gage on one sofa. Meredith and Julia sat in the other across from them.

"Why did Mama run from me?" Sapphire cried, visibly trying to control her distress. "I only wanted to tell her I was sorry. I behaved badly that day, but I was sorry. I wanted to tell her, but she ran away from me."

"She wasn't running from you," Theodore said, pulse throbbing visibly at his temples. "She was running from me."

A pin drop could have been heard in the silence that followed. Sapphire's mouth gaped open. Meredith could feel Julia's body stiffen beside her.

"It's not what you think," he added quickly. "I would never do anything to hurt her." He leaned forward, his voice husky. Dark shadows deepened beneath his eyes. "Never," he repeated.

Sapphire fixed her eyes, the color of a night ocean, on her uncle. *She adores him*, Gage had said. Glady Livingstone and Studs Wiley likewise had indicated that the relationship between them was one of deep trust. Meredith watched Sapphire. Was that trust about to be damaged beyond repair?

Theodore lifted his head to look at his niece. "Your mother would never have run from you. She loved you. But...she was going to run away from this ranch, from your father and..." Here he paused so long that Meredith wondered if he would continue. "And away from me."

"My father?" Sapphire whispered. "Why would she run away from Daddy?" Dry-eyed now, she sat up straight next to Gage, delicate hands in her lap. "She loved him. I know she did. What are you trying to tell me?" Her eyes flickered. "I'm not a child anymore, Uncle Teddy." She glanced in agitation at the other three people in the room, as though to relay that truth to each of them in turn. This was not the scared girl who had pleaded for help and stuffed a thousand dollars into Meredith's hand.

"I don't mean to treat you like a child," Theodore said. "But there are some things that wouldn't be good for you to know. Things that would be hurtful—"

"Please let me decide what's good for me! Don't I have that right?"

Theodore swallowed visibly and clasped his hands over the armrests. "Your father loved Garnet." As though he'd said something amiss, he amended, "Your mother. She and your father came from different backgrounds and experiences. It wasn't always easy for either of them. Your mother was often lonely. Preston had obligations, had to be away from home a lot. And his drinking...well, it made things a lot worse."

Sapphire bowed her head for a long moment before saying in a small voice, "I knew about the drinking. I wanted him to stop. But I didn't think it was really bad until after—after that day."

"You blame yourself for that too," Theodore said. "But his drinking had nothing to do with you or your mother. My brother had a weakness. He tried to quit. We all tried to help. It's one of the reasons I wanted to start the clinic here. But his condition got worse, and your mother became more and more restless and unhappy."

"Are you saying that my father…" Sapphire hesitated, her eyes widening in fear.

"No! No! He would never have done anything to hurt her—not on purpose, but his drinking did hurt her and you." Theodore thumped one fist into his open palm. "He blamed himself for her death, Sapphire. He never got over it. I wanted to spare you all this. I—"

An odd expression came over Sapphire's face, which may have been what made Theodore cut off so abruptly. "Wait," she said, narrowing her eyes. "You said my mother was running away from you. Why? What did you do?"

Exactly, Meredith thought, feeling acutely her position as witness to this very personal family drama. But Theodore had drawn them in. Now his discomfort was palpable.

"Your mother was going to leave. She packed her bags that day. She was going to take you and leave the ranch." Theodore put both hands to his temples, as though to still some raging inside his mind.

His eyes roamed to the wide bay window beyond them. "I remember it was raining. One of those dreary, heavy days in mid-July that makes the head swim. Preston had gone to accept a philanthropy award from the arts council. He wanted Garnet to go with him. He always wanted her at his side—so proud of her. She was so beautiful and elegant. But that day, your mother wanted to have lunch with Thelma. She refused to go with Preston."

Beyond them a light mist fell on the quiet landscape. A few drops quivered on a myrtle branch outside the window. Meredith watched them slide off the slender leaves and drip to the sill as the man's slow recitation continued.

"I took her to Thelma's little shop myself and brought her home when she was ready." He furrowed his brow, but a ghostly smile trembled at his lips. "She was wearing a blue dress with a white collar. I left a meeting early to take her home. You were with her. You had a red balloon in your hand."

Entrenched in memory, he spoke as though not completely aware of others in the room—or perhaps only of Sapphire. Meredith saw that Julia's face was riveted on him.

"Garnet was quiet all the way home," Theodore went on. "She said she was all right, but I could see she wasn't. She was so still and melancholy. When she was sad, her eyes went from blue to indigo. She asked Glady to wait on supper, but Preston didn't come home. He'd met up with some friends after the ceremony. Garnet didn't say anything when he came stumbling through the door. She just stood there with that look in her eyes."

It seemed to Meredith that Theodore Riverton aged before her eyes. There was about him nothing of the well-dressed executive or the rugged, outdoorsy persona she had imagined when they'd met at his clinic. The premature white hair around the handsome face now seemed sparse and yellowed like old paper.

"When I came downstairs again, she was standing there..." Theodore angled his head toward the grand hall which they had entered moments ago. "She was carrying two suitcases. I asked her where she was going. I was completely baffled. It was pouring rain, and the thunder was terrible. She was wearing a thin blue dress and those little sandals she liked so much. I asked her what she was doing. Told her she couldn't go out on a night like that. I was shouting at her, but I was afraid."

No one spoke, though Theodore had paused for what seemed an unendurable length of time.

"She was so distraught, said she couldn't find you." He cast an anguished glance at Sapphire. "She ran from room to room and flew upstairs calling for you." Theodore made a guttural sound like a groan. "She was crying, nearly hysterical, saying she had to get away. I begged her to calm down. I told her she couldn't leave, that Riverton Ranch was her home."

Theodore dropped his head in his hands. After a long moment, he straightened and calmed himself. "You see," he said quietly, "I loved Garnet from the first moment I met her. She didn't know. There was never anything between us but friendship as far as she was concerned. I knew she loved Preston."

His mouth clamped shut, and when he opened it again, his voice was flat. "I had always protected her, picked up the slack from my brother, tried to smooth things over. And now she was leaving. I just blurted it out, told her I loved her. That I had always loved her, and I could take care of her. That's when she ran. Just left the suitcases in the hall and took off toward the rock garden. I followed her, tried to say I was sorry, to make her understand."

"You and my mother!" Sapphire breathed, more amazed than scandalized.

"I only wanted to help her, but her heart was pledged to Preston. I knew that. I followed her to the lower part of the garden, but she kept running along the trail, going deeper into the garden. She yelled at me to go away, to leave her alone." He closed his eyes for a moment then opened them again. "I did go away. Oh, how I wish I hadn't. But I was sure she'd come back to the house and we could talk. I knew she wouldn't leave without you, Sapphie."

Meredith broke in. "But she didn't come back, did she?" The statement sliced the air, startling.

"No, and when it began to get late, I worried. I told Preston where she was. But not before I stormed into his study and told him what a cad he was for treating Garnet the way he did. As a psychologist, I understood. As someone who loved Garnet, I felt only contempt." He shook his head, and a wave of white hair fell over his forehead.

"And he went to find her," Meredith said.

"Yes. The coroner confirmed later that she was dead before Preston left the house to look for her. She must have tripped on one of the boulders in the upper garden."

"You didn't tell anyone that you were there that day," Meredith said.

"I was afraid they would think I had hurt her. Oh! I could never do that. I—" He stopped short of declaring his love once more. "I didn't want Sapphie to know—" He stopped himself, turned to his niece, whose tears streamed down her white cheeks. He shook his head despondently. "Preston blamed himself, of course. He even stopped drinking for a while, but he couldn't move forward."

"Poor Daddy," Sapphire whispered, knotting the handkerchief Gage had given her. After a few seconds, she said, "Poor Mama." She looked across at her uncle. "Poor Uncle Teddy."

Theodore suddenly stood and, assuming his authoritative manner, addressed Meredith and Julia. "I thank you ladies for helping me find my niece. I had no right to ask, but you came to my aid. I'm sure Sapphire and I can iron things out, now that…" He stopped and looked away to the bay window once more. Silence filled the little space, and Meredith recognized that Theodore had been about to dismiss them. But something seemed to change in his face. He stared into her eyes and said, "But there's more, isn't there?" Without breaking eye contact with Meredith, he said, "Gage, will you take my niece outside? She could use some fresh air."

When they had gone, Theodore invited them to sit down again, since she and Julia had risen during the emotion of the last few moments. "I thought once we got beyond those first couple of years after Garnet died that Sapphire would be okay," he began. "She only had occasional episodes. Later, Elena would call them hauntings." His lips twisted downward. "Sapphire needed a woman, especially during her teen years. So, after Preston died, I married my old acquaintance. Elena and Sapphire were okay together for the most part, and things went on at the ranch and the clinic. Sapphire was busy at school. Then Elena's daughter came to us from Texas. It was only going to be for a while. I knew the girls didn't get along, but I thought—" He drew in a breath. "Oh, I never imagined—"

Did Elena know, Meredith wondered, that she had been sought out, not as a lover for Theodore but as a mother substitute for Sapphire? In the best of people that could spell disaster.

And suddenly the lady herself entered the front door and hurried over to where Theodore stood. Her eyes were wet with tears as she linked an arm with her husband in a possessive gesture. "This has all been so hard on you," she crooned. "Are you all right, Teddy?"

Theodore disengaged his arm, an inscrutable expression on his face.

Elena turned to Meredith and Julia with a raised eyebrow. "We will be all right now. Thank you for your help finding Sapphire." She made a grand sweep of her arm that left no doubt that they should go.

"I want them to stay," Theodore said, bringing Elena whirling about to face him in surprise. "They will stay, and you will tell us the truth. Did you know?"

"What?" Elena asked, eyes wide.

"Did you know that Lara pretended to be Sapphire's mother calling from the grave? I want to know. Could you be that cruel?" His eyes flashed beneath the shaggy brows. "How many times has she done this?"

"Teddy, please! Lara is difficult... She—I know she was jealous of Sapphire, but...you must understand. Her father left her with nothing after she was put out of the university." Elena was suddenly overcome by tears, which did not appear to move Theodore.

Meredith watched the drama unfold. Lara had, in fact, flunked out of two private schools her father had paid for. Then when her funds ran out, she'd left the acting academy and appealed to her now very well-married mother. Meredith couldn't help but pity Lara, who must have felt that life had been desperately unfair to her. She turned to Theodore. "Is it true that Sapphire will inherit her father's estate when she turns twenty-one?"

"It is true," Theodore said. "Preston made no secret of that."

"And until then, you hold the estate in trust."

"That too is well known. But what you are really asking is if I am deliberately keeping her dependent on me to control the funds." He ran a hand over his chin. "I am not," he said succinctly. "And Elena has no reason either to—" He broke off as though suddenly struck. He stared at his wife for a long moment then said in a voice that left no room for argument, "Tell Lara to come in here."

"But surely these ladies—"

"Do it, Elena. Now."

Elena obeyed and returned momentarily with a belligerent Lara in tow. They stood in a haphazard circle as electricity crackled. When Theodore spoke, his voice was controlled. "Why were you calling Sapphire's name while she slept at the clinic last night?"

Instead of the injured retort Meredith expected, Lara began to wail. "She kept Cameron from me! He's all I ever wanted. He would care for me too, except for her. It's always everything for Sapphire, what she wants, what she needs. She has everything, and she had to have him too."

"Sapphire has no interest in Cameron Wiley," Theodore said with astonishment. "He's been her friend since they were children."

Meredith recalled Studs Wiley's words. *History repeating itself.* As Theodore had hopelessly loved Garnet, had Cameron Wiley yearned for Sapphire?

"But he wants her, and I'm sick of it!" Lara fumed, ugly in her rage. "He should see her for the spoiled child she is." Meredith marveled that Lara was foolish enough not to have known that Sapphire's bungalow would be monitored, especially at night, for the safety of vulnerable patients. This surely Elena had to know. Had jealousy robbed Lara of reason?

"You make me ashamed!" Elena broke in, adding a string of comments in a foreign dialect.

"My mother, the hypocrite," Lara said, her tears spent and sarcasm in full gear. "You're the one who worries that you'll lose Teddy's precious money—this ranch—and all the things he buys for you."

"Lara!" Elena whirled around, her hands flapping. She turned pleading eyes on her husband. "Teddy! It is not so! I think only of you. All those years you work this ranch—morning until night—while your brother dried out in some fancy rehab house. This—this…" She flung her arms outward to encompass the luxury that surrounded them. "Who knows what Sapphire will do—probably sell this ranch and buy flowers! And you will be left with nothing." A flood of tears followed, and Elena flung herself onto the couch.

Theodore looked down at her with the same inscrutable expression. "So, you had Lara do this! You told her to—"

"No! No, *mi querida*, I swear I did not know!" She stood up, reached for her husband again. "I only want what is good for you. What is yours. What you work so hard for!" She whirled around, reaching for the hands held rigid at his sides. "Please believe me, Teddy. Please believe that I love you."

Theodore walked to the window, shaking his head. Elena sank into the chair Teddy had vacated. She looked from Meredith to Julia as though they might convince her husband of her devotion. "It is true that in the beginning I wanted to marry Teddy for his money. Like it was with the others." She twisted her fingers in her lap, glanced at Theodore's rigid back. "But it was different with my Theodore. He was so kind. Always. He was good to me—to me and to everyone. I just wanted him to keep what he has worked so hard for. Oh, Teddy," she said sadly, speaking to his back. "Mi querida, please understand. I am sorry."

It was hard to know what Theodore understood. If it was true that Elena had not been involved in Lara's antics, perhaps there was hope for her future with Theodore. As for her daughter, it was hard to guess the next steps for the young woman who had caused so much distress in recent months. Meredith was struck by a new thought. In a way, Lara had been the instrument to bring Sapphire's fears into the open so they could be addressed. *Yes, God works in mysterious ways.* She glanced out the open door where Sapphire waited with Gage. "If you'll excuse us now," she said, standing, "Julia and I need to talk with our client."

They left Theodore and Elena standing apart in the grip of their private recriminations and the decisions that would have to be made. Sapphire, having faced her fear, would have to decide for herself how she would cope with her past and what direction her life would take in the future. Neither Theodore nor Elena spoke as the partners left the house.

Chapter Twenty

THE DAY AFTER THE ASTONISHING revelations at Riverton Ranch, Sapphire sat at the conference table in Magnolia Investigations next to Meredith and Julia. Her lips curved in a shy smile. "I want to thank you," she said, looking at each of them in turn. "My grandma said I could trust you, and Gage told me you would help me."

Carmen had hurriedly prepared the conference room when Meredith phoned to tell her they were coming. She and Julia had led the way with Gage and Sapphire following in Gage's Jeep.

Their trusty assistant had ordered sandwiches and drinks and brought in extra chairs for the little group that was being treated to a very late lunch.

"Are you all right, Sapphire?" Meredith asked, touching her arm lightly.

She dropped her head and twisted her fingers in her lap. "I don't know, but at least I know I wasn't imagining everything. It was so awful hearing Mama's voice. I know it was crazy. It was driving me crazy." She gave a small disparaging laugh.

Across from her, Gage nodded his head gently, as though to nudge her to continue.

"When Daddy died and Elena first came, Grandma hired Mr. Bellefontaine to check into things. She didn't trust Elena. She worried for Uncle Teddy—and for me, I guess." Sapphire pushed back a lock of light hair that had fallen over her eyes. "I never cared about trust funds and wills and all that, but she said if I ever needed help I should go to Mr. Bellefontaine."

"I see," Meredith said quietly, absorbing the sweetness of having finished a case Ron had begun.

"So when I started hearing my mother's voice again, I decided to come here." She toyed with the napkin in her lap and glanced at Gage, who sat across from her. "Gage and I went to see Grandma today. She gave me one of her stones—told me to be strong, to go to the garden. Most of the time her mind is all mixed up, but sometimes a window opens, and she's herself again."

Gage set down his can of soda and leaned in. "You always knew there was something about the garden—something you needed to know." He grinned at her admiringly. "And you found the courage to face it—with the help of Mrs. Bellefontaine and Mrs. Foley."

Julia cleared her throat. She rolled her eyes at him with a smile. "I guess you ought to be calling us by our first names after all we've been through together."

"Thank you, ma'am. Julia and Meredith then," he said, nodding his curly head.

Meredith stifled a grin at Julia's largesse. Apparently she had forgiven Gage for leading her on a merry chase through the neighborhood. She turned again to Sapphire. "So it was your grandmother who introduced us."

"Grandma always said everything would be all right. Then she got sick, and I wasn't sure it would be anymore. My thoughts got as mixed up as hers."

"What Lara did sure didn't help," Gage said. "It was rotten to trick you like that."

Sapphire lowered her head over her ham and cheese roll. "She thought Cam and I..." She shook her head. "I feel sorry for her—for all of us, really."

A gracious attitude from this young woman who had been mistreated on a variety of fronts. Meredith was touched by her spirit. "You have been very special to your grandma for a long time—and you still are." She smiled, seeing Carmen usher Maggie Lu into the room. "Sapphire, there's someone I want you to meet." She waved them toward the table. "This is Maggie Lu King. She knew both your grandma and your mother."

Gage stood and pulled out a chair for Maggie Lu, scooting to the side and giving her the place directly across from Sapphire.

A tender glow filled the wise woman's face. "Carmen tells me this is Miss Sapphire Riverton." Maggie Lu extended her hand. "I knew your grandma when she had her shop on LeGrand Street, and your mama too."

Sapphire nodded, curiosity marking her features.

"Mind you, when I met your mama she was a little girl. Your grandma and I often met on the street because I lived near her old shop. She had your mama with her. Your mama became a beautiful young lady, Sapphire." Maggie Lu closed her eyes in recollection then laughed her musical laugh.

Sapphire's blue eyes lit up. "Wait! Are you the 'God bless you' lady?"

Maggie Lu was taken aback but only for a moment. "Why, bless your heart, I suppose I am," and her tuneful laugh broke out again.

Maggie Lu always invoked God's blessing whenever she said goodbye to someone. "Grandma told me about you," Sapphire said with a look of awe. "Before she got sick, I mean." She shook her head wonderingly. "The 'God bless you' lady!" she repeated.

A tinge of happiness sprang into the girl's shining eyes. Meredith felt a lump forming in her throat. She and Maggie Lu had agreed that sometimes it was the small things a person remembers. That God listens to the sincere blessing given to one of His children in His name.

"And I'm Gage Gallagher, ma'am," Gage said, lightening the emotional silence that followed. He pumped Maggie Lu's hand gently. "Veterinary student and barn manager at Riverton Ranch. Uh, former manager, that is. I'm headed back to Texas in a few days to complete my studies, but I'll be coming back up this way now and again." He tipped an imaginary hat and exchanged a knowing glance with Sapphire.

Julia poked her head forward to see Sapphire. "What are you going to do now?"

"Well, I'm not sure, but maybe when Uncle Teddy thinks it's time, I'd like to go to art school. I've always wanted to, but things…" She let the sentence drift, and some of the frightened child seemed to threaten. After a moment, she shrugged, smiling shyly. "But Uncle Teddy needs me at the boutique right now."

Conversation flowed around the table as the little group ate their catered meal. Meredith glanced at her cell phone and saw that Quin had left three messages. She had a lot to tell him, and she wished she could hear his voice right now.

And suddenly, she did!

"I don't mean to interrupt," he was saying to Carmen, who had been dividing her attentions between the conference room and the outer office. Now she stood across the room with the handsome silver-haired lawyer.

Her heart drumming a quick cadence, Meredith got up to join him at the door. "You're not interrupting." She hooked her arm in his. "Have you had lunch?"

"About four hours ago," he said drolly, while his eyes said how glad he was to see her. He kept his voice down, motioning to the little group talking around the table. "I've been calling."

"I know. Sorry."

"Carmen said something was going on with the case and that you went out to Riverton's place. Is that—"

"Yes, that's Sapphire." She indicated with a nod of her head. "And Gage next to Maggie Lu." She smiled up at him. "I'll introduce you—"

"Wait. Of course I want to meet them—and to hear all about them, but first…" He placed a hand over hers still tucked in his elbow. "Are you all right? When I couldn't reach you, I was worried."

A tiny muscle in his left temple pulsed, and Meredith found it impossibly and illogically endearing. She felt an equally illogical, though restrained, desire to kiss that spot next to his brown eye. "I'm fine, and I'm sorry to worry you. Can I make it up to you?"

"What do you have in mind?" He lifted his chin in mock skepticism.

"Jumbo shrimp and grits at my place? Seven o'clock?"

"Well…"

"And the whole story of the rock garden and Sapphire's secret."

"You drive a hard bargain, but you're on!"

The look he gave her could melt butter. It certainly melted her— all the way down to her toes. She smiled, not only warmed by Quin's nearness but by the sight of Sapphire and Gage sharing animated conversation with Julia, Carmen, and Maggie Lu—the "God bless you" lady!

Courage had overcome fear, and faith had triumphed. It was a time for thanksgiving, a time to move ahead with confidence and joy.

Dear Reader,

What occurs in a child's life has a lasting influence, since in those early years we form the basis of intelligence, personality, social behavior, and capacity to learn and nurture ourselves as adults. We can all relate to some event in our lives or in the life of someone we know that has marked us—either for good or ill. Sometimes it is a secret fear rooted in the past. I wanted to explore a young girl's adventure in moving beyond a stultifying secret and finding courage to forge ahead with hope. I enjoyed imagining how our winsome and wily investigators helped Sapphire Riverton unlock her fear and find faith to overcome. Meredith and Julia reckoned with horses, a mysterious garden, handsome cowboys, and other interesting characters who made their own imprint on life. It's been an exciting ride made all the more satisfying with the help of those wise editors at Guideposts.

I hope you enjoyed the ride too!

—Marlene Chase

About the Author

MARLENE CHASE IS A LT. Colonel in the Salvation Army, having served people in various communities in the Midwest for forty-three years. She retired as Editor in Chief and Literary Secretary for the Army's National Publications, headquartered in Alexandria, Virginia. She continues to serve the ministry endeavors of the organization and to write from her home in Rockford, Illinois. She is the author of twenty-two books and numerous articles, poems, and stories. She has two daughters, four grandchildren, and two great-granddaughters. She holds a Bachelor of Arts degree from Mid-America Nazarene University in Kansas and is an ordained minister in the Salvation Army.

An Armchair Tour of Savannah

While Riverton Ranch is a fictional place, there are many ranches in and around Savannah where horses are bred and raised for profit and where horseback riding provides pleasant occupation for tourists. Horses have always been important in the South, particularly during the American Civil War, an infamously nightmarish experience not only for people but also for horses.

As gregarious animals, horses form bonds with others in their team, as well as with cats, dogs, and humans. During the Civil War, those bonds were routinely broken. Instead of spending their lives on a farm with friends and acquaintances, they found themselves crammed together with strangers in railroad cars and hastily assembled corrals. Bustling war camps and long marches offered few chances for the horses to form the social connections that herd animals depend on. They experienced anxiety and aggression and were frequently thirsty and underfed. Closeness with a rider can make up for the lack of connection with fellow equines to some extent, but many of the soldiers knew nothing about how to relate to the horses they rode. War sometimes forced them into cruelty to their mounts.

Confederate horses often fared better, since Southern soldiers generally rode their own mounts to war. Horses who knew and trusted their riders performed better in the chaos of battle.

There are many different breeds of horses in the Peachtree state today. These magnificent, hardworking animals generate millions of dollars for the state every year. There are even feral horses, about 160 of them, on Cumberland Island, Georgia's largest and southern-most barrier island.

From the rugged, mountainous north to the western coastal plains, horse trails are found everywhere, offering a refreshing gambol beneath Southern blue skies.

HARVEST TIME HOT CHOCOLATE

Ingredients:

2 cups almond milk
(or preferred choice of milk)
1 tablespoon blackstrap
molasses

1 tablespoon cocoa powder
½ teaspoon ground cloves
1 teaspoon cinnamon
Pinch of salt

Directions:

Heat milk in saucepan until just simmering. Stir in molasses until fully blended. Whisk in cocoa powder, cloves, cinnamon, and salt. Pour into mug and sprinkle with a little more cinnamon.

This hot chocolate tastes amazing and provides some real health benefits too. Cocoa powder is a strong antioxidant and is rich in magnesium and B vitamins. Cinnamon increases circulation and reduces inflammation in the body. Blackstrap molasses provides calcium and magnesium. If desired, you can substitute molasses with stevia or sweetener of choice, adjusting for preferred sweetness. But a real Southern cook would prefer blackstrap molasses!

*Read on for a sneak peek of another exciting book
in the Savannah Secrets series!*

Jingle Bell Heist

BY RUTH LOGAN HERNE

Four million desserts and counting…

Julia Foley didn't give her business partner and friend time to kick off her shoes inside the door on the early December Friday. She grabbed Meredith Bellefontaine by the hand and hustled her over to the basement stairs. On the way down she indicated the two plastic containers in Meredith's hands with a quick look. "Thank you so much for doing these, Mere. It's a big help."

"Always happy to—"

Julia turned when Meredith stopped talking.

Eyes wide, Meredith had stopped on the middle stair.

She was staring at Julia's finished basement.

Julia had set up long portable tables to help organize the church's annual Christmas bake sale. Each table was covered with stacks of plasticware, and each container held delicious desserts, guaranteed to please.

Meredith swallowed hard then came down the last few steps. "Julia, the New Beginnings baking committee has outdone themselves."

It was Julia's turn to take a breath, but Meredith wasn't done. Her gaze swept the wide range of containers. "This is wonderful! The sale will be a huge success. No wonder you chair it. How can I help you organize?"

Meredith's dive-in nature was exactly what Julia needed right now. "I want to tag everything, transport it to the hall, and have it ready for tomorrow, because I've got the Christmas Box Fund meeting on Tuesday night and I need to get my notes ready for that."

"Another wonderful cause." Meredith smiled as she set her plastic containers down. "Should we load up the car and drive these over?"

"After we go through my checklist." Julia handed Meredith a steno-style notepad and a pencil. "I want your opinion on the selection to see if anything is missing. Okay?"

Meredith flipped the notepad open. "I can't imagine we're missing a thing, but I'm ready. Let's go."

Julia tapped the first group of containers. "Carrot cake with cream cheese frosting, carrot cake with pineapple and walnuts and cream cheese frosting, and carrot cake with raisins and walnuts and the ubiquitous—"

"Cream cheese frosting." Meredith laughed. "You can never have too much carrot cake or too much frosting. Done."

"Four harvest apple cakes with burnt sugar icing, three oatmeal cakes with broiled coconut topping, and six of Grandma Waverly's fruitcake loaves for the stouthearted among us."

"I refuse to waste my calories on something as odious as fruitcake," said Meredith as she jotted things down. When she was done, she indicated a stack to her left. "But are those six containers all pralines? Who made them? You know that pralines and fudge are my downfall."

"I did," Julia said when Meredith looked up from her list.

"You've been busy."

Meredith didn't know the half of it, and Julia was embarrassed to have her know, but Meredith had been her friend for a long time.

"And we have twelve-and-a-half dozen chocolate chip cookies, minus one as payment." Meredith grinned as she savored a bite of the cookie she'd filched. "It's my pleasure to be the official taste tester. Are these Wanda's contribution?"

"Her recipe, yes."

A tiny furrow deepened between Meredith's brows as Julia pointed out two more plastic containers and said, "Lemon bars, a wretchedly awful thing for December, but at the request of Mortie Sims, and considering his age, I made them."

Meredith's pencil paused. She glanced right. Then left. Then right again. "Jules, did you make all this?"

Reckoning had come.

Julia swallowed a sigh. "Mostly. Yes. Except the things you just brought and three others."

"Julia, why?" Meredith didn't just look surprised. She looked shocked by the revelation. "I know New Beginnings isn't a huge congregation, but there are so many people willing to help. Why did all this fall on you?" True concern deepened the lines between her friend's brows.

"It's December." Julia shrugged. "Everyone's busy. When a couple of folks bowed out because of the flu, I jumped in to make up lost ground. And then I didn't stop. It seemed easier than calling around, begging for help. Let's just say my freezer became a close personal friend this past week."

Meredith frowned. "Except that New Beginnings is about the sweetest church there is, and I'm sure Naomi is baking for the kids."

Naomi was their beloved pastor's organized and kindhearted wife.

"And Myla loves to make cream cheese brownies."

Myla worked for Meredith's neighbor Harlowe Green, the oldest citizen of the city of Savannah.

Julia cringed.

"You haven't asked them to help." Meredith's brows shot up. "Why?"

"We had a committee, and I thought we were all set. Then it turned out that a few of the members weren't all that motivated. I didn't realize that until this last week, and I didn't think it would be right to call folks in December when everyone has so many commitments. Except I did call you because I knew you'd drop everything to help."

Meredith looked unconvinced. She tipped her reading glasses down. "Why take this on yourself, my friend? At this time of year?"

The very question Julia had been asking herself all week. A question that had no answers. "I'm already avoiding the calendar because there are so many things that crop up this month. Former jobs, organizations, old friends, and neighbors all seem intent on hosting some kind of holiday gathering. We're booked each of the next two weekends and two Wednesdays, one Tuesday and one Thursday. And everyone expects either a dish to pass or a box of cookies for a cookie exchange."

Meredith's frown deepened. "That's crazy, Jules. To tie up that much time? Is that what you want? To be run ragged with things all through December?"

Julia wasn't sure herself.

Any other time of year she was the delegator. She handed out jobs left and right, spreading the joy of many hands making light work, but not in December. Never in December.

Meredith looked about to say something else, but she must have thought better of it because she paused, clamped her mouth shut, and went straight back to the list. "Let's get this done, and then we can pack the car. Next?"

"Chocolate frosted peanut butter."

"Those were Ron's favorite."

Ron was Meredith's late husband. He'd begun an investigations agency decades before, an agency that Meredith and Julia reopened eighteen months ago—and what a wonderful year and a half it had been.

Julia really didn't want to be questioned about her reasoning, mostly because she hadn't figured it out herself. She'd been scolding herself for the last three days, a long seventy-two hours of baking, baking, baking. "Done." She pressed a label onto the large sealed plastic container and pointed to one of the containers Meredith had brought in.

"My totally Southern contribution of chocolate fudge bourbon balls, made famous by my late mother-in-law. The Bellefontaine family has declared them to be the best in the world, and as a young bride I learned to never argue with the Bellefontaine clan. In this case, they are probably right."

"Thank you for doing them." Julia pointed to another container. "And you did the fudge too?"

"Yes, ma'am, but looking at all you did, I feel like a slacker." Meredith smiled as Julia labeled the plastic container before setting it aside for transport to the church hall.

Julia opened her mouth just as the doorbell pealed and her phone lit up with her doorbell app.

"You've got your doorbell linked to your phone?" asked Meredith. "Since when?"

"A few of Beau's friends have this app. He decided we couldn't live without it and installed one yesterday. I'm not sure how I feel about it." She glanced at her phone and recognized her neighbor. "Tasha, hey," she said. "I'm in the basement. I'll be right up."

"Do you want me to finish?" asked Meredith.

Julia shook her head and muted the app. "Let's have coffee. Tasha's had a rough few months, and she looks like she might be having a bad day."

"Coffee it is."

Julia led the way up the stairs, and when she opened the front door, her thirty-something neighbor almost fell through the opening. Eyes wide, Tasha Alexander glanced behind her as if checking for pursuers, then shut the door snugly, flipped the deadbolt, and turned, ashen-faced.

"Tasha, what's happened? What's going on? Is it the boys?" Tasha had a seven-year-old and a nine-year-old, a pair of normal, busy boys. "Are they all right? Are you?" Julia asked as she turned to lead Tasha into the living room.

"My shoes!" Tasha pulled up short, aghast, a proper Southern woman to the max. "On your good rug? I can't even!"

"Everything here is washable," Julia reassured her, but she waited while Tasha toed off the cute boots she was wearing. "Are we good now?" she teased once the boots were squarely on the foyer throw rug.

"No." Tasha moved forward, sank onto the sofa, and put her head in her hands. "And maybe never will be again, but I didn't do it, Julia." Anguished, she dropped her hands, sighed, and looked straight at Julia while Meredith set up coffee in the kitchen. The open concept of the house left them visible to one another.

"Do you want privacy?" Julia posed the question softly. She would never hurt Meredith's feelings, but if Tasha had confidential news to share, Meredith would understand. "I'm sure Meredith—"

"No." Tasha shook her head. "I want you both here."

Julia glanced toward the kitchen.

Meredith arched both brows in silent question.

Julia shifted her attention back to Tasha. "What's happened, Tasha?"

"A theft at the museum."

Meredith left the coffee to burble and moved closer.

"Someone stole something from the museum?" Julia liked history all right, but she didn't pretend to be a regular visitor to the beautiful historical museum sprawled out at the intersection of Liberty Street and Martin Luther King Jr. Highway. History was Meredith's forte. "I thought the museum was undergoing some kind of major renovation and closed to visitors?"

"They reopened the tours to drive up annual memberships for the coming year. Memberships are a big Christmas gift idea, and it should have been all right because the rough spots were cordoned off, but it wasn't all right." She sighed deeply. "It was bad from the beginning, and it shouldn't have been, even if it was the first one I've done all on my own. We were only fifteen minutes or so into it when the power went out. It was black as pitch in the areas with no windows because they didn't have the backup system rewired into the new system yet. So when we lost power, folks screamed and began yelling and running back and forth. It was a mess. It's an old, multistory schoolhouse, so there are no big windows that give natural light in the entry like a modern museum might have. Without power and the emergency backup system there was hardly any light at all."

"So what happened?" Meredith moved into the room and took a seat.

Tasha shook her head. "I waited to make certain everyone had safely left the floor. One of our regular security guards, Jay Crawford, was up there too, and when it seemed like everyone was down the stairs, I met Jay. He followed me out and drew the rope across the stairs so no one could get back up there."

"Except a rope is only a visual reminder," Julia said. "Not an actual barrier."

"A good point, but Jay stayed there, watching, while I tried to calm the situation down. And when we finally got the lobby cleared and folks on their way, I went back upstairs with my cell phone flashlight. Jay has one of those bigger ones, and the construction foreman hooked up one of their big lights. Jay and I looked around. Everything looked fine until we got to the Settled in Savannah holiday exhibit."

Tears welled in her eyes.

Julia handed her a wad of tissues from a nearby box. "Here, sweetie. What happened then?"

"The bells were gone." She took a deep breath, squared her shoulders, and faced Julia and Meredith. "The Mulholland bells, a forty-three piece set of handbells donated by St. Kieran's Church down near the water. Bells that were brought here in the mid-1800s as an act in P.T. Barnum's traveling show. Absolutely irreplaceable."

"Mulholland Laces & Wovens?" Julia exchanged a look with Meredith. Everyone knew of the rich local family, not just because of their Fortune 500 textile company but because of their constant infighting that had resulted in lawsuits and countersuits over the years.

"The very same. They were individually made handbells in very nice condition. They were donated to the museum over a decade ago. But that's not the worst part." She clutched the tissues to her face for a moment then took a deep breath. "Councilman Webster is part of the family. Hank *Mulholland* Webster. And some of his own family were in the crowd, heckling him. I'm sure you know how the Mulhollands don't all get along," Tasha explained. "My boss always double-checks whenever she displays something related to their family history because some might be fine with it, but a cousin or brother or aunt or uncle somewhere might launch an objection. They always seem to be at odds. Maybe if I'd had more experience with them, I'd have been better prepared for what happened. But I was completely taken by surprise when Fiona Mulholland showed up with a whole crew of people protesting the city spending hundreds of thousands of dollars on Christmas lights when soup kitchens need help. She was leading chants about that while her cousin was trying to gain support for the city's Toys on Patrol campaign. Then the lights go out and the family's heirloom bells go missing. I can't think of a worse possible coincidence."

Coincidence?

Or plan?

Julia exchanged a look with Meredith. "This is awful, Tasha, but you couldn't have foreseen this. Things happen."

"But that's just it." She brought the tissues to her face again. "The police took me into a back room for questioning because I was the last person up there, and I'm afraid they're going to think I did it, Julia."

"Why would they do that?" Tasha was a hardworking, honest woman who helped elderly neighbors and saved lost kittens. The thought of her pilfering a pricey collection of bells was ridiculous.

"Because I'm broke."

Her sad expression underscored her fear.

"This divorce is costing me my house and my car," she confessed. "I was close to staying afloat, but then the latest ruling said I had to hand over half of my inheritance from my grandmother because it doesn't matter that Hayden cheated on me, squandered money on high living on his 'business trips'"—she waggled quote marks with her fingers—"and has skipped all the important days in his sons' lives. It came down to when Meemaw died and how long we were married, which means the cushion I thought I had is gone. If they're looking for someone who needs money"—she lifted tearful eyes to Julia and Meredith—"I'm their number-one suspect. And I need your help."

A Note from the Editors

WE HOPE YOU ENJOY THE Savannah Secrets series, created by the Books and Inspirational Media Division of Guideposts, a nonprofit organization that touches millions of lives every day through products and services that inspire, encourage, help you grow in your faith, and celebrate God's love in every aspect of your daily life.

Thank you for making a difference with your purchase of this book, which helps fund our many outreach programs to military personnel, prisons, hospitals, nursing homes, and educational institutions. To learn more, visit GuidepostsFoundation.org.

We also maintain many useful and uplifting online resources. Visit Guideposts.org to read true stories of hope and inspiration, access OurPrayer network, sign up for free newsletters, download free e-books, join our Facebook community, and follow our stimulating blogs.

To learn about other Guideposts publications, including the bestselling devotional *Daily Guideposts*, go to ShopGuideposts.org, call (800) 932-2145, or write to Guideposts, PO Box 5815, Harlan, Iowa 51593.

Sign up for the
Guideposts Fiction Newsletter
and stay up-to-date on the books you love!

You'll get sneak peeks of new releases, recommendations from other Guideposts readers, and special offers just for you . . .
and it's FREE!

Just go to Guideposts.org/Newsletters
today to sign up.

Find more inspiring stories in these best-loved Guideposts fiction series!